C000183097

"This is an adorable, heartwarming regency 1 you smile. I absolutely loved this book. I ado... most adorable, gentlemanly, caring guy who just wants the best for the woman he has loved forever. Gloved Heart is such a lovely, charming and romantic novel. Although it does have its fair share of heartbreak (I cried on more than one occasion!), you will smile and feel warm inside when you read this. If you love historical fiction, romance, regency romance or just want something to warm your heart then you should definitely check this out!"
Chelle - Curled up with a good book

"Gloved Heart is a different look at historical romance, one that strips away the pretences of the privileged and highlights what true happiness really is, not one's station in life, but one's perception of what a quality life is. A different take on historical romance, both fresh and full of heart, this one is a true reading treasure chest gem!"
Dianne from Tome Tender

"Gloved Heart had me hooked by the first few pages. This lovely romance set in regency times is perfect for fans of this genre. I adored this story."
Chells and Books

"The situation of Amy's unmarried state and other sensitive matters are handled very delicately. I recommend this story for readers who like a sweet romance."
Susan Pruett for the Historical Novel Society

"I truly enjoyed this book, and its sweet, touching moments (of which there are many) easily outshone the darkness of Amy's past as it leaks into her current situation. Just as Amy strives to uncover happiness despite it all, the reader is able to cherish sweet moments to find a truly lovely novel."
Juliette Sebock - Pencils & Pages

"This kind of book is not normally on my to-read pile but something in this blurb attracted me and I was sold. Honestly, when the story is good, the genre is less important. The author takes us back to 1803 but I have to say that the essence of the story can as well be a modern tale of love and trust. I often think the characters in historical romance novels are very naive and a bit foolish. In this case the author has created very loveable ones that made the book very real. I enjoyed reading it a lot. 5 stars."
Els from B for Book Review

"There are no straight lines in this novel, and the story takes off in unexpected directions. The beginning takes you directly, and without further ado, to the heart of the story of Amy and her baby. It is a different approach to historical fiction and makes for interesting reading. Charlotte's prose is beautiful and so easy to read, like a river slowly flowing through the landscape. Gloved Heart with its secrets and mysteries, keeps you wondering until the very end. Looking forward to her next story."
Lisa - The Content Reader

"Gloved Heart by Charlotte Brentwood is not the typical regency romance. Neither of the love interests are swimming in money and both are trying to get away from something. I really enjoyed this story. Amy could not have been written better and Henry's care for her and understanding puts him on a pedestal that maybe only Mr. Darcy holds (at least in my eyes). It has plenty of light moments inside what could be a very dark story and I deeply appreciate that. If you're looking for a regency romance that deals with some difficult issues, this is the book for you."
Sarah - Bookish Rantings

"Henry Russell is an absolute delight to spend a couple of days in the company of, and his love for Amy sings from the pages. I would highly recommend it to readers of Regency romance, or anyone who likes a romance at the sweeter end of the scale. It's beautifully written, and I thoroughly enjoyed it."
Jennifer C Wilson @ Historical Fiction with Spirit

THE **HEARTS OF AMBERLEY** SERIES

The Vagabond Vicar
Gloved Heart
Heart of a Gentleman (coming soon)

Go to www.charlottebrentwood.com and sign up
to my email newsletter for book news!

Chapter One

Amberley, Shropshire

June 1806

Screams echoed in every corner of the room, and in her mind.

There was agony, humiliation and confusion... Her dress torn, her skin ripped, and a man intent on possessing her, no matter the cost. She had never felt more helpless, worthless, or alone.

Amy woke with tears pouring down her cheeks, but the incessant cries she could hear were not her own.

It was the consequence of that hideous night: a baby born of sin. Motherhood had been thrust upon her, her life irrevocably altered.

The baby's cries escalated, and she forced herself from the bed. Her nightdress was saturated from the neck to the waist. Her milk flowed freely whenever he cried, or at the mere thought of feeding him. She couldn't even control her own body these days, let alone the course of her life.

She hurried down the hall to the nursery, but the crying stopped before she opened the door.

Good heavens! Is he alive?

She threw the door open. In the moonlight sat the wet nurse, already feeding her child. Amy's heart nearly burst out of her chest with relief when she saw her son, healthy.

The woman looked up and saw her, then focussed her attention on the child again.

Amy stepped forward.

"I'll take him, please."

The nurse didn't move. "He needs feeding, miss."

"I can do that. I want to."

"Nonsense, miss. You're to leave that to me."

"But–"

"Mrs Fortescue wouldn't hear of you feeding him. Go back to bed. You need your rest."

Amy nodded wearily. She did not want to disturb her son by fighting over him. She rubbed her pounding temples, on the edge of giving up. Benjamin was only a few weeks old, but he was already fodder for battle. Despite her guardian's orders, Amy had often managed to feed Benjamin herself, at all hours of the day and night. She was so tired she didn't know who she was anymore. It would be easier to go back to bed.

But her breasts ached, and there was a longing somewhere deeper inside her, too. For what purpose did she need rest? Lord knew Mrs Fortescue wouldn't let her lift a finger with any household duties. She felt impotent and purposeless. Tending to her son was the one thing she *could* do.

She unbuttoned the top of her night-rail and reached for him, saying with as much authority as she could muster, "Give him to me."

The baby started at the sound of her voice, detaching from the nurse's breast. Amy scooped him up and he began whimpering. She rushed to the chair on the other side of the cradle and settled into it, cuddling him and nudging him to her throbbing breast. He opened his mouth wide, latched on, and began to suck vigorously.

She sighed and began to relax as sweet release came. Little Benjamin wriggled closer to her, and her heart skipped a beat. She had been so afraid she would resent or despise this little wonder of a creature, but a seed of love had been planted in the first moment she held him in her arms. It had only grown since.

The nurse also sighed and trudged from the room.

Amy barely noticed. She gently caressed Benjamin's cheek with her fingertip, stroked his wisp of hair, and tapped the tip of his tiny nose.

"Hello, little one," she whispered. "You take as much as you need. I'll look after you."

When he was satiated, Benjamin opened his eyes. A connection sparked between them, visceral and sweet. A few moments later, he fell asleep, and Amy pulled him in close to her. She rested her head back and closed her eyes as fulfilment, love and contentment flowed through her. She had never known something this powerful could exist.

Now, he was the only reason she had to live.

ಶ‍ೃ

Later that morning, Amy ran a finger down her gleaming silver hairbrush as she sat in front of her dresser. She had never possessed anything so beautiful before coming to live in this house. There was a comb of tortoiseshell, hair pins of ivory and silk ribbons so smooth they slipped through her fingers in glossy waves.

Her dresses consisted of cast-offs from the Barringtons, which fit well enough, and some gowns from Mrs Fortescue herself, many of which Amy still needed to take in to fit her leaner frame. The fabrics were all so much finer than she was used to, some with delicate lace or intricate embroidery. Far *too* fine for someone like her.

They were all lovely things a lady should have – not an imposter who didn't belong.

A large mirror was affixed to the back of the dresser, and Amy's deep green eyes stared back at her, clear as day. Previously she'd had only a small, rusted pane and an approximation of her likeness.

She reached for the hairbrush again, her fingers curling around the shiny silver handle.

"I'll take that!"

The hairbrush was whisked from her hand. She gasped, whirling around on her seat. "Jenny!"

"Good morning, miss," the maid said crisply. She began to remove the curling papers from Amy's hair. Her auburn curls were ill-formed, at best. The maid tut-tutted, as if Amy had purposely underachieved, and then started to brush her hair with strokes that were not altogether gentle.

Amy reached above her head. "Give me that, please. I can do it myself."

"Poppycock." Jenny sniffed. "You're a *lady* now." Her tone indicated she believed the opposite was true.

And well Amy knew it. Though she had been given her own room on the first floor, though she had freedom from earning wages, she was still the adopted daughter of a tenant farmer, her true lineage a mystery. She had lately been a lady's maid herself and had never dreamed she would ever have someone else brush her hair or help her dress. Jenny was a parlour maid who had been tasked with attending to Amy, and it was clear she resented the extra work. Or perhaps she felt that Amy did not deserve to be attended upon. Amy wished the Fortescues had not thought to give her the help. It only served to remind her that she did not fit in.

She remained silent while she was helped into stays, a petticoat and a morning gown. Jenny then arranged her hair in a simple chignon, leaving her crinkled hair carefully exposed.

The maid reached beneath the bed to retrieve her chamber pot. Glancing at the contents she asked, "Will that be all, miss?"

"Yes, Jenny," Amy croaked. "Thank you."

Once alone again, she took a few deep breaths in order to recover her composure before leaving the room. She went directly to the nursery to check on Benjamin, who was slumbering sweetly under the watch of a nurse. Her heart warmed, she was now able to face the breakfast table with a degree of equanimity.

Amy had come to live at Briarwood, the Fortescues' home, when her swelling figure had made her position at the big house untenable – and she had been desperate. If not for their charity, she would be in a workhouse, and she dreaded to think what would have become of her baby.

Surely the Fortescues had only taken her in to make a show of their benevolence. How long before their goodwill turned sour? She had told herself time and again she should be grateful and bend to their ways, but her natural temper was quick, her hackles easily raised. It was sometimes very difficult to hold her tongue.

She had not been seated with her toast and ham for more than ten seconds when the lady of the house, the only other person in the room, addressed her from directly across the table.

"I hear you are in the habit of dismissing the night nurse and attending to the babe yourself."

Amy looked her straight in the eye. "Yes, I have done so."

Mrs Fortescue heaved a sigh. "I have given you nurses so you may rest. Why would you choose not to take advantage of that?"

Indignation rose up within Amy, and she spoke with measured words so as not to lose her temper. "Is it fair to stop me from feeding my very own child?"

"The nurse will not be able to continue nursing if you do not allow her to do it with regularity," Mrs Fortescue shot back. "Is *that* fair?"

"I cannot sleep while he cries," Amy protested. "I need to be with him. He needs *me*."

Something flashed in Mrs Fortescue's eyes. Amy braced herself for the next reproach, but it never came. The older woman swallowed and returned her attention to her breakfast.

She will never understand. How could she? She never had a child of her own. An awkward silence followed, punctuated only by the clinking of knives and forks against plates and cups on saucers.

Amy gobbled up her food, then shoved her chair back and stood. "I will go and see if Benjamin needs anything."

Mrs Fortescue also sprang up. "Nurse Agnes will notify us in that case." She came around to stand in front of her charge, blocking the way.

Amy sucked in a breath. She was not going to give in today. Every fibre in her body yearned for her son. "I have every right to see him whenever I like," she said, then she dodged around Mrs Fortescue and dashed from the room.

"Don't coddle him!" the woman roared after her.

"I'll do whatever I damn well please," Amy muttered, as she ran across the hall and up the stairs. As she reached the landing, she looked towards the nursery and saw Agnes walking into the hallway clutching a chamber pot. The nurse ducked into a neighbouring empty bedroom to relieve herself.

Amy sprinted down to the nursery and within a few seconds had picked up Benjamin and cradled him in her arms. He had been asleep but he stirred, made a little gurgling sound, and his eyes fluttered open.

Entranced by those deep, dark pools, her heart flooded with love anew. She was suddenly overwhelmed with the desire to be alone with him for as long as she wanted. After putting him back in his cradle, she darted about the room, packing necessities in a large cloth. She slung this around her shoulders, picked Benjamin up again, and darted to the door.

There was no sign of the nurse in the hallway. Seizing her chance, Amy walked as fast as she dared down the passage and to the servants' stairs. By some miracle, she made it to the back entrance undetected, and after flinging the door open, she dashed towards a hedge that ran down one side of the house.

Tears filled her eyes, blurring her vision. She hardly knew where she was going, half running across the back garden, through a gate and out into the fields beyond. As she drew in more fresh air, her anger began to dissipate and instead a heady optimism filled her. *Freedom!*

❧❦

Henry Russell drove his mallet down hard upon the fencepost, crying out with the effort. His anger drove him to execute his task with rather more strength and fervour than was required. He'd volunteered to repair the fence just to get away from his father.

If he contradicts me one more time…

The post was soon in place, and he worked on securing the horizontal railings to it.

He was no longer a child but a man of six-and-twenty. He knew his own mind. But if he dared to express his opinions, they were crushed every time. Was his father really so threatened by him? He slung the mallet over his shoulder and began to trudge back to the farm house.

They were two roosters, cooped up together for far too long. How much longer would he have to put up with this? He longed for his own space, to be able to make his own decisions and control his own fate, as much as a tenant farmer could.

Still incensed, Henry changed course, deciding to go home around the perimeter of the lands his family had leased from the Barringtons for several generations. Surely he should check the health of other fences as well.

Sheep scattered as he traversed a paddock. He then headed up a hill and came to a crest whereupon he could look back across Amberley village. The little huddle of buildings nestled along the valley floor, with the church at one end. In the opposite direction, the main street petered out into houses and the small estates of the landed gentry. The view hadn't changed in his whole life; he doubted it ever would.

He jumped over a gate and started down across the next field, scanning the fences in the meadows. The sight of someone under a tree in the distance made him stop short. Who could that be? It looked like a woman with some sort of bundle. Perhaps she needed assistance. He set down his mallet and began to jog down the hill towards her. It looked as though she was sleeping.

After only a few steps he stopped short and swore softly. It was Amy Miller, as he lived and breathed. He hadn't seen her since she'd had her baby, and hadn't talked to her for many months before that.

His heart pounded, and he began to sweat. He had half a mind to turn around and run in the other direction. Their last proper conversation had been years ago, and they hadn't really been alone since she'd matured into a woman.

What would he say to her? What did she think of him, if anything? He had so much he could tell her, but he knew not how… and this was not the time. She must still be going through so much. His heart ached, throbbed for her.

His feet began to move again, almost of their own volition. He wanted to see her. He needed to. Being in her presence had given him the most happiness he had experienced in his life.

She was not asleep; she merely had her head bowed over her infant. Nearly upon her, he slowed his steps as she hadn't noticed him yet. He was suddenly apprehensive, feeling as if he were intruding even though it was she who was on his land. He drank in the scene. The little child was snuggled into her, its hand grasping her dress. Amy gazed down at him with an expression of wonder and peace.

A twig snapped under his foot and her head whipped up towards him. "Oh! I–" Her arm flew over the child in a protective gesture, and she reached for her bag with the other hand. "Oh, it's only you, Henry," she said with a huge sigh of relief.

Henry's heart sank. He took some tentative steps forward. "Yes, it's only me. Good day, Miss Miller."

She glanced down at the baby and then back up at him. Even at this distance, her green eyes seemed to see right through him. He saw those eyes in his dreams.

"Can I… help you?" He hovered in front of her, desperately awkward.

She broke the eye contact. "No… that is, I am probably… beyond helping."

His breath quickened. What kind of trouble was she in? How could things be worse? Had someone hurt her? His fists clenched, and before he knew what he was doing he was kneeling before her in the grass. "What is it? Are you hurt?"

She raised her face to him once again, tears in her eyes.

"No, I am feeling better than I have since little Benjamin arrived," she said, her voice breaking. "I have… run away." She said this with a shrug and then a little laugh, but she looked as if she might cry. He longed to reach out to her.

"Run away?" he repeated. "What do you mean?"

"I am not supposed to be mothering him, if I am to be a lady. That is what she says. But I cannot stay away from him. He is… a part of me."

Henry tried to absorb all this. "So, you stole him?" He smiled a little.

"Yes, I suppose I did." Her mouth quirked.

"Does anyone know?"

"They likely will by now. I expect I will be in trouble." Her steady stare spoke of defiance, as if she did not care if she was in trouble. Her spirit made him ache all the more. She'd always had that spirit.

A comfortable moment of silence passed, and a breeze swirled around them. It caused the sleeping baby to stir, and he made a few burbling noises before settling down again. Amy caressed his cheek and bent down to kiss his head.

The tender moment took Henry's breath away. How incredible, that this woman had been through such horror and yet was so loving and gentle towards this child.

"How have you been, Miss Amy?" he asked gently. "Are you all right?"

She did not speak immediately, her head still bowed. He wondered if she had heard him. But after a few seconds she raised glistening eyes to

sorry, or justify any feelings or actions. Given all you've been through, I'm stunned by your composure."

She smiled. "I suppose motherhood must agree with me." She indicated they should walk on, and Henry fell into step with her, returning her smile.

"Of that I'm glad. You certainly seem to be taking to it in a natural way." He paused and drew in a breath. "I'm not of the same class as the gentlemen you're now used to being around," he said. "I understand if you think I am beneath you, or if you would rather not acknowledge our friendship in public."

Amy gave a shout of laughter. "Oh my dear Henry, what a thing to say! You could not possibly be beneath me. I am sunk to the very lowest order as a result of my – well, you know. I am a charity case and have been taken in as a sullied orphan. I rather expect you would not want to be seen with *me*!"

She looked over to see Henry's eyes darken before he looked away. Amy's smile faded. Was it true? "I would never think such things of you," he finally said. "I've known you your whole life. I know who you really are."

These words unsettled Amy; she didn't know herself anymore. "And who am I, Henry?"

He sought her eyes. "You are the most honest and kind person I know. You bear life's calamities with good grace – though a more stubborn girl I have never met!"

They both laughed at that.

"You were a devoted daughter, and although I've hardly seen you since you became a lady's maid, I'm sure you would have been a loyal and hardworking servant. You put your whole heart into everything you do."

Amy's heart swelled, and she longed for the simpler days of youth. At least there was someone who didn't think she was repugnant. A reminder of her good qualities was just the tonic for her battered soul. She didn't quite know how to put her gratitude into words and had to settle for simplicity. "Thank you, Henry," she said. "That means a lot."

After a moment, Henry replied, "You can trust me, Amy. You can always rely on me for anything you need – always." They'd reached the barn, and as Henry opened the final gate, he caught her gaze and they shared a smile of understanding.

He led her inside the large building to a series of pens, and she heard the grunts of the piglets before she saw them. A row of little pink bodies were huddled up to the mother pig, feeding.

Off to the side, another piglet lay on its own. Henry got into the pen and picked up the tiny creature, gently stroking its back.

He brought it near his face and whispered something to it, and then he put it down in front of one of the mother's nipples and nuzzled its nose against it. The little pig eventually managed to latch on and began sucking away, its curly tail twitching.

"The poor little thing," Amy said, touched. "I do hope he pulls through." Benjamin stirred at her chest, and she turned away to let him find her breast. She rearranged her shawl so she was covered, and turned back around to find Henry cuddling another one of the piglets, regarding it affectionately.

"You always were so good with the animals," she said. Another memory came to her, not as welcome as the first. "How do you get on... with your father?"

Henry's head snapped up, and he frowned at her before looking down again. "Much the same," he muttered.

"I am sorry to hear it," she said sincerely. She was suddenly mindful of her own domestic situation. "I should be on my way," she said, reluctant to leave the comfort of this place and return to her cloistered existence. "Thank you for letting me see the piglets, and for your company."

He was at her side in an instant. "You're welcome back any time," he said, his eyes clear and earnest. He led her out to the yard and towards the lane which would take her back to the village. "We could always use an extra pair of hands."

She smiled. "I'm a bit busy with Benjamin at present, but I'll keep that in mind."

Henry gestured towards the cart in the yard. "I'll drive you back to Briarwood."

Amy began to walk with purposeful strides. "Oh, that's really not necessary. I shall enjoy the walk."

He kept up with her. "Surely you're tired? And you must be keen to return as soon as you can."

She smiled and shook her head. "I am quite content to walk, and I'd like to remain beyond the house for a little longer to have Benjamin to myself while he sleeps."

To her annoyance, Henry stepped in front of her. "Miss Miller, I'm afraid for your safety. You are alone and unguarded."

Amy softened when she saw how serious he was. He was genuinely worried about her. It bothered her that she should probably be worried for herself, given her history. But she had always enjoyed coming and going on her own, without the restrictions placed upon those in the upper classes. Surely no one would dare to interfere with her while she carried Ben… She shivered.

But her resolve was firm. A life not lived freely was not worth living. "I thank you for your concern, Henry," she said. "I understand your intentions. But I only need go down the lane and a short distance beside the road before I reach the property. I would rather go on my own."

Henry sighed and stepped aside. "Always so independent, so obstinate. Take care."

"Thank you, I will." She started off down the lane, and called over her shoulder, "Good day!"

As she headed towards the main road, she gulped in shaky breaths. Damnation. Despite her bravado, she was afraid.

Henry's warning played in her mind. She was alone, and by virtue of her sex she was in danger. She had never been scared when out by herself before she was attacked.

As soon as she was out of sight of the farm buildings, Amy began looking behind her, off to the sides, and back to the front, again and again as she walked along the road. It was like being in a prison, in the same setting where she had felt so free just an hour earlier.

A man had done this to her. And not any man – not a stranger, not someone who preyed upon her and then disappeared. No, it was the very man she had fancied herself in love with, and a gentleman to boot, who was supposed to abide by a code of honour and respect.

John Barrington was the brother of the lady she had been employed to wait on, and after some months of being in his company, he became her chief source of happiness. He flattered her, listened to her, made her think she was worth spending time with, even though most of their times together had been in the presence of his sister. He was charming and quick-witted, and he challenged her. He made her hope that someone of his rank could be interested in a lowly orphan like her.

Clearly, she had been mistaken. He had only been toying with her. Once he'd had his fun, he never spoke to her again. His disdain and avoidance were all the more apparent because they lived under the same roof. She had thought that after he found out she was with child, he would offer some measure of assistance, or show some remorse or empathy. But there was none. She could not have had a more brutal lesson in the true nature of men.

Something cracked. Amy whirled around, bracing to defend herself and Benjamin. There was no one there. She let out a breath, close to tears. The paranoia was exhausting.

She hurried on with new determination. One thing was for certain: she would never, ever again trust any man.

And she was quite sure that no one would ever want her anyway. She was ashamed of the recent changes in her body – she had already lost the sparkle of youth. She was a mother now; she would never be a maiden again.

Regardless, she had to keep her guard up to protect herself. Now men would see her only as an easy target. She would never let herself be vulnerable, never let anyone get close to her.

By the time she reached Briarwood she was nearly running. But she could not run from her fears.

એજ૰૭

Henry watched Amy stride off down the lane with a heavy heart. If anything happened to her, he'd never forgive himself.

Guilt weighed heavily on him for failing to intervene between her and Barrington. He should have warned her, but he'd had no idea what was really going on. She and Barrington had never been together publicly; Henry got only an inkling of her feelings when he saw her staring at the man one day after church. It hadn't occurred to him that the rat would take advantage of her, but now he blamed himself for not seeing the danger that had lain in front of her.

After learning what had happened, Henry had burned with a need to take revenge on Barrington, but he couldn't think of a single thing he could do which wouldn't put a target on his back. If he offended Barrington or his family, it would be nothing at all for Lord Ashworth to evict the Russells from the farm, leaving them destitute. He couldn't risk endangering their livelihood. Generations of Russells had worked that land, and as the only son, Henry would continue that tradition. He wished he could have defended Amy's honour called the scoundrel out, as an equal. But sadly, he couldn't mete out justice himself.

What he'd really wanted to do was wallop Barrington so hard that his arrogant eyes smacked into the back of his skull. Even now his fist tightened at the thought of some kind of pain being felt by a man who seemed oblivious to the pain he had caused the woman Henry held most dear.

He could not fail her again. He certainly couldn't watch over her all the time, but when he could protect her, he would.

He waited around the corner of the barn until she was out of sight and then sprinted down the lane after her, ducking behind the stand of dense trees which ran along the road. He caught sight of her between the branches, a little ahead of him. He followed along as quietly as he could, keeping behind the trees, stopping to check on her through gaps in the foliage.

Suddenly a branch snapped under his foot, and he watched as Amy frantically scanned the road, clearly worried someone was after her.

Henry's heart thumped painfully as he hid himself behind a tree trunk, wishing her innocence hadn't been robbed and that he could soothe her wounds. If only she'd let him take her home… But he knew her independence was of great value to her, and she would resent him if he tried to impose protection on her.

Henry remembered her saying that perhaps he no longer wanted to know her. Others might have been cruel to her, and she might see herself as an outcast, but his perception of her hadn't changed – at least, not for the worst. He saw only more beauty in her strength.

He stayed alongside her until she turned into the Fortescues' lane. There was nowhere for him to remain hidden, and besides, he could see the house at the end of the straight path. He waited until she rapped on the main door and then turned back towards home.

Once at the farmhouse, he went straight through to the kitchen, where the rest of the family was assembled around the table.

When he saw Henry, his father jumped up from his chair, his thick ginger brows knotted together. "Where the bloody hell have you been? I had to dock all those lambs on my own."

Henry took a deep breath and forced himself to speak calmly. "I'm sorry, Pa, I got held up mending the fence." There was no way he was going to reveal what he'd actually been doing.

"Well, I hope you did a good job then. Got back just in time for your nuncheon, of course."

Henry declined to engage with him further, as he'd learned nothing good would come from talking back. He simply greeted his mother and two sisters, picked up a sandwich and an apple, and sat at the opposite end of the table from his father.

Clara, the elder of the girls, eyed him with a frown, and he sent her a wink. She smiled and resumed eating.

As Henry chewed on the gristly mutton filling, resentment stirred in his belly. His mind was still full of Amy, and he was yet to forgive his parents for what had happened the previous year.

When the news of Amy's pregnancy had broken, his immediate thought had been to marry her, to save her from a life of destitution and hardship. She may be reluctant to marry someone she didn't love, but given the desperation of her situation he'd hoped she would accept his assistance.

He'd made the mistake of declaring his intentions to his parents. They were vehemently opposed, proclaiming in no uncertain terms that they wouldn't accept a hussy as a daughter, or a bastard as a grandchild. They were also hoping for a dowry when Henry married, which could then be used as dowries for their daughters. As it was, they wouldn't have a penny to offer potential suitors.

His father had said that if Henry were to proceed, he would see to it that Henry would not have the lease on the farm. Henry didn't think his father as strongly opposed to Amy as his mother was, but this was just one more thing to be held over him, to make sure he knew his place.

He should have just gone and married her and let them deal with it after the fact, once he and Amy were already settled. In fact, he'd been considering eloping with her, trying to figure out how on earth he could afford to do such a thing, when the Fortescues had stepped in and saved her.

Now she was elevated higher than him, as the ward of a gentle family. She would be better off there anyway – they could give her far more than he ever could. He'd given up hope, deciding to shelve his feelings and leave her to a better life than one with him.

And now, there was still no hope of a life with her, but there was the promise of perhaps reigniting a friendship, and that chance would be enough to sustain him through his darker moments.

Chapter Three

"Where have you *been*?" Mrs Fortescue's question was a verbal assault.

Amy had hoped to enter the house quietly, but she'd been intercepted on her way to the nursery. She had only made it only two steps up the main staircase when Mrs Fortescue came rushing down, and now she towered over Amy and Benjamin with a face of thunder.

Amy grabbed onto the bannister, desperate not to wake the slumbering baby.

"I went for a walk," she said, with as much lightness as she could muster. She looked Mrs Fortescue straight in the eyes.

"A walk?" Clearly this answer would not suffice.

Mr Fortescue also came down the stairs, but at a more dignified pace than his wife. He put one arm around her and glanced at the hovering butler, who was not altogether succeeding in his attempt at a neutral expression. "Let us go into the drawing room, my dear," he said quietly. He raised his eyebrows at Amy and escorted his wife to the room.

On entering the drawing room, Amy sat opposite her guardians, but a moment later Mrs Fortescue leapt to her feet and yanked on the bell pull. Then the lady began pacing about the room, giving flight to her injuries.

"Agnes was frantic when she discovered Benjamin was missing. We turned the house and grounds upside down looking for you both."

"I was–"

"And then we searched in the village, the church, asked at the Brooks', even enquired at the Hall, and no one, *no one* had any idea as to your whereabouts."

"I am–"

"What choice did we have but to return and wait for you, sick with worry. Only think about what could have happened to you?"

Amy took another breath but then kept her mouth closed. Once more she was confronted with the threat of being violated a second time. It was too dreadful to think she could be targeted again, when she had always felt so safe in Amberley. The source of her past danger was in a different county, as John Barrington had been sent away by his family. Still, Henry Russell's words echoed in her ears, and the fear which had plagued her short journey home was all too present.

Mrs Fortescue's words had lost their ferocity towards the end, and she now stood in front of Amy, shaking her head sadly.

"I am sorry to have caused you trouble," Amy said. "I'm not used to having to report on my whereabouts." She stood as well. "You must understand, ma'am, that I only wanted to be free of the house for a while, and to enjoy the feeling of being a mother to my son."

Agnes entered the room and came over to her mistress, bobbing a curtsey.

Mrs Fortescue pointed at Benjamin. "Hand him over at once."

Amy raised her chin and placed her arm across the baby. "I will not."

Her sharp tone caused Benjamin to stir. He opened his eyes and began to cry softly.

"He must need his napkin changed." Mrs Fortescue's eyes flashed with a challenge.

The air left Amy's lungs. In her haste and then distraction, she had indeed forgotten to check Benjamin's napkin. She bounced him in an attempt to settle him, but his cries grew louder. She would have checked him if she'd been able to go straight to the nursery, of course, but now she was here in the middle of yet another argument. She also knew there was more to be said.

She unwrapped Benjamin from the sling and gave him a kiss before placing him in Agnes's arms. "I'll be in to feed him shortly," she told the nurse.

Agnes took the sobbing infant from the room, leaving Amy bereft. She turned back to the others to find Mrs Fortescue seated and her husband pouring glasses of claret.

She resumed her seat as well. "You must have known it was I who had taken him, when you realised I was also gone. I am his mother. I can take care of him."

"We are responsible for you both," Mrs Fortescue said. "It would have been our fault if something had happened to either of you." She accepted a glass from Mr Fortescue as he sat down, and took a tiny sip.

Amy frowned. "I don't know why you feel such a responsibility. I understand you have a strong sense of charity..."

Mr Fortescue interjected. "We do care for you both."

Amy let out a breath, unsure how to navigate these waters. She had lived with these people for five months now, and the conflict between them was getting worse, not better. Now she had dared show a small measure of independence, and it had turned the place into an uproar. She could understand they had been worried, but if she had told someone she was taking Benjamin out, they would have tried to stop her. What kind of existence was this... a home, or a prison? She was suddenly very, very tired.

"This arrangement is not working," she said. "I shall leave."

Mrs Fortescue nearly dropped her glass, and bright red liquid splashed onto her gown. She hastily swallowed her mouthful. "And where will you go?"

Amy resented the reminder that she was in a desperate situation, and that nobody wanted her. She was sure the woman loved to rub her nose in it, probably to remind her of her sins. "I'm sure Cecilia will help me."

Mrs Fortescue shook her head. "You know perfectly well the vicar cannot be seen housing an unwed mother and her babe. He was in enough strife last year as it was. It would be cruel to ask them."

Amy sighed. She knew Mrs Fortescue was right. Mr Brook had been embroiled in such a scandal it had almost compromised his position and his ability to marry Cecilia. Even though she was sure they would not deny her solace, it was not fair to ask it of them.

"I'm sure you will soon tire of housing us," Amy said, annoyed at the tremor in her voice. "I have caused you far too much trouble."

It was Mrs Fortescue's turn to sigh. "Don't be ridiculous, child."

Amy scowled. *I am not your child.* "Surely we cannot keep up a charade of domesticity forever."

There was a silence, during which Mrs Fortescue appeared to contemplate the contents of her glass. "Are you really so miserable here?" she asked, not looking up. "Are we truly so horrible?"

Something about the lady's countenance moved Amy to compassion. "No, indeed. I am much obliged for all you have done for me. I only wish not to burden you any longer."

Mr Fortescue cleared his throat. "We would be uneasy if we knew you were at the mercy of the world," he said, in his quiet, measured way. "It is better for you to be safe, here."

There was really no alternative in any case. Finding a situation while mothering an infant was nigh on impossible, and she had no funds to travel. "I will try to be more considerate in future," she said.

"That is all we ask," Mr Fortescue said.

Amy began to get up, but Mrs Fortescue spoke again. "Will you at least let me help you in learning the ways of being a lady?"

Amy's eyes narrowed. "What do you mean?"

"Well…" She put her glass down on a side table. "You may like to learn how to paint miniatures, or play the piano. You know how to sew, but a lady can embroider beautiful patterns. You can practise your penmanship and learn how to craft letters properly. Perhaps, when Benjamin is more settled, you can help me manage the household."

"And how will these things serve to make me a better mother?"

Mrs Fortescue sighed. "They will help to keep your hands occupied during the afternoon hours and keep you out of trouble. They will also make you more attractive as a wife."

"Ha!" Amy fairly shouted. "So you wish to tame me, so I cannot get into any mischief. This is your low opinion of me, that I am a rebellious hellion who needs to be occupied."

Mrs Fortescue began to speak, but Amy spoke over her.

"As for being attractive to men – that is of no consequence to me whatsoever. I understand you may wish to be rid of me as soon as you can, but I do not wish you to have false hopes about marrying me off. Not only do I never wish to have any kind of relationship with a man again, there is no one who would take on a woman with someone else's child. And I won't give Benjamin up, not for anyone."

Mrs Fortescue held up a hand. "Now, Amelia…"

"It is the truth," Amy continued, on the edge of emotion. "You should not waste your time trying to make me into something I am not. I am a farmer's daughter; I am a servant. I will never be a lady."

Mrs Fortescue looked down at her lap for several moments, her hands clasped tightly together. When she raised her face, her eyes were shining. "I only wish to help you, my dear," she said. "Will you not see that I am suggesting these things out of… concern for you?"

The lady's sudden softness threw Amy off, and she knew not how to respond. Amy exhaled, disarmed. "Believe me, I am sensible of what you have done that others would not," she said. "I am still none the wiser as to why you would make such a sacrifice. I don't mean to be difficult. I only wish for us to exist together in peace."

Mrs Fortescue pinched the bridge of her nose and then shook her head. For the first time, Amy saw her not as her governor but as a woman trying to do the best thing she knew how. "I want us to more than exist, Amelia," she said finally. "Is it too much to ask that we could live together as a sort of… family?"

This was too much for Amy. She couldn't even imagine how that could be, given how different they were. "I don't know what is possible," she said, "or how long I will remain here." She paused. "There is one thing that would help me feel more… at home."

"What is it?"

"My name is Amy. Not Amelia."

Mrs Fortescue's face fell. "Oh, I thought you were christened Amelia," she said, an odd tone in her voice. "It is a lovely name."

"That may be," Amy said firmly, "but my parents always called me Amy, so that is my name. Please use it."

Mrs Fortescue exchanged a glance with her husband and then nodded. "As you wish."

❧❦

Henry and his father were on opposite sides of the cattle herd, directing them into an adjoining field. Mr Russell was heavy-handed with the beasts, slapping them with his cane and shouting.

Henry could feel their discomfort; he'd felt it often enough himself at the hands of his father. A man used to getting his own way, his Pa was not one to be contradicted. And when he'd had a few at the pub, he was wont to imagine contradictions, and dish out retribution with his fists.

Henry preferred to gently nudge the cattle, gaining their cooperation through trust and compassion. But he knew his father's blood ran in his veins, sometimes hotter and faster than he would like. Despite that, and perhaps in spite of it, he'd made himself a promise many years ago that he would never abuse his own son the way his father had him.

It got worse when Henry matured and began to form his own opinions on how things should be done on the farm. Even on the occasions Mr Russell was not physically violent, he would belittle Henry in front of the rest of the family.

The ironic thing was that Mr Russell was usually kind to the general populace. He saved all his venom for his son. Shouldn't he have been the most benevolent with his firstborn?

There were times when Henry had been tempted to fight back – to actually hit his father – but he'd never had the gumption to do it. Several times his father had goaded him, daring Henry to strike him, but that was a line Henry wouldn't cross. He didn't have it in him to abuse his own sire in that way, but that didn't mean he didn't fight back verbally when provoked. It also didn't mean he had such scruples with his peers.

Damn and blast! Before he knew what had happened, Henry had slipped in some mud (at least he hoped it was mud) and fallen on his backside.

Laughter echoed from the other side of the field. "Wool-gathering, was ye? Get back up before the cows trample you!"

Pushing himself up from the ground, Henry muttered, "I'm all right, thanks for asking."

He nudged the remaining cows into the neighbouring paddock and then closed and secured the gate. As he brushed the dirt from his breeches, a pleasant memory filled his mind.

He was twelve years old and teasing one Amy Miller because her big toe was poking out of her worn boots. She was seven, and already an independent little miss with a short fuse. She took exception to his gentle ribbing and shoved him with all her might. He'd toppled backwards into mud as he had just now, and once the shock had worn off he'd burst out laughing. Her giggles rippled through the air as she came to stand over him, offering both her hands to help him up. He still remembered the simple joy of that moment.

A smile played around his mouth as he jumped up onto the cart next to his father. Mr Russell snapped the reins and the cart lurched into motion.

Henry was so wrapped up in his thoughts, he didn't notice at first that his father was taking a different route. The jolt of the cart stopping pulled him back to reality, and he squinted at unfamiliar surroundings. They had pulled up in front of a small cottage. "Where are we?"

Mr Russell grunted. "Took you long enough. In a world of your own." He gestured around them. "We're in the middle of a smallholding here, about ten acres."

Henry took in the surrounding paddocks. "Aye, it's Ashworth's land. Aren't we trespassing?"

Mr Russell jumped down from the cart and motioned for Henry to do the same. "Until yesterday, we would've been. But I've signed an agreement with Ashworth to take up the lease of these lands to extend our farm."

Joining his father in walking towards the cottage, Henry raised an eyebrow. "Have you, now?"

His father nodded. "And along with these lands comes this place, the croft house." He jerked his thumb at the little building then fished in his pocket.

Henry examined the cottage more closely as his father jiggled a key in the lock on the front door. The two-storeyed house was built of red brick, with a steep sloping roof. It was pleasingly symmetrical, with a window on either side of the front door and three windows above. All five were covered with wooden boards.

It took more than a little shoving to get the front door open. As he followed his father inside, Henry said, "Looks like it's been empty for a while?"

"Aye," said Mr Russell, "nigh on twenty years I think."

Stairs went up to the second storey, with a door on either side of

Chapter Four

The tea-cup clattered down onto the saucer, tea slopping over the rim. Cecilia Brook's eyes were as round as the saucer. "You did what?" she sputtered.

Amy shrugged with an impish smile. "I stole Benjamin away. I had to get out of that house."

"Goodness me." Cecilia set her cup and saucer down on a low table and gave her friend's hand a sympathetic squeeze. They were settled together on the couch in the parlour at the vicarage. "How did Mrs Fortescue react?"

A laugh escaped from Amy's lips. "As you might imagine she would. I was left in no doubt of her displeasure."

"Yes, from what I've seen she is not one to hide her opinions. She has a good heart, though."

"Dear Cici, you can always see the best in everyone. You are well suited to your role as a vicar's wife."

Cecilia frowned. "Are they unkind to you?"

Amy considered this, and then shook her head. "I believe their strictness is kindly meant. It is just that I am so unused to this sort of life." She glanced out the window at the waiting carriage. "I feel terrible making the coachman and footman wait for me, but Mrs Fortescue did insist I travel escorted, as a lady would."

"Do not worry yourself, dearest," Cecilia said, with a reassuring smile.

"If they were not here waiting on you, *they* would be stuck at the house, would they not?"

Amy smiled back. "I suppose so."

Cecilia picked up her teacup again and took a sip. "Tell me what you did after you left the house with Benjamin. Where did you go?"

Amy's breath quickened at the memory of her escape. "I went around the back garden and through the wood, then once I came to open fields I began to tire. I stopped under a tree to rest and feed the baby."

Cecilia nodded. "And then what happened?"

"Oh, I was chanced upon by Henry Russell. As it turned out, I was on their farm."

"Henry Russell?" Cecilia's eyes danced. "I daresay you failed to mention *that* to Mrs Fortescue!"

Amy chuckled. "Indeed! All alone with a gentleman unescorted…"

"If it were any other man, she would be right to be worried."

"Aye, and I wouldn't want to be alone with any other man, either, thank you very much."

Amy shivered. "But there is no harm to come from Henry. I know him as well as if he were my own brother."

Cecilia smiled. "Yes, and he is now such a friend to William I cannot help but think kindly of him. I have wondered about him on occasion though – I know he wanted William's living. He stands to inherit the lease on the farm, does he not? Why would he seek an alternative means of employment?"

Amy considered how much to reveal. She had been privy to certain events in Henry's past which he might not want made public and which could explain why he would want to abandon what he was due to inherit. She decided to err on the side of caution. The man had his pride and deserved to save face. "Perhaps he feels he wants to make more use of his mental powers," she said, "or to strike out on his own rather than do what his family has always done."

Cecilia nodded, accepting this. Finishing her tea and setting her cup and saucer aside, she turned to face Amy more squarely. "Now, dearest," she began, "I have something of great import – and sensitivity – to tell you."

"Oh yes?" Amy's heart began to pound. Had Cecilia decided she no

But she smiled, her eyes sparkling. "I shall keep that in mind."

He gave a start, realising he hadn't enquired about the subject that would matter to her the most. "Uh, forgive me... is your baby well?"

"Oh yes." Amy's face became radiant as she looked down at the little bundle. "He is... an angel."

When she looked up, Henry drank in the warmth of her glowing eyes. For a moment, he fancied there was a connection between them.

Mrs Fortescue came back to claim her companion, and the spell was broken. "Come now, Amelia, we should be going."

Amy directed a long-suffering look at Henry, and he cleared his throat to restrain a laugh. "Yes, ma'am," she said.

"It was..." Henry began, but they were already gone. *It was lovely to see you. Love.*

He turned to the window and watched them walk down the street. Though Mrs Fortescue was quite portly compared to Amy, their proportions were otherwise very similar. Amy had always been so much taller and more strong-boned than her parents. There were so many likenesses between these two women, so many that they pointed to only one conclusion... He pushed his hands into his hair and let out a long, slow breath.

Amy must be Mrs Fortescue's daughter. He thought of Mr Fortescue. The gentleman was of small stature and had blonde hair and rounded features. There was nothing about Amy that was remotely like him.

That would explain a few things.

Henry left the shop and walked away in the direction opposite the ladies, even though this also took him further from his farm. His mind was spinning. Amy didn't know. Surely she would have said something if she did? Her interactions with her guardian would have been different had she an awareness of the true nature of their relationship.

Should he tell her? His assumption might not even be true. What effect would the knowledge have on her, when she'd already been through so much?

Surely now that the women were being seen in public together, he wouldn't be the only one to draw this conclusion. It must be only a matter of time before rumours would begin to fly. And would it not be kinder for her to find out from someone who cared about her?

His dream came back to him, so clear in his mind. Amy and her son, settled with him in his cottage.

As fanciful as it may have been, it now seemed even further beyond his grasp. Mrs Fortescue was more than just her guardian in name… and she would never accept someone of his station to provide for her daughter. Didn't Amy say the Fortescues wanted her to act as a lady? He was by no means a gentleman, and never would be.

Suddenly the barriers in the way of his marital happiness seemed very large indeed. Did he have any chance at all?

"I see. Well, perhaps we might give you lessons, then. In the meantime, I cannot see that you can walk all the way to the Russells' farm. You will be driven in the barouche." Mrs Fortescue folded her arms across her chest.

Amy matched the posture. "Fine, but I will have the driver set me down at the roadside by the turning so I may walk down to the farm from there." She couldn't bear the thought of all the farmworkers watching her arrive in a fancy vehicle. She wanted to appear as their equal.

Mrs Fortescue shook her head in exasperated surrender. "As you wish. I shall have him return for you later in the afternoon."

"Thank you, ma'am." Amy walked towards the door. "I shall check on Benjamin now."

"One more thing," Mrs Fortescue said sharply, causing Amy to turn on her heel.

"What is it?" *Please not a lecture about the tea service.*

"I would prefer it if you ceased referring to me as 'ma'am', as if I were your employer, or the queen."

"Oh." This flummoxed Amy. She had thought her deference would be appreciated. "But what should I call you? Mrs Fortescue?"

The lady appeared to be considering something else, but then she nodded. "For now. Perhaps in time you may use my Christian name."

Amy doubted that would ever happen. "Yes, ma – yes, Mrs Fortescue."

⤶⤷

At church that Sunday, Henry strained his neck to catch sight of Amy and Mrs Fortescue, who were several pews in front of him. His newfound knowledge weighed heavy on his heart, and the ever-perceptive vicar, his friend William Brook, must have seen signs of his dilemma.

As they shook hands at the rear of the church after the service, William said quietly, "How do you do… is everything all right?"

Henry smiled at him sheepishly. "I suppose so."

"It is far too long since we talked properly, Henry," William said, dropping his hand and speaking loudly enough that Henry's parents could hear. He exchanged a glance with his wife. "How would you like to come to the vicarage for lunch?"

Henry looked to his father, who gave him a dismissive shrug. Mr Russell would find luncheon with the vicar a torment. "Thank you, I will," Henry said to William.

He waited outside while the other parishioners exited the building. When the Fortescues came into view with Amy, he held his breath. He had no reason to approach her.

However, when Amy saw him, she spoke briefly with her guardians and then came directly to him. He began breathing rapidly.

"Henry, I have some news!"

The Fortescues caught up to her and traded hellos with Henry. He bowed awkwardly, and Amy bounced a half-hearted curtsey after receiving an elbow from Mrs Fortescue.

"What is your news, Miss Miller?" Henry asked Amy. They smiled at each other, and he hoped she was also thinking it was amusing to be so formal when they knew each other so well.

"I'm going to help your family with cutting the hay," she fairly squealed, a grin lighting up her features.

"You're what?" Henry gaped at her.

"Miss Miller has expressed an interest in assisting with the works on your farm, Mr Russell," said Mrs Fortescue. "We will allow her to do this, so long as she will be well looked after. Is that clear?"

Henry looked at the older woman in amazement, then closed his open mouth and swallowed. "Yes, Mrs Fortescue, she will be safe – my mother and sisters will see to that." He turned to Amy. "Do you really want to spend a whole day working on the farm?" It was too good to be true.

She nodded. "Several days, if I am needed. I'm eager to help if I can."

"Well," Henry said, a smile spreading across his face. "You'll be most welcome. We start an hour after dawn tomorrow."

"I shall be there." She locked eyes with him, and he got a sense of how earnest she was, of how she longed for something. Whatever it was, he hoped he could provide it for her.

Before Henry could think of what to say next, Mr Fortescue bade him goodbye and the ladies accompanied him to their waiting carriage. "Oh, goodbye!" he called after them.

Henry could barely touch the delicious lunch Cecilia Brook and her

Chapter Six

Once again, Amy woke with screams echoing in her ears. But this time, the screams were her own.

It wasn't the usual dream in which she relived her violation. In this one, John Barrington ripped Benjamin from her arms, swept him up onto his horse and galloped off with him.

"Amelia, wake up!" She was suddenly aware of being shaken, and of Mrs Fortescue's voice.

Her eyes flew open. The dream was too horrible, and far too real for her battered feelings to bear.

"Whatever is the matter?" Mrs Fortescue asked softly, concern visible in her eyes even in the darkness. The sight of the woman standing over her in her night-rail and hair curlers was at first a shock but then surprisingly comforting.

Amy pushed herself up to a sitting position, her arms shaking. "It was him," she sputtered through trembling lips. "He took Ben from me."

Mrs Fortescue nodded and reached out to take Amy's hand. "It was not real," she said. "You are both safe here."

The expression of sympathy pushed Amy's emotions over the edge, and she began to cry.

Mrs Fortescue came closer and began to reach out with her other arm, but Amy pushed the covers aside and swung her feet to the floor.

"I must go to him. I need to check he is well." She moved past Mrs

Fortescue to the open door and stumbled down the hall to the nursery.

Benjamin was there, sleeping peacefully, one tiny arm thrown across his forehead. Amy exhaled as her heartbeat began to slow.

"My precious little one," she whispered, lightly stroking his stomach. "I'll keep you safe with me."

She picked him up and padded back to her room. Mrs Fortescue was gone. She got back into bed and propped herself up with pillows so she could gaze down at her baby as he slept. They stayed this way for the remaining hours of the night, Amy letting Benjamin feed when he stirred.

❧❦

Several hours later, the pungent, earthy aroma of hay filled Amy's nostrils. It was a smell that took her instantly back to her childhood, when she would help her mother gather up the hay and bind it together. Fellow farmers would help, indeed Henry and the other Russells frequently assisted them, and they would help others in turn. There was something wholesome and comforting about doing work on the land, toiling with others to ensure the animals would have enough to eat during the winter. It was gruelling work but satisfying all the same.

She worked in a line of women and children, behind the men who were cutting the hay. She bent to gather stalks into her basket and then transferred them to huge piles at one end of the field.

She'd arrived at the farm just in time to join several other workers on the cart, to be transported to the field. The Russell family were already there working, and it was only after she started gathering that she ran into Henry's mother.

"Miss Miller," Mrs Russell acknowledged her briefly, and then turned her back and resumed working.

The cold civility cut through Amy. She was the target of spite and even hostility from many of the villagers, but she had been on friendly terms with all the Russells throughout her life. Did they hate her now because she had been gullible and trusting?

She went back to work, disconcerted. She had hoped to feel a level of acceptance amongst those she considered to be her own kind. Did she not even belong here anymore? Where on earth *did* she belong?

She glanced up as she put more hay in her basket and caught sight of Henry. He was one of the men moving through the fields, reaping the hay with a scythe. Amy remembered when he had first been entrusted with wielding this tool as a teenager. He had been apprehensive at best, dangerous at worst! Now, he handled it with confidence and ease, sweeping through the dry grass with long, bold strokes.

Impressed, she smiled to herself and bent down again. They had both grown up, but he'd had a specific role to grow into, and it appeared he was doing a fine job. It must be so heartening to have a clear destiny, a straightforward path in life, to be able to achieve things and look to a secure future. *Dear me*, she thought. *Am I jealous of Henry Russell now as well?*

Around noon, they paused to rest for a half hour and ale and pies were produced. Amy found herself sitting next to Clara Russell, who, at seventeen, was the eldest of the two Russell daughters. They exchanged polite smiles and then Amy tucked into her pie hungrily.

"We were surprised you offered to help with the haymaking, Miss Amy," Clara said between mouthfuls.

Amy nearly choked. She cleared her throat. "Is that so, Clara? Why would that be?" They had spent many an afternoon working together in the past.

"Well, it's been a couple of years since you've done any kind of real labour. I suppose we all assumed you would think yourself above this kind of thing now."

Amy stiffened. "That's your assumption, not mine." She resented the notion that her job as a lady's maid wasn't real labour.

"They're not making you go out and work, are they?" Clara asked, wide-eyed. "The Fortescues, I mean."

Amy laughed. "Of course not. They're scandalised by the very idea!"

Clara sniggered and drank a mouthful of ale. "Well, I hope to be above all this one day soon."

Amy paused with her pie in mid-transit. "What do you mean, Clara?"

Clara studied Amy for a moment then leaned forward and took a breath.

"How are we getting on, ladies?" Henry sat down in the space between them and smiled at each in turn.

"Really, Henry." Clara directed an exasperated look at Amy.

"Oh, am I interrupting something?" Henry asked, his brows raised.

❧

"Never you mind!" Clara got up, brushed flakes of pastry from her apron and flounced over to her younger sister.

Henry laughed. "She's a mystery!" he said to Amy, then muttered, "Along with most of female-kind." He glanced at her, a little coy. The exertion of her work had brought a glow to her cheeks and a spark to her eyes. Her hair had fallen out of the fancy style she had worn at first, and though she'd retied it in a low bun, much of it wafted about her face charmingly. To him, she appeared far more beautiful now than when she'd arrived this morning looking polished and groomed.

Amy shook her head. "It seems I am destined to never understand men, so you're in good company." She took a bite of her pie and chewed glumly, and Henry cursed himself. He'd made her think of *him*.

He cleared his throat. "Will you stay for the afternoon?"

She nodded. "Yes, if I am welcome."

"Of course!" *You can stay forever if you wish.* "We do so appreciate the help. But you must be missing the babe?"

Her eyes flew to his with a flare of emotion. "Yes. But it's good to feel useful again."

"Useful?" he asked, incredulous. "I can't think of a more noble occupation than being a mother."

She smiled at him. "Thank you. It is certainly more all-consuming than I could have imagined. But I'm lucky, I suppose, to have the help the Fortescues have arranged for me."

It was help he couldn't have offered. "Yes, that is fortunate," he said lamely.

She finished her pie and took a sip of ale, her eyes sweeping over the fields. "I'm enjoying working outside on the land again, being part of the process of making food and the cycles of life. It reminds me of… happier days." She continued to stare into the distance.

Henry sighed with relief. Watching her work all morning, he'd wondered if Amy had remembered how tiring physical labour was, and if she regretted her decision to work on the farm. It did his heart no end of

52

good to know she wanted to be here.

He looked at her resolutely. "I'm sure you will be happy again." She met his eyes, and he didn't look away, hoping to communicate to her that he would do whatever he could to ensure her happiness. More than anything, he craved her trust.

She took a deep breath, and said finally, "I hope you are right."

ন্দ্ৰ০০্জ

Amy returned home from her day on the farm exhausted but contented.

Mrs Fortescue came into the vestibule and began to greet her, then recoiled. She steadied herself. "Hello, Amy. How was your day?"

Amy removed her wrap and handed it to the footman, who took it from her as if it were poisoned. "It was wonderful, thank you. How was yours?"

Mrs Fortescue blinked, and her mouth quirked. "Perhaps not as wonderful as yours."

Amy barely heard her. "I'll go up to see Benjamin now," she called, already heading to the staircase.

She entered the nursery, and Agnes gasped then put a finger to her lips.

"He's sleeping. And if you don't mind me saying so, miss, you may want to wash up before you see him next?"

Amy stared at her. Wasn't that a bit presumptuous? She went to the cradle and leaned over to see Benjamin's peaceful little face. She watched his chest rise and fall, and something good and right settled within her. He was well. She should change her clothes for dinner.

"See you soon, little one," she whispered. Then she went to her own room and sat down before the mirror.

She immediately burst out laughing on seeing her reflection. What a state she was in. Her hair was mostly loose around her shoulders, and there were streaks of dirt across her face, no doubt from her hands, which were several shades darker than usual. Her apron and dress were a shambles. No wonder Mrs Fortescue had seemed so appalled.

She remembered the friendly affection with which Henry had regarded her, even when she must have looked like a vagrant. The knowledge that he didn't care about her appearance was a kind of reassurance.

She rang the bell, and a few minutes later Jenny came in. "Evenin', miss. Shall I... oh." She observed Amy's face and hands. "You'll be needin' some hot water, miss."

"Yes, please." Amy unfastened what was left of the bun in her hair and shrugged out of her apron.

Jenny returned with a steaming bowl and helped Amy undress and wash. She sighed and harrumphed as if Amy had gotten herself into this state for the sole purpose of making her life difficult.

Amy continued to help at the farm for the rest of the week, feeling more like herself again with each passing day. On the Friday, the men finished cutting the grass. It was now only a matter of taking all the dried hay back to the barn.

Amy stretched her arms behind her back as she stood amongst piles of hay in the last field to be worked on. Her back had been increasingly sore since she gave birth to Benjamin, and several days of bending and straightening had taken a toll.

She gathered as much hay as she could carry and began to walk towards the cart at the bottom of the field. A few steps in, she regretted picking up so much but continued on doggedly, wanting to show those Russell women she was made of sterner stuff.

"Here, let me help you with that." Henry Russell gathered up most of her hay as if it weighed nothing at all and fell into step beside her.

"Thank you." Amy smiled at him.

He gave her a shy half-smile in response, which warmed her heart. He was so unlike the self-assured aristocrats and gentlemen she had lately been in company with. He had so many worthy attributes, yet he retained modesty and generosity. While the men she had known in the higher orders always had something to recommend them, most seemed to think it necessary to lord their position over others, to always appear confident even when they likely didn't know any better than anyone else.

There was also something in Henry's coy gaze that made her heart beat just a little faster. They had shared several conversations during the past week, and she was on such easy terms with him as to feel quite herself, and quite relaxed.

"Will you ride with me in the cart back to the barn? I can take you home once we unload this heap. We'll be finished a few hours before your carriage is due to arrive."

How did he know about the carriage? Her careful subterfuge hadn't fooled him.

She wondered about the propriety of riding alone with him in public, but she would prefer risking her reputation to walking alone on her aching feet. "That would be very much appreciated. Thank you, Henry."

Chapter Seven

Henry dropped the hay into the cart then jumped up onto the vehicle, pushing the stalks forward so he and Amy would have room to sit on the end. His father hitched the horse to the cart and then waited for everyone to finish putting the last of the hay into it.

As Henry sat down on the back of the cart, Amy pushed herself up onto it and smiled at him, heaving a tired sigh. She had proven herself to be a hard worker, and he was both proud of her and worried that she'd overdone it.

He gasped. "Your hands, Amy!"

She turned her palms up and examined them before throwing them behind her back. They were red, bruised and blistered. "It's nothing," she said. "It's just that I'm no longer used to farm work."

"I hope they heal up quickly," he said. "You're very brave, but I think you should stop handling hay from now on."

"If you insist, doctor," she said, a teasing smile playing on her lips.

As the cart sprang into motion, Henry marvelled at the change in her. She had a carefree kind of lightness about her and seemed to no longer be bearing the weight she'd carried for nearly a year. He hadn't seen her like this since before she went to work at the big house.

He longed to scoop her up into his arms and share the lightness in his own heart.

The companionable silence of the ride was broken only by the singing of Mr Russell, whose inability to stay in tune produced some chuckles from the pair.

Henry was inwardly bubbling with anticipation at the idea of spending some time with her as he took her home, completely alone. But first there was a job to be done, and it was more challenging than shifting hay.

The possibility of Mrs Fortescue being Amy's mother weighed heavily on Henry's heart. He felt as if he was keeping something from her, and he wanted to always be truthful with her, to show her some men could be trusted. But how to begin? He must somehow find out if it was true, or if she suspected it herself.

They both jumped down from the cart, and Henry let his father know he'd be using it to take Amy home. Mr Russell agreed, reluctantly, on the condition that Henry unload all the hay himself.

Henry picked up several tools from the cart and nodded at Amy to indicate she should walk with him into the barn.

He cleared his throat. "How are you getting on with the Fortescues?" he asked, hoping he sounded nonchalant.

Amy wrinkled her nose. "It's... different," she said slowly. "I am not used to, well, so many things. I am not used to being waited on or having my own fine things. It embarrasses me. I know the servants think ill of me. Mrs Fortescue insists I am to learn to be a lady, and..."

"Yes?" He smiled and gestured she should enter the barn before him. He joined her inside. A farmhand was mucking out one of the animal pens in the far corner. Henry placed the tools on their designated hooks on the wall and turned to her expectantly.

"Well," she said, "let's just say their way of life doesn't come naturally to me. I am used to routines in life – first on the farm, and then with my duties as lady's maid. I cannot fathom spending my time on... on *hobbies*. Thank goodness I have little Ben to focus my attentions on. And even *that* has been a struggle with them."

He frowned. "Still? What is it they won't let you do?"

She stepped closer and looked straight into his eyes, her own on fire with emotion. "They want me to leave him in the care of nursemaids all the time," she said, with quiet intensity. "I'm not supposed to be feeding him, or bathing him, or attending to any of his basic needs. As if he doesn't belong to me!" Her passion was endearing, captivating. Like that of the Amy of old.

He had wondered if she would want to have some distance from the child, given what had happened with its father. But she was clearly as protective and loving as any mother would be.

"Have you stood your ground?" he asked.

She gave a wry smile. "Of course."

He laughed softly. That was definitely his Amy, not afraid to stand up for herself or those she loved.

He had to somehow lead the conversation to the question. "It was kind of them, wasn't it, to take you in?"

Amy's face clouded over and her eyes narrowed. "Yes, it was. Do you also think they are mad to be taking on a fallen woman?"

"What? No, of course I don't think that!" This wasn't going at all well. He had to turn this around, fast. "What I mean is, I wonder why they've chosen to help in this way. Have they mentioned having ties with your parents?"

Amy shook her head. "No, nothing of that sort. I only know Mrs Fortescue is friends with Lady Ashworth, so perhaps she persuaded her it was the right thing to do."

If Amy knew the secret, she wasn't going to tell him. Perhaps he should hint at something that might make her think along those lines. But then he looked at her face again and thought better of it. She looked a little troubled, a little anxious. He had no idea how she might react to such a suggestion. He remembered William's warning. It was between her and the Fortescues, and it wasn't his place to meddle, or upset things.

He would have to keep his suspicion to himself and allow her to discover the truth on her own – or not at all. He wasn't going to cause trouble or, worse, give her pain. It wasn't his secret to share.

"Why do you ask?" she asked suddenly. "Do you know something about them?"

Henry panicked. "No! That is, I just wondered why they would take such a keen interest in your… learning."

Amy shrugged. "I can only surmise that they took me in as a charitable endeavour and now they are embarrassed of me. They want to make me into something I am not in order to save face."

Henry could push no more. She was becoming melancholy, and it was his fault. If she saw it on her own in the future, or, of course if she was told by the woman herself, that would be the natural way of things. But it wasn't his place to announce "it seems likely Mrs Fortescue is your mother". Whether he was wrong or right about that, he couldn't be the one responsible for hurting her if the truth wasn't welcome. He could even jeopardise Amy's place at the house if the knowledge made her confront Mrs Fortescue and cause a scene. No, it was safest for her, emotionally and physically, if he kept his mouth shut. As hard as it was to keep something from her, doing so would protect her.

"I think," he said slowly, drawing a little closer, "they must take such pleasure in your company that they have decided they would like to have you as an equal. Mrs Fortescue wants to share her ladylike activities with you and help you to feel like you belong there."

Amy considered that, then smiled at him. "You are too good. It is impossible that I should be their equal, nor do I wish to be. I would rather be with people who accept me as I am. Like you."

Those last words were light, almost thrown away, but they lifted Henry's heart so high he thought he might lift off the ground. She couldn't know the effect she had on him, or how he had longed to hear her say she belonged with him. She hadn't said that, quite, but something almost like it. And he would treasure that, as a starving animal would cherish its last meal.

☙◦❧

Amy was glad of the ride back to Briarwood. She was so weary she thought her legs might give way. Her emotions were close to the surface, threatening to brim over. Henry had touched more than one nerve with his innocent line of questioning. He was right to wonder why a respectable couple such as the Fortescues, to whom she had hardly said a word in her life, would stoop so low as to house an unwed mother when no one else wanted her. She had asked herself that question many times; it was reasonable for him to wonder too.

She wanted to believe his assertion that they intended to make her more like them so she would belong. But she couldn't bring herself to foster such a happy illusion; she was no longer an innocent young girl

59

who saw the best in people first. She knew most people were hiding something and their actions were not always good indicators of their motivations or intentions. In fact, sometimes they acted to deliberately deceive. She couldn't believe the Fortescues would intentionally hurt her, as there was undeniably an altruistic motive for most of their actions. But their efforts to remake her in the image of a lady were an affront to her very identity.

"Miss Miller?"

Amy turned to see Henry waiting for her on the cart. She laughed at him. "Come now, Henry, don't address me as if you were my chauffeur. It's only Amy, and it always has been."

She stepped towards the box and he automatically offered his hand to help her up. She stared at it, dismayed.

It was perfectly natural for him to help her up into her seat, but despite her recent familiarity with him, she still could not stand to let their hands touch. She tried to fight the irrational terror which overtook her. Nothing bad would happen. It would be over in a matter of seconds, and Henry was not going to abuse the situation, was he? But she could not bring herself to put her hand in his.

"I'm sorry," she said.

He shook his head as if to dismiss her apology. "It's nothing. Just put your foot here, and hold on here and you can pull yourself up."

She nodded, did as he instructed, and managed to hoist herself up onto the seat.

Henry took up the reins. "Are you comfortable?"

She met his eyes and nodded again, startled by how close his face was to hers. "Thank you." Her voice came out as a squeak and she immediately felt herself colouring. She focussed on the lane ahead as Henry brought the cart around and steered the mare down towards the road.

He sat as far as he could to the right of her, but the seat was not very wide, so their thighs were still only inches apart. She could see his muscles flexing within his buckskin trousers. Suddenly she was unbearably warm.

Comfortable? Perhaps *too* comfortable.

She could not resist taking sly glances at him as they bounced along towards her home. The freckles across his nose had multiplied, giving him a boyish charm. His shock of fiery hair was tossed about in unruly waves like a turbulent sea. He caught her looking at him, and threw her a bashful smile, which she couldn't help returning before forcing her eyes to her lap. She caught a whiff of his scent; he smelled of the grasses and earth and a rich, masculine aroma.

As they rounded a corner, the motion of Henry's hands guiding the reins caught Amy's attention, and she took in his strong, toned forearms. He had rolled up his sleeves above his elbows, and even beneath all that fabric his upper arms bulged. His chest strained against his waistcoat. He was a robust working man. Of course he would be… strapping. It was just that she'd never had such leisure to observe all this before. Or perhaps she had just never taken notice, never appreciated him in his masculinity. She had been a slip of a girl when she'd last spent any length of time with him, without any notions of forming attachments. Now, she was all too aware of him, and the nearness of him. She began to feel a little light-headed, and her heart seemed to be pulsing through her entire body.

She hadn't felt like this since… Her breath quickened as a painful pang hit her heart. She'd rather not remember the last time.

"Amy? Are you all right?"

Henry was looking at her seriously as he guided the cart through the gates that led to Briarwood.

She tried to slow her breathing, but the rising panic could not be quelled.

The last time she had felt this way, it had nearly destroyed her. It had made her giddy, blind, defenceless. She'd been a gullible fool, and she had paid the price for her infatuation with her innocence.

Fear closed over her heart in a vice-like grip, and she clutched the sides of the seat with white knuckles. She could not explain it to him, could not summon any words lest she begin to cry.

The cart came to a stop outside the house, and she leapt to the ground, nearly falling over.

"Amy!" Henry cried, dismounting in a flash and coming around to her side. "What on earth is the matter?"

She darted away from him, wishing she hadn't let her fancies get the better of her, that she could go back to the simplicity of their recent friendship. Perhaps she still could if not tempted in such a way.

"Goodbye, Henry," she called, as she began walking away from him. "Thank you."

She took quick steps up to the front door and banged on it until she was granted admittance. The house felt like a safe place for the first time. She was in no danger of being overcome by treacherous feelings here. She went to her room and closed the door, leaning back against it. She would have no reason to see Henry again, and it was just as well. She could not risk putting her heart in danger.

❧

Henry stared at the closed door after Amy disappeared into the house. What had just happened?

A wave of queasiness passed over him, and he grabbed at the cart to steady himself. He had a horrible sense of something being pulled out of reach.

When he could see clearly again, he pulled himself back up onto the box and picked up the reins. She had seemed happy, even pleased, to be riding with him just now. What had he done wrong?

He pushed his hands through his hair, shook his head, and snapped the reins. Just before turning away, he glanced up at the house and saw movement in one of the upper windows. There was Mrs Fortescue, watching him. A chill ran down his spine.

Henry was hardly cognisant of his surroundings as he drove home, distraught. Instead of the pleasure he'd expected to be feeling after their time together, he was confused, frustrated. Why had she run from him almost as if he'd dealt her a blow?

His father berated him as soon as he got home. "Took you long enough." The man was standing in the doorway as if he'd been waiting there the whole time.

Henry took a breath as he jumped to the ground. "I came straight back, Pa," he said, then turned his back and started untying the horse, muttering under his breath, "Not now!"

Mr Russell advanced on him. "I've seen you, fawning over that Miller girl all week. You've been lazy and thoughtless. You're trying to court

62

her, aren't you, even though you know we don't want her in this family! Do you honestly expect us to accept that child as one of our own?"

"So what if I am courting her?" Henry didn't stay for the answer. He marched to the stable with the horse, bringing the animal around in such a way that Mr Russell had to jump out of its path. His father didn't follow him, which was just as well. With his feelings in such turmoil, Henry might do something he would later regret.

When Henry was finally in bed for the night, his mind immediately returned to Amy. He thought they had come so far this week, that she might have come to trust him a little, and perhaps come to value his friendship. Even as they rode together, he thought he'd sensed a new level of closeness between them. How wrong he had been. Whatever he thought had been there had shattered at some point before they reached their destination. Her eyes had become veiled, her shoulders had stiffened, and she had turned away from him.

He tossed in his bed. His first instinct was to seek her out, even visit her at home. He must know what he'd done to offend, and beg her forgiveness.

He turned the other way. She might see such bold behaviour as an attack, and it might make her withdraw even further. No, he needed to remain gentle and let her come to him – always. He would have to wait until he saw her again.

He hoped he would be able to attend church this week, if all the chores were done. He would insist on going – or just leave the house undetected. Would she think him too forward if he happened upon her in the churchyard after the service?

He beat his pillow furiously. How had a woman turned him into such an indecisive mess? She had taken over his life, again, and now his love burned with such a bright flame he was sure it would never be extinguished. He renewed his determination not to rush her or push her. He would not for one moment have her feel put upon. If she was ever to be his, and he hoped with all his might she would be, it would have to be on her terms, and her timing. Even though it might kill him in the meantime!

Chapter Eight

There was one ladies' luxury that Amy relished: sinking into a steaming bath.

She felt the now-familiar guilt as Jenny and another maid trudged up and down the stairs with pots of boiled water to pour into the bath, but she was covered in dirt from head to toe, so bathing was a necessity if she was to present herself for dinner with the Fortescues.

Jenny picked up a cloth and dipped it in the water. "Will you have your back washed first, miss?"

Amy was still deeply embarrassed to have someone wait upon her when she was naked. With one hand covering herself, she reached out with the other. "I'll wash myself, thank you, Jenny. You may go."

Jenny hesitated for only a moment. There were dark circles under her eyes, and her posture stooped. "Thank you, miss," she said, handing the cloth over. She must have decided it wasn't worth insisting on attending Amy when she was so tired.

When the maid was gone and she was alone, Amy lay back with a sigh. All of her aches from the physical work on the farm seemed to melt into the soothing water, and she exhaled again as her eyes fluttered closed. Henry Russell immediately occupied her mind's eye.

She cursed herself and wrenched her eyes open. Could she not think of someone else, something else – anything at all?

She reflected on the day's activity and wasn't ashamed to feel proud of her contribution, however small. She felt more herself than she had in a very long time.

Henry's kind smile came back to her; she sensed he was proud of her as well. She was confronted by the vision of his eyes only inches from hers as she sat beside him. They were somewhere between light brown and hazel, his eyes, like the colour of autumn leaves just before they fall. There was something calming and good in them, which gave her a sense of finding a safe place to rest.

Except now, other feelings were beginning to stir within her, unwelcome feelings. Excitement, admiration and anticipation threatened to derail her new, fragile sense of being. She could not be sure he also fancied her, but something in the way he had been looking at her recently made her stomach flip over. It was enough to make her want to hope... if she wasn't so terrified.

She took in a gulp of air as tears gathered in her eyes. She cursed the name of John Barrington for the hundredth time, for taking this away from her. She should be able to think about another man without fear. She should be able to indulge in feminine fantasies and allow her mind to wander. Why should she not let the butterflies in her stomach fly wild?

It was clearly too soon to be contemplating anything of the sort. She should just cut off all contact with Henry Russell, before she put her heart in more danger. The corn harvest was imminent and that would occupy him for weeks. For her part, not only did Amy have Benjamin to look after – her industrious guardian had already organised a series of lessons for her in hopes of her developing ladylike accomplishments. God help her.

She sank down further into the waters.

❧

Jenny returned later to help Amy dress for dinner. The maid clearly wanted to get things done as speedily as possible so she could get to bed. She was hurried and rough as she tightened Amy's stays and she threw the dinner gown Amy's head carelessly. When Jenny reached for the hairbrush, Amy intercepted her. She did not wish to be hammered with it.

"Is everything well, Jenny?" she asked mildly.

"Yes, of course, miss," Jenny said, reaching again for the hairbrush. "Allow me."

Amy was already pulling the brush through her hair, rapidly. "There, all done," she said. "I can manage putting it up on my own, you know. I don't wish to detain you if you've had a busy day." Besides, creating an even hairstyle was not exactly the maid's strength.

Jenny sighed and began pulling at various sections of Amy's hair. "No busier than most, miss," she muttered. "It's just that I didn't get much sleep last night, on account of Molly's snoring."

"Oh!" Amy tried to hide a giggle. "That is unfortunate." Amy had shared a bedroom all her life – first with her parents and then with another lady's maid. Sleeping on her own had taken some getting used to. The silence was unnerving at first. Now, she was reminded it was yet another blessing.

The style taking shape on her head was lopsided and messy. Jenny heaved a frustrated sigh and began undoing it.

"Will you let me show you a different style?" Amy cried desperately. "There is something I learned at the big house that I would love you to do for me."

Jenny's eyes narrowed but then she nodded wearily. "All right. If it pleases you, miss."

Amy got to work at once, pinning off some sections first and then plaiting part of each side. She pulled most of her hair into a chignon and then wrapped the remaining strands diagonally across her head, pulling the ends around the bun before tucking them in. Finally, she took the plaits and crossed them on the top of the chignon, pinning the ends underneath.

"There!" she said. "I can't see how tidy it is at the back, but that should give you the general idea."

Jenny nodded slowly. "That's very good, miss, very pretty. You must have made a fine lady's maid."

It was the first kind thing she had ever said to Amy. Praise was something she was seldom given by anyone... Certainly not the Fortescues. She smiled, her heart swelling with unfamiliar pride.

"Thank you, Jenny," she said. Then she turned around to face the maid. "You know, I'm not here to make your life more difficult. I didn't choose this situation for myself. I never had ambitions beyond my station." ·

Jenny chewed on her bottom lip. "I know that, miss. And I know even though some things are easier for you now, you have suffered for it... and I don't envy you that."

Amy stood and impulsively threw her arms around the maid. Drawing back and smiling at the sight of Jenny's shocked expression, she said, "Thank you. You may go now. I hope you sleep better tonight."

"Thank you, miss." Jenny bobbed a curtsey and left the room.

Amy picked up her shawl and glanced at her reflection one more time before heading for the door.

A quarter-hour later, she was seated at the grandiose dining table with her guardians before two huge candelabras and a wide selection of dishes. She picked up her fish knife and the sound of it hitting her plate seemed to reverberate around the room. Conversation was sparse at best.

How she craved the warmth of the family suppers she had known for most of her life, sharing the day's highs and lows in a small, loving circle. She even missed the lively banter of the servants' hall. She thought back to everyone she had known at Ashworth Hall. Likely they all hated her now.

Amy looked up to see Mrs Fortescue's eyes on her, and she smiled politely before dropping her gaze again. If she ate quickly, perhaps the following courses would be served without delay...

Mr Fortescue cleared his throat. "You have finished your, er, commission at that farm, then?"

Amy swallowed some trout. "Yes, sir, I have. The hay cutting was completed earlier this afternoon."

Mrs Fortescue frowned at her. "I saw that young Henry Russell dropped you back."

Amy nodded, waiting to hear what it was the woman disapproved of. "Aye, he did. It was very kind of him to do so."

"Good sort, is he?" Mr Fortescue asked.

Amy's brow furrowed. "What do you mean? He is a decent farmer and – and a very good friend."

The Fortescues exchanged a glance.

"You do seem to be on easy terms with each other," Mrs Fortescue said, after a moment. "I do wonder if it is *wise* for you to be travelling about the countryside with him unchaperoned."

There it was. She had known there would be some sort of consequence. "It's a short distance, as you know," she said, her tone measured. "I would not have troubled him to come and fetch the coach when he could have just taken me with him. Would you have had me walk alone instead?"

She knew she was starting to sound defensive, and she took a deep breath to calm herself.

"You know perfectly well I would rather you had not gone at all," Mrs Fortescue snapped.

Amy opened her mouth but then closed it again. There was no point in having that argument all over again. She sighed deeply and pushed her plate away. "May I be excused?"

Mrs Fortescue put her hand out on the table in a restraining gesture. "Not just yet, if you please." She turned to a footman, instructing him to clear the table and fetch the next course.

Amy sat back in her chair with her arms folded. "I am... almost completely certain that you have nothing to worry about with Henry Russell."

"I gather you enjoy his company," Mrs Fortescue replied. "I only hope he is not the kind to... abuse your trust, if given the opportunity."

Against her will, Amy's mind flooded with horrible images which were nothing to do with Henry. She squirmed with the memory of the pain.

"Forgive me," said Mrs Fortescue. "We do not mean to distress you. We only want to protect you from harm."

Amy regarded them both in turn. "I understand that. And I thank you for your concern. I certainly would not want to find myself alone with any other man, even for a short while by accident. But Henry Russell is another case altogether – I have known him since I was a little girl, and we have been in each other's company for years. I think I can trust him. He may be hot-headed at times, but he's a gentle soul. You have nothing to fear."

The couple exchanged another glance. "That is reassuring," Mrs Fortescue said. "However, it is still best to avoid being alone with him, even in public. We don't want anyone else to think something is going on."

"Oh, you don't have to worry about that!" Amy said with a laugh. "I cannot see us being together at a ball or any such thing." The very idea of being romanced by Henry Russell was absurd.

Then she blushed... inexplicably, infuriatingly. She kept her gaze on the dishes of food being placed on the table. When she met eyes with Mrs Fortescue again, the woman was observing her keenly. "Besides," she went on, stupidly, "all the other Russells hate me."

Mrs Fortescue arched an eyebrow. "Oh, do they?"

Amy nodded. "I don't think they'll ever want anything to do with me, so you don't have to worry about *them* encouraging a courtship." She shoved a potato into her mouth and glared at the gravy boat as she went redder still. *Stop talking, Amy!*

There was a silence, and then Mrs Fortescue reached for the platter of beef. "Do not forget you have your piano lesson in the morning."

Amy coughed on her potato. "Er, thank you."

❧

Henry tried to think of an excuse, any excuse, to delay his family's departure after church so he could speak to Amy. He didn't want to scare her, but he did want to try to get back to how things had been.

As the Russell family walked out to the churchyard, Henry took his mother's elbow, and said, "I think I heard Mrs Stockton saying she went to Milton this week. Did you want to find out all the news before we go?" This was a gamble, as he hadn't heard any such thing. The falsehood made him sweat; he never lied to his mother. He would be unlucky to be wrong: Mrs Stockton generally went to Milton at least once a week.

Mrs Russell's eyes lit up, and she spotted Mrs Stockton in front of them. "Why yes, Henry, I should like to hear the goings-on." She smiled at him. "Thank you, dear."

As she bustled off, Henry let out a slow breath. What kind of fool had love made him? Subterfuge of any kind was against his nature.

As his mother fell into easy conversation with her friend, the rest of the family also dispersed, and Henry turned to wait for the Fortescues to make their exit.

When they appeared with Amy, he was surprised to see her sharing a laugh with Mrs Fortescue. How could he get her away from them so he could talk to her? This would require further tactical manoeuvres on his part.

Henry approached his targets. "Good day," he said, addressing the little group. Both Fortescues greeted him with polite smiles. Amy merely glanced at him and then surveyed the ground, which only made his heart ache more. She had her baby bundled up in a sling at her chest.

An awkward silence followed. The birds chirped in the trees above and the general chatter around them increased.

Mrs Fortescue caught his eye and then looked at Amy. She looped her arm through her husband's. "Mr Fortescue, I should like to have a word with Mrs Grant."

"Of course, my dear." He gave Henry a nod and led his wife to where Cecilia's parents stood conversing with other villagers.

Henry stared at them – had Mrs Fortescue really just engineered a way for him to talk privately with Amy? Surely not.

"Will you be starting the harvest soon?" Amy asked quietly, regarding him from beneath her lashes. She cupped her hand around Benjamin's head.

His heart began to pound at the sound of her voice. "Yes," he croaked. "We'll start preparing this week if the weather is fine."

She nodded and looked over to the church, where Mr and Mrs Brook had appeared. "If you don't mind–"

He couldn't let her escape, not yet. "Your help with bringing in the hay was very welcome," he blurted. "I did enjoy being able to talk with you again, as well." He took a breath. "Things seem to be improving with the Fortescues?" He started to walk slowly through the trees which interspersed the graveyard.

She nodded again and granted him a little smile, following his footsteps. "A little. I have more freedoms where Benjamin is concerned, at least."

Henry stopped strolling and turned to regard the little bundle. All he could see was a tiny nose poking out from the sling.

"How does he get on?" he asked. He knew nothing about babies, barely remembering what it was like when his sisters were small.

70

Amy gazed at the babe, and a true smile stretched her lips. "He is wonderful," she said. A moment later, she looked back up at Henry. "Would you like to see him?"

Henry glanced back over to the group of parishioners, now a small distance away. His parents were still conversing with their friends. "Yes," he said to Amy, "if that won't disturb him."

His breath caught in his throat as she drew closer and loosened her sling so that the baby rolled away from her chest a little.

Henry saw Benjamin's little face fully for the first time, and it was perfect. Some dark downy hair poked out from his cap, and long eyelashes lay against the chubby curve of his cheeks. His chin was dimpled, and his body seemed to start straight below it.

"He is handsome," Henry whispered, and then he met Amy's eyes. This time she didn't look away, and a new and different spark seemed to pass between them.

The baby squirmed, drawing his attention again. One of Benjamin's small arms escaped as he stretched, and a huge yawn took over his face. Then he opened his eyes and looked directly at Henry.

The shock of those huge dark brown orbs staring up at him stirred up something raw and powerful within him. Before he knew what he was doing, he reached out to the little infant, offering his index finger. Benjamin immediately reached out and grabbed it, his smooth pink fingers tiny in comparison to Henry's calloused one.

The world seemed to fall away, and Henry swallowed hard against the rising tide of emotion. Benjamin looked at his mother and made a gurgling sound then smiled. He let go of Henry's finger and pawed at Amy.

"What a special little boy," Henry said. "I can see how he brings you joy."

"He certainly is," Amy said, beaming. She wrapped him up tightly again. "I should take him home and feed him."

Henry nodded. "Before you go, Amy, I wanted to ask you something."

Her eyebrows lifted. "Yes?"

"Well…" He cleared his throat. "It's only that, when I drove you home on Friday, you seemed… out of sorts. I don't know what I did wrong, but I'm sorry for whatever it was."

CHARLOTTE BRENTWOOD

Amy sighed. "Oh Henry, it wasn't anything you *did*..." She closed her eyes for a moment, as if remembering. "I was very tired after such a long week, and – and I'm not used to being in such close quarters with someone. It was... overwhelming."

He tried to take in what she was saying. Was she *blushing*? "Oh, I see," he said, although he really didn't. Her words hadn't quite explained what had happened, but it seemed as if she didn't blame him for whatever it was.

She looked back towards the thinning crowd of villagers. The Fortescues now stood watching them. "I really should go. I hope you have a bountiful harvest. Everyone must be looking forward to the fair."

"To be sure. It will be a few months of hard work to get there." He walked back with her. "I may not see you for a while, Amy. I hope all will be well for you. Don't forget, I'm here if you ever need anything."

"I won't forget." She smiled at him before turning away.

72

Chapter Nine

A week later, Amy sat beneath a large oak tree in the back garden attempting to copy a painted miniature in pencil. It was one of the Fortescue forebears, dressed in an army uniform.

As Amy tried to draw the man's shoulders and arms, cursing her inability to keep things in proportion, she was reminded of another man's arms, and she wondered what it might feel like to be held by them. Then she blinked hard and cursed again, this time under her breath.

"What was that?" Her drawing tutor peered at her over his glasses.

"Nothing," Amy said, feeling her cheeks colour.

So much for putting Henry and his masculinity out of her mind. When she last saw him, at church, he had been dressed in his Sunday best and clean shaven with his wild red hair in some sort of order. His almost gentleman-like appearance had thrown her further off guard. And the crisp white shirt he wore had worn only served to make him more appealing.

His tenderness with Ben had really melted her heart. She had not expected a rugged farmer to be so gentle, and so clearly taken with him at first glance. Of course she thought her baby was beautiful, but to have him admired by someone she had such a growing respect and esteem for pleased her beyond measure.

She wasn't sure how long she could keep her feelings restrained, if she could at all. She took a deep breath to steady her pencil, and resumed her concentration.

After a light luncheon, she set Benjamin down in the nursery to sleep with Agnes in attendance and then went to visit Cecilia.

After they were settled in the parlour, Amy asked Cecilia how she was feeling.

"I am well, thank you," Cecilia said with a smile. "I think I have felt this little one begin to kick." She patted the small mound on her stomach.

"Oh really? That is good news." Jealousy again sparked in Amy, unwelcome but undeniable. The first stirring of her own offspring within her had caused panic rather than joyous anticipation.

She squashed the feelings down and took Cecilia's hand, forcing a smile.

"Tell me more about your adventures on the farm," Cecilia said. "I hope it was not too taxing for you. Did you have leisure to socialise with any old friends?"

Amy nodded, trying to contain yet another blush. "One old friend in particular," she said coyly.

Cecilia grinned. "Oh yes?"

Amy proceeded to confide her recent turbulent emotions regarding Henry.

"Dearest, I think it is wonderful," Cecilia said, her eyes misting over. "After the upheaval you have been through, it is lovely to have the potential of someone to care for you."

"But I'm scared, Cici. Even if I wanted to give him some kind of encouragement, fear is holding me back. I am worried my heart – even my soul – is irreparably damaged."

Cecilia squeezed her hand. "It is perfectly natural to feel apprehension, given all that has happened. It is healthy, I think. You do not want to commit yourself until you know you are safe."

"I cannot stop thinking about him," Amy confessed.

"I well remember those early sensations," Cecilia said, smiling. "But tell me, dearest, if it doesn't pain you too much… how does this compare to how you felt… last time?"

Heaving a sigh, Amy pried into the places in her heart she had tried to hide from. It was a fair question. She didn't want to enter into anything blindly. If she was ever going to trust again, it would need to be with a bold and discerning spirit.

"I think it's a different feeling," she said slowly. "With… *him*, it was exciting in part because it was like a forbidden territory, and there was something mysterious and enigmatic about him. Like a moth to a flame." She shook her head sadly. "With Henry, it is like a quiet fire which is slowly building. He is strong and straightforward, and I think he is honest. I would love to be able to let myself trust him."

Cecilia nodded. "You deserve to be loved by someone good. There is certainly no rush to take any action on your feelings. They may grow or subside in time. Has Henry said anything?"

Amy shook her head. "No, I can't say he has. He may not even feel a thing beyond friendship for me."

There was a knock on the door, and the maid entered with a tea tray. Cecilia thanked her and reached for the teapot. "We shall see," she said. "I have a notion you will know one way or the other before too long."

Cecilia poured the tea and then filled Amy in on various items of news from around the parish. As the vicar's wife, she had frequent visits with everyone in the village.

Amy laughed as Cecilia recounted calling on Mrs Croxley. The widow had produced several devices to divine the gender of Cecilia's baby. Satisfied it was to be a girl, she had already matched the poor unborn child with a local boy.

"She cannot help herself," Cecilia said. "And I already have more lacy outfits for the baby than I should ever wish to use." She finished her tea and set it down on the side table. "What else have you been doing, dearest? How do you get on with your musical endeavours?"

Amy chuckled. "Terribly. And this morning I disappointed another master, this time with the fine arts." She paused, and a smile dawned on her lips. "I should have thought of this before. Will you help me, Cici?"

"How so?"

"Will you teach me to paint? If I can show at least some skill, I may be able to ask Mrs Fortescue to dispense with the drawing master."

"Why, of course I will, dearest." Cecilia's face lit up. "But you've never shown any interest in art before."

"I can't honestly say I am that interested," Amy said with a laugh. "But it might give me a little peace with the Fortescues if I can show some kind of accomplishment."

"I know!" Cecilia clapped her hands. "There is a project I have been meaning to do, and you can help me with it. Come with me."

Amy followed Cecilia as she procured a jug of water and then went upstairs to retrieve her paints from the bottom of her wardrobe. They went into the neighbouring room, in which the only furniture was a cupboard and a small table.

"This will be the nursery," Cecilia announced. "I am going to paint the wallpaper."

"Oh?" Amy surveyed the old yellowed paper on the walls. Its floral pattern had mostly faded.

"Yes, I enquired at Jones's in order to replace the paper, but the cost is far too high. So I will simply paint over it in watercolours."

Amy smiled. "What a good idea. What do you have in mind?"

Cecilia moved to the far wall and began to describe a scene with much animation of limbs. "'Tis to be the ruined abbey where William and I first… declared our love." She flushed. "There's a rainbow arcing across the sky, lush green grass, and the abbey itself with all its cloisters soaring up. Would you like to help me?"

"Oh, Cici, I do not wish to ruin your precious scene."

"Nonsense!" Cecilia started unpacking her paints. "You can help me with the sky, or grass, or anything I outline for you. Let's begin!"

Amy held back a smile as Cecilia's pencil flew in broad strokes across the faint dainty pattern. "Cici, are you quite sure Mr Brook is… aware of your plans? He approves?"

"Oh yes," Cecilia murmured, deep in artistic fervour, "he said I can decorate however I please."

Perhaps William had imagined Cecilia might make a quilt for the baby's cradle, or hang a sampler on the wall. Amy doubted he would be prepared for a work of this… scale.

Cecilia handed her friend a paintbrush. "Shall we start?"

Amy took the brush and grinned. "Yes, do let's."

The women were putting the final touches on the design when the vicar strode into the room. "Cecilia, my love, how have you… oh my." He stopped suddenly, and his mouth dropped open as he took in the masterpiece. Then, a smile overtook his features, and he took two long strides towards his wife, gently wrapping her in his arms. "It's beautiful, my darling," he said with a chuckle.

She beamed. "Do you like it, William?"

"Of course I do; it's extraordinary. A poignant reminder of that special place, and a lovely scene for our little treasure to look upon." He dropped a tiny kiss on the end of her nose.

"Amy was a great help," Cecilia said, nodding over William's shoulder.

William spun around. "Oh, Miss Miller! I didn't see you there – my apologies." He affected a quick bow. "Thank you, as ever, for your valuable companionship."

Amy smiled. "Your wife is a true friend." She was glad he couldn't read all the envious thoughts racing through her mind.

"I should be getting back to my baby," she said. "I can see myself out."

She stepped up into the carriage for the ride home, all too conscious of being alone. Painting with Cecilia had been wonderfully fun. She liked to think she had even achieved a degree of creativity.

But that carefree feeling had been cut off sharply by seeing the Brooks together, so happy. It made her wistful, and it fanned the tiny flame of longing that she might have such happiness one day.

What sort of situation could she possibly fit in now? She was not lady or servant, not worldly or pure. And what sort of man could overlook her past and accept Benjamin as his own?

Even if someone like Henry Russell could love her, how would she ever know that she could trust a man the way Cecilia trusted Mr Brook?

❧⚘

After a long day of harvesting corn, Henry was on his way back home. He came upon a paddock of cows not far from the house, where his sister Clara was finishing up the afternoon milking. Her long red hair was loosely tied into pigtails which hung down in front of her shoulders.

He tiptoed up behind her. "Afternoon, Miss Russell!"

She jumped up, knocking her stool over and nearly kicking the milk bucket as well. "Henry!" she cried, as the cow also let out an irritated moo. "When will you learn not to do that? You scared me half to death!"

Henry laughed and picked up the stool. "You're an easy target." Then he patted the cow fondly and said, "I'm sorry, old girl, your mistress is a good sort, and I'm a rascal."

Clara resumed her position and continued milking. "I'm nearly finished here," she said, with her head to the side. "I'll come back with you."

A few minutes later, she hauled the bucket out from underneath the cow and Henry took it from her, his sickle in the other hand. He fell into step beside Clara.

"Good day?" she asked.

He shrugged one shoulder. "We were cutting today, need to start threshing tomorrow. How about you?"

"Just the same as usual," she said, and smiled at him. "Time to fill the bellies of you menfolk now."

"Oh yes, please," Henry said. "I'm starving. Did I see you rolling out pastry after breakfast? Maybe a berry pie for afters?"

"Maybe," she said with an impish laugh.

They both caught sight of Mr Russell by the house, digging over some dirt in the vegetable patch.

"He's in a foul mood today," Henry muttered. "Lord knows what kind of offence he'll conjure up to blame me for."

"I'll talk to him while you go in," Clara offered.

"Thank you," Henry said, giving her an appreciative smile. "What would I do without you, Clara?"

She chuckled.

"I mean it. Life here is far more bearable with you around."

Her smile faded. "I won't be here forever, Henry."

"I know that, but it'll be a while yet." Clara was still a girl in his eyes, and a constant in his life. He couldn't imagine her being a wife and mother for some time. He'd never witnessed anything more than juvenile flirtation on her part.

"If I had my way," she said, "I'd be gone tomorrow."

A shadow fell over his heart. "What do you mean? Is Pa being cruel to you?"

"Nothing like that." She shook her head. "I'm ready to have my own home and start a family."

Henry stopped walking and stared at her. "Are you?" She nodded and he blew out a breath. "I thought I was the only one looking for an escape."

She regarded him thoughtfully for a moment and then shrugged before running down the hill to the garden. He watched her, disquiet taking over his stomach. There was something about what she'd said, and something about the way she'd looked at him just now... He couldn't quite put his finger on it. She was hiding something.

Henry persuaded his mother to make his dinner into a substantial sandwich, and he took his tools to the croft house... His house. Now that it was still light after supper, he spent most of his evenings there working, as his daytime hours were completely monopolised by the harvest.

He also preferred to be here alone than to endure awkward family conversation or be isolated in his tiny bedroom. There was a different kind of loneliness in this small cottage. It was tied up with the hope that he would one day share this abode with a loving family, and the creeping dread that it would never happen. He could only ever imagine one woman living here with him.

As he mended floorboards, he remembered their last meeting, a few weeks before. There had been something new and special in Amy's eyes in the moments before she bade him farewell, and a radiance in her complexion. Dare he hope it was because of him? And yet she had still seemed eager to escape his company. It was baffling.

Then there had been those precious moments with baby Benjamin. He hadn't expected to feel such an instant connection with the little person, and with so brief an encounter. He couldn't explain it, but it felt real and right.

There had never been a question in Henry's mind that he would accept and care for the child. Benjamin was Amy's and he wanted Amy to be his. Devotion to both of them was a given. Love for the child he hadn't expected, not at first anyway, given the baby's sire. Henry worried he might feel resentment towards Benjamin, but now he was certain that was impossible. Benjamin was his own person, and his life didn't need to be coloured by his accidental ancestry. He could have a father who would cherish him for who he was. Amy was already setting a fine example of unconditional love.

It was getting dark as Henry finished mending a beam in the parlour.

He stretched his arms behind his back and surveyed the leftover bits of timber scattered about the floor. Almost unbidden, the memory of little Benjamin holding his finger filled his mind. He smiled and made a silent promise to show the boy the animals on the farm when he was old enough.

He picked up a piece of wood and turned it over in his hands thoughtfully. Then he picked up his chisel. He had an idea.

Chapter Ten

The summer heat was at its sticky height as Amy sat at the piano in the drawing room one evening, with the Fortescues as her audience. She attempted to pick out the latest piece she'd been taught, but her fingers would not cooperate.

After Amy had struggled with the same passage for a quarter of an hour, Mrs Fortescue said loudly, "That will do, child."

Amy wanted nothing more than to get up and close the instrument, never to open it again. But she stayed where she was with her fingers poised over the keys, obstinate. Didn't her guardian want her to perform ladylike arts?

"Mr Blackley says if I am to get better, I must practise," she said. "You *do* want me to get better, don't you?"

"Very much," said Mrs Fortescue. There was a pregnant pause, and then she erupted into giggles. She covered her face with her hands, but it was too late. Her shoulders shook, and when she uncovered her face there were tears of mirth in her eyes.

Amy exchanged a shocked glance with Mr Fortescue at the sight of his wife's dignified façade dissolving. Then they both joined in with the laughter. It was ridiculous – Amy knew she would never be an accomplished pianist. Wishing for her to magically become competent was a waste of time.

She crossed the room and flopped down on the couch with a sigh.

"Posture, Amelia."

At Mrs Fortescue's censure she immediately sat up straight but seethed inwardly. Did the woman never stop? Did she have to wreck a moment of levity? She again looked over at Mr Fortescue, and he shrugged a little. The gesture told Amy he knew his wife was a tyrant but there was no changing her. She considered him for a moment; he did not seem to become irked by his wife's nagging and controlling nature... And he seemed happy enough. How well matched they were.

"I collect, Amy," Mrs Fortescue said, "you are more at home making hay in the fields than you are in front of that instrument."

"I am indeed, ma'am," Amy replied earnestly. "I grew up on a farm. I suppose it is where I belong."

"Indeed," murmured Mrs Fortescue.

Amy picked up her book and thought nothing more of it, until she glanced up a few minutes later and saw that the other woman still wore a pensive expression. Amy frowned and returned to her book. She had a sinking feeling her guardian was cooking up a new scheme.

❧❦

While the ladies were at breakfast the following morning, letters were delivered. Mrs Fortescue opened each in turn, and when she came to the last she looked up at Amy.

"What is it?" Amy asked, her mouth full of crumpet.

Mrs Fortescue glowered at her, no doubt due to her lack of manners. Then she looked back at the letter and took a deep breath. "The Barringtons have returned to Ashworth Hall," she said. "Mrs Croxley told me this the other day, but now I have a letter from Lady Ashworth herself."

"Oh." Amy took a moment to process this information. Of course the local landowners would return to their country estate at the conclusion of the London season. She had, however, grown used to their absence, and comfortably so. She could do without complications in her life at present.

A new thought struck fear into her heart. "He's not, is he – that is..."

"Not to worry," Mrs Fortescue interjected smoothly, "the second son is still far from home. I believe Lord Ashworth has him under strict orders to remain in Hampshire for a year at least."

Amy nodded, but sweat had already broken out on her brow. She began to mentally calculate when the year would be up.

"In her letter," Mrs Fortescue went on, "Lady Ashworth invites us both to visit her and the girls on Friday."

"Oh?"

Mrs Fortescue nodded. "Lady Ashworth is a dear friend, you know. It will be wonderful to see her again and hear about what transpired in London this year. She has corresponded with me a few times during the Season, but nothing is quite like personal conversation, is it?" She smiled, perhaps trying to calm Amy's jitters. "You will come with me, won't you?"

Amy closed her eyes for a moment, considering. "Yes," she said, at length. "I should love to see Catherine."

"Perfect. I shall write and let her know."

"Thank you." Amy frowned. Perhaps there was no real reason for her not to go, but she had an inkling she was about to walk into the lion's den.

❧

Henry stood on the doorstep of Briarwood clutching a small cloth sack. He raised his hand to knock then dropped it again. What was he doing? A man of his position had no right to be calling on the gentry uninvited.

After weeks of constant graft on the farm, without leave to even go to church, he'd finally managed to escape on some errands. It was late afternoon, and the air was thick and close.

Losing his nerve, Henry turned to leave. He would be unwelcome, and his humble offering judged unworthy.

Suddenly the front door was thrown open. "What are you about, young man?"

The butler stood on the threshold, tall and imposing.

"Oh, hello!" Henry said lamely. "I am a friend of..." He cleared his throat. He didn't want the shame of having to present his modest gifts to the lady herself. She probably didn't want to see him anyway. The last thing he wanted was to upset her. He held out the sack. "I came to give these to Miss Miller."

The butler eyed the bag with one eyebrow raised and then sniffed derisively. "What is that?"

"Is that you, Henry?" Amy's voice floated across the vestibule, and in moments the woman herself appeared in the doorway. "Oh, it *is* you. I thought I heard your voice."

Henry's world stood still as he took in the vision of her. She was in a white cotton dress, and her hair was piled on top of her head in a russet sea. A number of strands had escaped to rest about her face, which had become more tanned since he last saw her. Was it possible that she was even prettier than she'd been at their last meeting?

"'Afternoon, Miss Miller," he rasped, struggling to get enough air into his lungs.

Amy gestured to the butler and he withdrew. "Well, come in," she said with a smile. "Whatever can have brought you here?" She led him inside then turned to face him in front of a large staircase.

Henry took in his surroundings. It had been a long time since he was in such a house, and the grandness overwhelmed him. How could he possibly think he could provide for her, when she was used to such a life as this?

She was waiting for an answer. He cleared his throat… He might as well be honest. "I made something for your baby," he blurted out, jiggling the bag.

"Oh, how lovely!" She clasped her hands together. "Why don't you show it to him yourself? I was about to collect him and take him outside. He's just woken up from a nap."

"Uh… okay. If you think I won't bother him…"

She was already ascending the staircase. "Wait there," she called over her shoulder. "I'll be back down in a moment."

He knew Amy would be gone for five minutes at most, but standing alone in this strange place was excruciating for Henry. What if someone happened upon him? Perhaps the lady of the house? He'd probably be ordered from the premises.

Luckily, Amy reappeared before he was detected by anyone else. She carried Benjamin on her hip, and a woollen blanket was rolled up under her other arm. At the sight of the child, Henry was met with the same warm emotions he'd experienced the last time. Benjamin's cheeks seemed chubbier, his dark hair longer.

"Hello, Benjamin," he said cheerily, and was rewarded with a smile. He reached for the blanket. "Let me take that. Where are we going?"

Amy smiled her thanks as she handed it over. "To the back garden. Ben likes trying to roll over, and I like him to get some fresh air."

He followed her down a hallway and into a salon crowded with potted plants. At the other end of the room, glass doors opened out to a patio. A large lawn lay beyond, framed with a flower garden.

Amy walked several yards onto the grass and pointed. "Put it here, please."

He spread the blanket in the spot indicated, and she carefully put the baby down in the middle of it.

"Make yourself comfortable," she said with a smile, and she lay down on her side next to Benjamin.

Henry mirrored her on the baby's other side and smiled back at her. How lovely and natural it was, to be in so relaxed a situation with her. As she watched over her baby, she looked as if she was exactly where she was meant to be. Benjamin gazed up at the sky making cooing noises, his eyes wide with wonder.

It was what a future could potentially be like, and it made Henry ache for it. He wanted to belong with her, with them.

He suddenly remembered his purpose. He put the sack down and undid the twine holding it closed. He glanced up and saw Amy watching him with anticipation. Colour began creeping up his neck as he tipped the bag upside down and five small wooden figures fell out on to the blanket.

"Oh!" Amy gasped. "Little animals! May I?" She reached out a hand, and Henry gave her the horse he'd carved out of the floorboard offcuts.

"They're nothing, really," Henry muttered.

"Nonsense, I love it!" Amy cried, running her fingers over the mane it had taken Henry an hour to create with his chisel. "What else have you got there?"

"Oh… there's a cow, a pig, a duck, and a sheep." He dropped all but the sheep next to Amy, and then he pretended to make it run up and down Benjamin's body, bleating as he went. The baby reached out and batted at the toy, then let out a delighted giggle as Henry made it run all the way up to his chin. The sound made both Amy and Henry laugh, too, and their eyes met.

"Thank you, Henry," she said. "This is very thoughtful of you."

His face now well and truly red, Henry replied, "He's special to you and… I care about you both."

Amy's eyes widened, and Henry's heart began to beat wildly. Why had he said that?

"You do?" she whispered.

He nodded. "Your little man has made a big impression on me," he said, "and I–"

Benjamin chose that moment to fling himself on to his side, only to get his arm caught under his middle.

"Oh!" Amy cried. "You're so close, my love, just a little further!"

Henry blew out a sigh of relief. Thank heaven his ridiculous outburst had been interrupted. He'd been on the verge of revealing what was in his heart, and he was terrified such a confession would scare her off … Or that she would reject him.

He put his focus back on Benjamin. "You can do it!" he encouraged, and he put the sheep on the blanket just out of the boy's reach. Benjamin's eyes lit up as he stared at the wooden creature, and he began to rock towards it. All of a sudden he flopped onto his stomach and grasped the sheep.

"Well done!" Amy exclaimed, clapping. "What a clever boy." She leaned over and gently pulled Benjamin over onto his back. She was so close, Henry could have easily kissed her. "He hasn't figured out how to roll back yet," she said with a smile. "He gets upset if he's left on his tummy."

As she settled back on her side, her slipper knocked against Henry's boot.

"Sorry," he said, jerking his feet backwards. He knew how much she hated touch of any kind.

"Don't apologise," she said with a laugh. "I kicked you!"

He smiled back at her, relieved. Perhaps she was a little less frightened than before. He willed himself to breathe normally again, frazzled by the range of emotions he experienced in her presence. It was worth it though – or he hoped it very soon would be.

"The Barringtons are back."

Amy's statement brought him crashing back to reality. "Are they?"

She nodded. "I'm to visit with the ladies tomorrow."

He sat up. "Do you want to?"

Her brow creased. "I feel different now to how I did then. I'm not sure how to feel about seeing them. Certainly I am still fond of Catherine. I only hope they receive me well, and that they don't mention…" She trailed off.

He nodded, trying to tell her with his eyes he understood. "I hope they'll respect what you've been through. Take no notice if they say anything cruel. You don't need their approval."

She sat up as well, and nodded solemnly. "Thank you, Henry."

He was reminded of his only interaction with the Barringtons, when Lord Ashworth had told him in no uncertain terms that he wasn't suitable to be a vicar. He wasn't welcome in their world. Was it where Amy belonged?

"I should be getting back," he said, standing. When Amy started to rise, he put out his hand. "You stay there," he said. "I think Benjamin would like to be here awhile longer."

She smiled. "He loves the animals you made, as do I. Perhaps I'll see you at the harvest fair?"

"I hope so," he said, and he waved goodbye to them both.

As he walked away through the garden, avoiding the house altogether, he had a feeling he was being watched. But when he looked back up at the house, he saw no one.

Chapter Eleven

When Friday morning came, Amy was exhausted. She had been up most of the night with Benjamin. When Mrs Fortescue came to her room to see if she was getting dressed for their visit, Amy shook her head from the bed.

"I can't go. Benjamin is colicky and he won't settle for anyone but me."

Mrs Fortescue was only momentarily disconcerted. "Bring him with you, then."

Amy looked at her sideways. "Do you think that's wise?"

Mrs Fortescue shrugged one shoulder. "Lady Ashworth has seen infants before; she cannot be shocked. She said in her letter that she hopes you are both well. She will likely be pleased to see him for herself." She sat on the bed next to Amy. "Besides, Lady Ashworth has a kind heart."

"I know," Amy said softly. She was well aware of the lady's beneficence. In fact, it seemed Lady Ashworth had somewhat of a soft spot for her. She had not immediately forced Amy from the house on the discovery of her pregnancy, continuing to give her shelter until her condition was too obvious. A girl of Amy's status shouldn't even have been a lady's maid, but Lady Ashworth had offered her the position despite her complete lack of experience as a servant.

Amy sighed, her emotions and fatigue getting the better of her. "Why do you not just go on your own this time?"

Mrs Fortescue studied her for a moment. "I know you are tired, dear. I will understand if this is too much for you. But I would very much like to have you with me. I know the Barringtons will think you most positively altered."

Amy frowned. "They will see a girl pretending to be someone she is not."

"Do you not see, Amy?" Mrs Fortescue asked, her eyes imploring. "I am proud of you."

Amy swallowed. "What do you mean?"

"You have been through so much, and you have borne it magnificently. Think about how you were when you first came to live with us, and how much confidence you have gained. It is quite remarkable, and I think the experience of being in the company of these ladies will show you how far you have come."

Amy took in a sharp breath, unprepared for these kind words. Suddenly, she did not want to disappoint this lady. "At least I will not have to serve tea," she said.

Mrs Fortescue laughed, and for the first time Amy sensed they shared an understanding. "There are other qualities of a fine woman," she said. "And you have those in abundance."

"Thank you." Amy pushed herself out of bed and over to her wardrobe, hiding her face and the tears which would no longer be contained.

Half an hour later, trepidation overwhelmed Amy as the carriage rolled towards Ashworth Hall. Mrs Fortescue made several attempts at small talk, but Amy just stared out of the window as the lands of the estate passed by, paralysed in her distress. She had not been back to Ashworth Hall since leaving in disgrace. The house had been the scene of some of her happiest and most horrid moments.

She'd entered through the front door before, in her capacity as lady's maid, but this would be the first time she'd enter as a guest. Surely they would think she was an imposter.

"They do know I'm coming?" she asked Mrs Fortescue.

"Of course they do." The woman laid a hand on Amy's arm in comfort, but Amy flinched. Mrs Fortescue frowned and sat back. "Lady

Ashworth specifically asked us both to visit."

"And Benjamin?" The baby lay sleeping in a Moses basket next to Amy. The motion of the travel seemed to calm him.

"He may be a surprise," said Mrs Fortescue, "but a welcome one I am sure. They are women, after all, Amy. We are predisposed to like babies."

The remark puzzled Amy. If Mrs Fortescue thought it was natural to like babies, why did she not have any of her own?

The entrance hall seemed larger and grander than when she had seen it last. Her every whisper seemed to echo, and when Benjamin whimpered, she was so startled she nearly dropped the basket.

"Her ladyship will see you in the drawing room," the butler announced. He gave Amy a brief nod with cold eyes. The man had never warmed to her, given her sudden rise in the ranks of servanthood, and now he probably thought her beyond the pale. She remembered Henry's advice and tried to put the butler's deprecation out of her mind.

They were announced, and Amy took a deep breath as she followed Mrs Fortescue into the room.

"Good morning, ladies," Lady Ashworth said warmly, as she rose from her chair. Her daughters, Lady Louisa and Lady Catherine, also stood.

"Good morning," replied Mrs Fortescue, "and thank you for the invitation."

The Barringtons and Mrs Fortescue dropped into curtsies, and Amy hastily followed suit. Her curtsey was a little wobbly with the Moses basket looped over one arm.

"Do come and sit down," Lady Ashworth said, indicating the sofa. "I see you have brought the baby with you – how charming!"

Amy smiled at her as she took her seat and put the basket down beside her. "Yes, he has been poorly, so I did not want to leave him behind."

Lady Louisa recoiled as she sat down. "Is he contagious?"

"No, of course not!" Amy replied. "I should not have come at all if that were the case."

Lady Louisa sniffed and regarded mother and baby with narrowed eyes.

Amy met Lady Catherine's gaze and they shared a smile.

"Dear Amy," said Catherine. "How good it is to see you, and you're looking so well!"

"Thank you, my lady," Amy said. Then she paused awkwardly, not sure if it was appropriate to return the compliment. It had never been her place to appraise her mistress's appearance. Catherine was prettier than ever. She had a pleasing openness about her which her sister lacked, and her dark hair contrasted with her porcelain-like skin beautifully. Louisa had fairer hair and more olive skin, like her mother.

"I trust you are all well?" Mrs Fortescue enquired.

"Oh yes," Lady Ashworth replied. "We are all in excellent health. Excepting that I have not recently heard from… well."

Amy stared at her hands and her cheeks burned. It was clear whom she was talking about.

Mrs Fortescue cleared her throat. "How was the remainder of your time in London? Did you enjoy Ascot?"

The ladies launched into an animated discussion, during which tea was served. Amy was content to be a spectator, exchanging the occasional friendly glance with Catherine.

Benjamin began to stir, and Amy placed a hand on his chest.

"Oh look," Catherine said, "he's waking up. May I?" She came over to the sofa and gestured towards the basket.

Amy nodded, and Catherine knelt down before Benjamin.

"Oh, he's precious!"

Benjamin squirmed, blinked and then opened his eyes fully.

Catherine gasped. "Oh my." She looked up at Amy.

Amy nodded. She knew. She reached down and picked up the baby, cuddling him close.

Those eyes – his father's eyes. There was no escaping it.

She had been deathly afraid that she would resent this child, who had been created in lust and fear. She had wondered how she could ever really look him in the eye, when it would be her mistakes looking back at her. But Ben's eyes were part of the whole miracle of him, and she could only adore every part. Perhaps she would forget the misfortune in time. But she would always have Ben.

As Catherine resumed her seat, her eyes still wide, Amy's thoughts wandered to what she had thought was the best time of her life, when

John Barrington had made her feel like the most special woman in the world.

Catherine had always talked of John so highly, of what a kind and loving brother he was. The three of them had spent a lot of time together, even in this very room. John and Catherine had a close relationship, and Amy got on so well with her mistress that she was almost constantly in her company. John could be cheeky, sometimes mischievous, but he always made them laugh. This combination of attention and playfulness – not to mention his dark good looks – had made her fall in love with him.

"Would you mind terribly if I held him?"

Amy's head snapped up at Lady Ashworth's words. *Would* she mind? Something in her was instantly fearful, but she told herself she was being silly. Naturally a mother would want the joy of holding a baby. But if the baby was her illegitimate grandchild… What would that mean?

"Of course you may," she said, forcing out the words. She went over to where Lady Ashworth sat and carefully transferred Benjamin into her arms.

"Hello, little one," Lady Ashworth cooed. Then her mouth dropped. "He has–" She looked at Amy, then Mrs Fortescue. "Beautiful eyes." Her chin wobbled and her eyes glossed over.

Pride swelled in Amy as a hush fell over the room. She could not deny the authenticity of this moment: a woman meeting her own flesh and blood for the first time, and being completely besotted with him.

But when Lady Ashworth began to bounce Benjamin about and sing him a song, Amy grew impatient to take him back. Anxiety seeped into her body, and she hovered near her son uncomfortably.

Benjamin began to cry softly, and Amy immediately stepped in. "I must feed him now," she said, scooping him up.

"Come up to my room, Amy," said Catherine, "where you can be comfortable."

Amy nodded, relieved to leave this scene. "Thank you," she said, following Catherine from the room.

Once in her chamber, Catherine helped Amy settle in a chair, and promised to return in a short while.

While Benjamin drank his fill, Amy took in the familiar surroundings.

She had laid Catherine's dresses out on the bed just there, and she had helped to lace her stays in the centre of the room. On the other wall was her dressing table, where Amy had brushed Catherine's tresses until they shone. How strange to be sitting still in this room, and not bustling about with a list of tasks. She took a deep breath in and out, and relaxed back into the chair. The stillness was welcome, albeit strange.

When Catherine returned, Amy had finished the feed and had just stood up.

"Come," Catherine said, crossing the room towards her. "Sit on the bed with me and we can talk."

Amy did as she was bid, laying Benjamin in the middle of the bed and keeping a hand on his stomach.

"Oh Amy... my dear." Catherine grasped her hand, her face a study in melancholy.

Amy frowned. "What is it?"

"I do not think I can express to you... that is, there is no way to explain to you how sorry I am for what John did."

At the sound of his name, Amy could not restrain a gasp. "You do not need to–"

"But I must. In those months afterwards I suppose I was too shocked and saddened to really share my regrets with you. I watched as he charmed you, not knowing how deep an effect he was having. I had no idea you really fancied yourself in love. You did, did you not?"

Amy nodded and looked away. "I am ashamed to admit it. I was such a fool."

"Please, my dear girl, do not talk of shame. It is he who should be sorry. He took advantage of your innocence. I could not have believed he was capable..." She wrung her hands. "Please know I wish I could have protected you in some way, and that I could have provided the assistance you dearly needed when we knew you had to leave us. I could not think of any way I could support your future."

Amy squeezed her hand. "Lady Catherine, don't worry about me. I will make my own way. I've never been one to fret about the future, and at present I only have the energy to live day by day."

Catherine shook her head and smiled. "If there is anything I can do, you must not be afraid to ask me. When I am married, I may perhaps have some financial power. I can assist you then."

Amy smiled ruefully. "It is unlikely your husband would be so charitable, but I thank you for the thought."

There was silence for several moments, and then Catherine spoke again. "We will be hosting the annual ball soon."

Amy nodded. It was to be expected.

"Would you like to be invited?"

"Pardon?" Amy had never been to a ball in her life. "Do you really think Lady Ashworth would invite me?"

Catherine nodded. "If I asked her to. As the Fortescues' ward, there is no reason why you should not attend."

"Oh." Amy considered this. Would it be exciting to wear a ball dress and dance to a real orchestra?

She imagined being announced into the ball, and her heart sunk when she thought about how she would be received by the guests. She was sure to be judged wanting, undeserving, improper. She was quite certain no one would ask her to dance, and the only person she would feel at ease with would be Cecilia – and she would have her husband.

Besides, she didn't know all the dances, and the only man she would feel remotely comfortable dancing with would not be on the guest list.

"I am still attending to Benjamin during the night," she said. "The ball would be at such a late hour as to render me unconscious. While I very much appreciate your consideration, I must decline your offer."

Catherine smiled. "I understand."

There was something else about the ball, something that made Amy shiver from head to toe. It was the night of this ball, the previous year, that John Barrington had forced himself on her. Catherine probably didn't know that.

The lady was gazing at Benjamin. "He really is a delightful little creature," she said. "I hope I may see a lot of him as he grows up."

"Yes, I think he is wonderful too," Amy said, not sure what to think about their possible future relations. She picked up Benjamin and pushed herself off the bed.

"You do look well, my dear," Catherine said, also getting to her feet. "Happy. Motherhood becomes you. I am so glad."

"Thank you, my lady," Amy said, looking down at her son. She *was* relatively contented, she supposed. Henry appeared in her mind's eye, and she found herself colouring.

"Has something else happened?" Catherine asked with a lift of her eyebrows.

"Perhaps," Amy said, hiding a smile. She left it at that, and Catherine pried no further.

Amy was much more relaxed in the carriage on the way home, and she mulled over the end of her conversation with Catherine.

She recalled Henry's visit and the lovely presents he had made for her son. It had been the most natural thing in the world, to have him in repose next to her and Benjamin. She had felt comfortable, at ease. The sight of him interacting with Benjamin so readily had made her feelings for him deepen. And he had said he *cared* for them. He would make a wonderful father. But would he accept Benjamin, if she asked that of him? It was too perfect an idea to dwell on, lest it take hold in her heart.

It was later in bed that night when Amy thought about Lady Ashworth and *her* tender moments with Benjamin. She could not shake the disquiet which had consumed her as she'd watched them form a bond.

"What if..." she whispered into the darkness, and the fear made her jolt upright in her bed.

At first she'd been worried that Benjamin would be a target of malice for the Barringtons because he was a smear on their good name. They could even dispute that John was the father, calling Amy's character into question. But now that Lady Ashworth could see so clearly that the child was in fact John's, what would this mean for Benjamin's future?

Lady Ashworth had looked at him as any grandmother might. Then there was Lady Catherine's comment that she hoped she would see him frequently.

What if they wanted to take him away from her and raise him as one of their own? Or what if they didn't want the reminder of John's folly and stole him from her to be sent away? They could also persuade the Fortescues to banish both of them and leave them to life on the streets. John would surely return one day soon, and they would give his comfort priority over his by-blow's.

Her nightmare came back to her – John Barrington stealing the child from her very arms. Perhaps it would not be him but his family.

She would put her own life on the line before she would let that happen.

☙❧

At the conclusion of the corn harvest, the Russells prepared to celebrate at the fair. Cakes and marmalades were produced in the kitchen, enormous vegetables were carefully plucked from the garden, and their finest beasts were groomed for judging.

Clara sang a merry tune as she helped Henry brush his bull's coat in the barn. Henry picked up on her optimism, feeling anything could happen.

"What a handsome lad you are, Jimmy," Henry said to the bull, who replied with a long-suffering groan. Clara caught his eye and they laughed.

"Your suffering is for a good cause," she said to the beast. "I'm sure your master will give you some treats when you win the prize ribbon."

"He can eat the prize turnip as a reward," Henry said, then ducked behind the bull as Clara tried to whack him with her brush.

"You wouldn't dare!" she cried. "Not my turnip!"

Once Henry was satisfied with Jimmy's appearance, he ushered him into an adjoining pen and helped Clara tidy up.

"Are you going to try to dance with anyone in particular at the fair, Henry?" She twirled around with the broom she was using and then winked at him.

Henry gaped at her, trying to keep a straight face. "Maybe…" How much did she know?

"Come on," Clara said, setting the broom against the wall. "Let's practise, so you don't completely embarrass yourself."

Henry began to protest, but she had a point. He wasn't exactly famous for his dancing skills, and he didn't want to ruin his chance to impress Amy if by some miracle she agreed to dance with him.

"Go on, then," he muttered, taking her hands.

She grinned and began to sing again, skipping with him around the barn.

After a couple of minutes, Henry asked breathlessly, "Do you know who I might dance with?"

She threw back her head and laughed. "Of course I do, you ninny."

Henry went a shade of scarlet. "How long have you known?"

Clara twirled once more as she ended her tune, then turned to face Henry. "Oh, I don't know, a couple of years."

Henry stared at her, incredulous. "Years?"

Clara nodded. "Do you think I don't know you at all, brother dear?"

He shrugged. It had been over a month since he saw Amy, with long days in the fields and long evenings at the croft house. She had probably forgotten all about him, but the flame in his heart still burned brightly.

"Will you dance with anyone, Clara?" he countered, as he opened the barn door for her.

She squinted in the bright sun as Henry joined her outside. "I don't know, it depends who asks. I daresay," she said archly, "there will be more fun to be had around the bonfire."

They had reached the farmhouse, and Clara raced up to her bedroom before Henry could ask her what she meant.

Chapter Twelve

The familiar ache of grief settled over Amy as butter-coloured ribbons were threaded through her hair. Amy missed her parents so, and the annual fête was a strong reminder of them. It had always been the most joyful time of the year, a chance to celebrate good fortune with her family and their friends. Mrs Miller's Shrewsbury cake was a contender for a ribbon every year, and baking it with her was one of Amy's dearest memories.

She lifted her arms so Jenny could tie a ribbon of the same colour around her white muslin dress, just below the bust. Once the maid had gone, Amy picked up the jewellery box on her dresser. From it she retrieved a short piece of deep blue ribbon, only a few inches long. Amy's mother had sewn the ribbon around the bottom of a dress she'd made. Amy had worn it to the last harvest fair before her mother died.

She wrapped her fingers around the ribbon and closed her eyes. She saw an image of her parents together, the last real happy time before her father's health began to fail. They were having a family picnic under a huge plane tree in their yard. As they devoured sandwiches and cake, Amy's parents were relaxed and affectionate. At the time Amy had no idea this idyllic existence would soon disappear, but she had known she wanted their happiness for her own life. She could not have begun to imagine what would happen to her in the next few years, and that her future would be so radically changed.

Amy opened her eyes and dried the tears rolling down her cheeks. She took up her shawl and bag and headed for the door.

Mrs Fortescue had not made anything herself for the fair, of course, but she had taken great pains in organising the event in conjunction with the parish vestry. Indeed, much of Amy's time over the past month had been taken up helping with the plans for one thing or another, from laying out the design of the food stalls to keeping track of who was judging what.

The Fortescues had left for the site on the Ashworth estate early, to oversee proceedings. Amy had stayed behind to tend to Benjamin, and due to his feeding schedule, she would miss the afternoon games of strength and skill.

The evening sun was dropping low in the sky when she arrived at the fair in the carriage with a footman as her escort. As she weaved through the crowds of villagers, from labourers to gentry, Amy remembered how she had felt last year. She had begun to suspect her pregnancy and hadn't yet given up hope on her connection with Mr Barrington. She had been, in fact, desperate to ask him for help. She shook the horrible memories from her mind.

As she searched for Cecilia, she greeted some friendly faces, and avoided malicious ones. She saw Mrs Fortescue presiding over events from the main tent in the middle of the fair, and although she kept her eyes peeled for red hair, none was apparent. Before Amy could find her friend, she was intercepted by Lady Catherine Barrington.

"Good evening!" Catherine greeted her warmly and dropped a kiss onto each of her cheeks. It was the first time Amy had been greeted thus by a member of the aristocracy, and she was taken aback.

Recovering, she awkwardly kissed her back on one cheek. "Hello, Lady Catherine."

"What a jolly evening," said Catherine, looping her arm through Amy's, "and still so warm! I hope you and the little one are well?"

"Yes, quite well, thank you," Amy replied. She was sensible of the stares of passers-by – a member of the highest born family in the area was choosing to consort with one of the lowest as an equal. Was this a deliberate tactic on Catherine's part?

"Have you eaten?" Catherine asked.

Amy shook her head.

"Will you let me treat you? The aroma from that suckling pig is divine!"

Amy laughed. "By all means."

Catherine chatted to Amy about her recent time in London while they visited various food stalls. As Amy had been to London with her the year before, she knew some of the names and places. Given she'd never travelled further than Milton before that, her time in London had been eye-opening to say the least.

"Mama is despairing that neither Louisa nor I are wedded by now," Catherine confided with an indulgent smile. "However, Louisa has several invitations to spend her summer at other estates, so perhaps she will be engaged by the end of the year."

"And you?" Amy enquired boldly, as they sat on a bench with jam tarts.

Catherine paused before replying, an almost mischievous glint in her eye. "I have had my share of admirers, and have admired some in my turn… but thus far, preference and suitability have not united. I expect Mama is secretly pleased to have a reason to attend all the balls of the season, and I may enjoy another year before I am really pressured to get a husband."

Catherine was eighteen, and in the prime of her bloom. Amy had no idea what her dowry was like, but with her lively and kind personality, she would surely have her choice of suitors.

"We are very lucky, I suppose," Catherine went on, "in that we do not need to marry to acquire further property. Mama will let us choose someone we like, as long as the gentleman in question can provide for us in the manner to which we are accustomed."

"Yes, very lucky indeed," Amy said, trying to keep her wistfulness out of her voice. Catherine must have her own challenges, but in this moment Amy wished she had some of her privileges.

"I am going to visit John," Catherine announced abruptly.

Amy dropped her tart, her mouth falling open. "Your – your brother, John?" she stammered.

Catherine nodded, brushing crumbs from her skirt and turning to face Amy more squarely. "I wanted to tell you myself. I still cannot forgive his actions, but I feel sorry for him being there without friends or family. I miss him."

Amy nodded, unable to say anything.

"I have had a letter from him," Catherine continued, "and while he did not request my presence, I can sense his loneliness. Papa has said I may go."

Amy could not understand the bond of siblings; she had none. But she had seen with her own eyes how close John and Catherine were, and with Catherine's giving heart, Amy should not be surprised that it was the lady's instinct to be with him if she thought herself needed. Despite this knowledge, Amy still felt as if she was losing an ally. Would he poison Catherine against her?

"There you are!" It was Cecilia, now properly swollen with child. "Hello, Lady Catherine," she said with a quick curtsey.

"Mrs Brook." Catherine smiled at her and stood. To Amy she said, "I am unsure when I will be back – perhaps not before the Season. I hope your plans succeed, whatever they may be. Goodbye." She curtsied to them both and left.

Cecilia took her place next to Amy. "What was all that about?"

Amy frowned. "Oh, nothing of consequence. Lady Catherine is going to do some travelling." She looked her friend in the eye, taking one of her hands. "Now, tell me, dearest, how are you getting on?"

❧◈❧

Darkness had well and truly descended, and music started playing. A joyful, spirited melody filled the air. There were shouts and hoots of excitement, and groups of people immediately ran to the area in front of the musicians which was lit with a circle of torches.

Amy loved to dance. In younger days she would dance herself into giddiness... but it had been a while since she danced like that, and she wondered if she ever would again.

Still, she found herself drifting towards the dancers. She stood off to the side, watching them, and couldn't help but smile as their intoxicating merriment rubbed off on her.

"Miss Miller?"

She jumped. It was Henry, suddenly at her side. "Hello," she said, her breath quickening. "Are you having a good evening?"

"Aye, thank you, I am." He paused, and she looked at him properly.

He had shaved, and he was wearing a jacket she hadn't known he possessed. The firelight danced on his eyes and lit up his flame-red hair, which he had tried, unsuccessfully, to flatten down. She felt a little flutter in her heart – had he made a special effort just for her?

He cleared his throat. "Will you dance with me, Amy?"

"Oh! I…" She looked away with a bashful smile, flattered. Was this the first time a man had ever asked her to dance with him? It had to be. How it must feel to be a lady, and to have a dance card and many suitors. The flutter became a pitter-patter. The idea of dancing – and dancing with him – excited her. Couldn't she just let go and enjoy herself? Didn't she deserve that much?

She smiled at him and then noticed his hands. No gloves, of course; he only wore them for working. She looked down at her own hands, which were also bare. She hadn't even considered bringing gloves to the fair. The very thought of having her skin touched still struck fear into her heart. She couldn't quite bring herself to do it. "No!" she cried suddenly. "I can't dance with you."

In embarrassment and confusion, she ran from him, back towards the food stalls. She almost collided with Mrs Fortescue, who was in conversation with Mrs Grant. "Oh, pardon me," she mumbled.

Mrs Fortescue broke away from Mrs Grant and pulled Amy to the side. "Are you quite all right, my dear?"

Amy was so rattled she forgot to be offended by the term of endearment. "Oh yes, I suppose I am. I only feel like… I will never be myself again. As if I can never enjoy the things a woman should."

Mrs Fortescue raised her eyebrows. "Such as?"

Amy sighed. "Henry Russell asked me to dance just now."

"Oh, did he? I saw him heading that way. He appeared to be quite polished, compared to his normal attire." She contemplated Amy. "You do not want to dance with him?"

Amy bit her lip. "I do want to. But I have no gloves."

Mrs Fortescue smiled. "This is not a ball, my dear. Many people are not wearing gloves."

"You don't understand. I don't want him to… touch me." She

emphasised the words, hoping she wouldn't have to explain further.

But Mrs Fortescue sailed on, uncomprehending. "I appreciate your regard for propriety, child. Given the informality of the setting, you wouldn't be reproached. It is only your hands that will touch."

Amy hung her head. "That's too much."

Mrs Fortescue nodded slowly, understanding finally dawning. "I see." She began to remove her own gloves. "Here, you may use mine."

Amy stared at her. "You don't mind?"

"Not in the slightest." She handed the gloves over. "But you will stay in the light, won't you?"

Amy nodded, taking the proffered gloves. "I will, I promise. Thank you, Mrs Fortescue."

Her heart began to beat madly as she pulled the fabric over her hands and coaxed her fingers in. She took a deep breath, trying to calm her nerves. "How well they fit," she murmured absentmindedly.

"Enjoy yourself," Mrs Fortescue said, surprising Amy. They exchanged a smile, and Amy went back towards the band. Had there been tears in the woman's eyes? She must have imagined it.

She reached the circle of flames, but Henry was nowhere to be seen. Had she missed her chance? Now that the prospect of dancing with him was real, she wanted to more than anything.

Searching for him, she bumped into cavorting children, gossiping matrons and strolling lovers. Had her rejection of Henry caused him to go home immediately? At last she found him amongst the pens of animals being exhibited.

"Mr Russell?" she called from behind him.

He whirled around. "Oh! It's you, Amy."

"I do hope I'm not disturbing you."

He shook his head. "I was only talking to Jimmy here, telling him he must walk home quietly." He indicated the bull in the pen behind him.

"Ah. Do you anticipate he will make trouble?"

He nodded gravely. "I expect nothing less. He caused a proper stampede on the way here."

Amy turned to the bull. "Jimmy, sir, do please mind your master on the journey home," she said, as seriously as she could. "For my sake. But I am afraid I must detain you a little longer, so I can dance with your master."

Henry threw her a puzzled look. "I thought you didn't want to dance with me?"

Amy shook her head. "I did want to, but I was… well, it's silly, I suppose. But now I have these" – she wiggled her gloved fingers at him – "I feel more at ease."

He regarded her hands and then looked back at her face. "If you're sure."

She held out her hand. "Let's go."

He smiled and took her hand, pressing her fingers gently before leading her back to the music.

Her heart drummed loudly in her ears as anxiety began to take hold again. He wouldn't be actually touching her skin while they danced, but there was still the intimacy of being so close.

As they faced each other within the whirling dancers, she told herself firmly there was nothing to fear: she knew him. He offered her his other hand and she took it. Then he held her eyes with an expression of such affection and reassurance that all her fear melted away.

And they danced.

かんかん

Henry could barely believe what was happening. His entire being pulsed with joy as he twirled Amy around and weaved her through the other couples, revelling in her energy and nearness. Her beauty was magnified by the movement. He couldn't take his eyes off her.

He'd spent the whole evening working up the courage to talk to her. She hadn't been alone until the moment she'd gone to watch the dancing.

He'd hoped she would dance with him, of course, but he'd always assumed, deep down, that she would refuse. When she had, it had confirmed what he'd always believed to be true: that they would never be more than friends, and that she was still too traumatised to even consider anything romantic.

But she'd changed her mind, albeit with a concession to her security: the gloves. He didn't care what she needed to do to make herself comfortable with him – just so long as she was. When she'd held her hand out to him, he knew they were crossing into new territory – a new trust. And he hoped with everything in him that it was the beginning of a journey to everything his heart had desired for so long.

The dance was a public declaration of sorts. Even in such an informal setting, taking a partner signified an intent. And spending several songs dancing with the same partner was almost tantamount to an engagement. The whole village would know he fancied her.

After some quarter-hour of dancing together, they were both panting and tired. The song the musicians were playing ended, and as cheers resounded, Henry guided her off to the side.

Even in the flickering torchlight, he could see her colour, heightened by the exercise, and her eyes glowing brightly. "Thank you, Henry," she said, smiling at him.

He chuckled, the bliss in his heart spilling over. That she should thank *him* seemed preposterous, when she had made his year. "The pleasure was mine."

"It's an age since I last danced," she said. "I hope I didn't embarrass you."

"Far from it," he replied instantly. "I've never been more proud."

There was a silence, and they both smiled at each other coyly. What could he say in order to spend more time with her? "Can I get a drink for you, Amy?" he blurted out.

"Yes, please," she said. She put her hand in the crook of his elbow and let him lead her away. It was another wonderful sign that they were becoming a couple.

He caught his mother's eye, and saw a distinct note of disapproval. Did his parents really still think Amy so horrid? Well, they would just have to get used to the idea. There would never be another woman in his life.

He purchased two mugs of cider, and guided Amy to a bale of hay by the bonfire.

Henry's mind became a jumble as they sat down. There was so much he wanted to say, but even if he could find a way to express himself, would she be receptive to him?

She raised her mug to her lips and gazed out over the crowds. He had to say something soon or she would think he was an idiot.

He decided on a banal comment about the clear, starry sky. "Isn't it–"

"Don't you–"

They both laughed, having chosen to speak at exactly the same moment.

While her eyes were downcast, he took in the waves of her hair, which intertwined with a golden ribbon, and the strands which fell around her creamy neck and collarbone.

"You look beautiful, Amy," he said, his voice thick.

"Thank you for saying that, Henry," she said, regarding him from beneath her lashes. "I like your jacket."

It pleased him that she'd noticed it. He'd borrowed it from William especially. But there was something in the way she'd thanked him that he didn't like. "I'm not just saying it," he said. "I always think you're beautiful, inside and out."

She smiled, but in a sad kind of way, and then stared at her hands without speaking.

Henry could tell something was wrong... Had he already said too much? Was she struggling with the right words to tell him she didn't share his feelings?

Finally, she looked up at him with tears in her eyes. "I wish the world would see me as you do, Henry."

He frowned. "What do you mean?"

"I'm not good enough," she whispered, her eyes radiating hurt. "I can see it in the way everyone looks at me, in little things they say. Even your parents hate me. I saw the way your mother looked at me just now."

Damn, she'd seen it too. Henry's heart throbbed. "I think you're good enough," he said hoarsely. "No, no, not good enough – perfect. I can't see a single fault. If anyone chooses to see flaws, it's a reflection of their own character, not yours. You've suffered, and only because of your trusting, innocent nature. I for one don't see why you should be bullied because of it."

"But don't you see, Henry?" she said, her expression desolate. "I've been abandoned so many times, there *must* be something wrong with me. My real mother gave me up." Her voice cracked. "My parents died, and I was alone in the world. I was evicted from Ashworth Hall. And now I am a burden to a respectable couple who wish I were someone I am not. I feel as if I will never belong anywhere, that no one will ever *choose* me."

How Henry longed to take her in his arms and comfort her, to show her his love. Her speech had made him want to weep. He knew he couldn't demonstrate his affection as he wanted to, but he wasn't going to let her leave without knowing that someone cared about her unconditionally. It was time to risk his heart, to save hers.

Chapter Thirteen

Henry reached out a tentative hand and slowly placed it over hers, which was still sheathed in a glove.

She blinked but didn't flinch.

"I would choose you, Amy," he said, "if you'd let me."

His heart pounding, he looked into her eyes intently, searching for some sort of assurance that she wanted to choose him, too.

She held his gaze but remained silent for what seemed like an eternity. "How do I know I wouldn't be... hurt again?" she asked.

A dark shadow passed over his heart. Could she really compare him to that heartless aristocrat? Could she really believe him capable of abusing her?

"I can't think what I can say to convince you to trust me," he said. "Only that I hope I've proven myself in all the times we've been together. But I don't want to rush you, or give you any sense of obligation if you don't... want the same things I do."

She shook her head. "It's just that I feel so... ashamed of what happened. People judge me because they think I encouraged him, because I didn't get rid of the child, or because I didn't find somewhere to hide away. God knows I tried..." She wiped away a tear. "When people see me, they see immorality and weakness."

He curled his fingers around hers, unwavering in his gaze. "You have nothing – nothing – to be ashamed of," he told her, swallowing back the

108

emotion rising in his throat. "All I see when I look at you is courage, and beauty, and kindness."

She took a breath and gave him a wobbly smile. "Thank you, Henry." She tightened her hand around his, and they remained in comfortable silence for some time.

Henry hoped he had eased her suffering, even to a small degree. In the back of his mind there was a nagging thought. Would it help her to know that her mother, the very person at the root of her feelings of rejection, might have been the one who had chosen to save her and Benjamin? He couldn't guess at the reason why Mrs Fortescue had given up Amy in the first place, but it was apparent to him that she must have watched over her this whole time. After all, it would have been easy for her to leave Amberley and try to forget she ever had a child, if that was what she had wanted.

As Henry struggled again with how he might suggest this notion, Amy finished her cider and placed her mug down.

"I should really be getting home," she said. "Benjamin has some teeth starting to come through and will need me tonight."

His heart sunk a little, and he lost his courage. He didn't want the wonder of this night to end. And he certainly didn't want to detain Amy when there was a chance his words could cause her pain.

There was no way of knowing when he would have more time with her; certainly any opportunities for such close, unguarded conversation would be few and far between. But he had monopolised her long enough, and whatever was between them had to be on her terms.

He stood and reached down to help her up. Smiling, she placed her gloved hands in his and squeezed his fingers, mirroring his earlier gesture, before she rose.

There she remained, inches away from him, staring deep into his eyes. He felt as if something was shifting, falling into place. There were no words, but there didn't have to be. He held her gaze, trying to show her the love and care in his heart. He drank in those magical green eyes, those strong cheekbones, that rosy mouth. He lingered, considering what it might feel like to caress those lips with his. It would be so easy – too easy – to drop his head and melt into that softness... but he couldn't. It was her gift to give, in her own time, if at all. He must not take anything for granted. The precious moments of this night had seemed impossible only a few months ago.

"Goodnight, then," he said hoarsely. "I hope you've had an agreeable evening."

She grinned. "More than agreeable, Henry. The best night I've had in a very long time." She let go of his hands and turned away. After taking several steps, she turned back and waved, a smile on her lips.

He waved back and watched her disappear. Then he sank back down onto the hay bale and drained the rest of his cider. The future was suddenly unbelievably bright.

Some time later, Henry whistled a jolly tune as he prepared to escort his animals back to the farm, hardly knowing what he was doing. As he rounded the end pen, he heard laughter and stopped dead in his tracks. Clara.

He whipped around, looking for her. The moonlight illuminated the whole area, but a nearby stand of broad trees created a labyrinth of shadows. Then he heard a male voice, and he sucked in a breath. Surely it wasn't...

He rushed towards the sound, his heart in his throat. And there, pressing Clara up against the trunk of an oak tree, was bloody Mick Stockton. The bastard.

"Get the hell away from my sister!" Henry charged at Stockton. The scoundrel had his mouth on her neck, his hands all over her. Henry grabbed him from behind and yanked him off her before shoving him backwards.

"Russell," Stockton said, raising his palms, "I know what you must think, but–"

"Damn right I know what to think!" He shrugged out of his jacket and tossed it on the ground.

"Henry," Clara cried. "Don't!"

But a veil of rage obscured Henry's vision, and he was intent on only one thing: hurting Stockton.

❧

Once settled in the carriage, Amy peeled the gloves off her hands and gave them back to Mrs Fortescue, who was sitting opposite with her husband.

"How did you fare with the dancing?" Mrs Fortescue asked, putting the gloves in her reticule.

Amy blushed. "Quite well, thank you." Her words belied the incredible lightness in her spirit. Dancing with Henry she'd felt completely happy and carefree for the first time in over a year. The wonderful things he'd said to her were starting to penetrate her heart, beginning to thaw that which had been frozen by hurt and rejection.

Mrs Fortescue sent her a sly smile. "You seemed to be quite comfortable from what I could see. As did Mr Russell."

Amy couldn't hold back a return smile. "I would not have danced with anyone but him."

Mrs Fortescue nodded. "I thought as much. Your actions will certainly set tongues wagging – dancing with him for so long and then engaging in a cosy tête-à-tête afterwards."

"Were you *spying* on me?"

Mrs Fortescue sighed. "No, not spying, merely looking out for your safety."

Amy pursed her lips in response.

"Now." Mrs Fortescue exchanged a glance with her husband. "Please do not be offended by the question, but for your sake I must know... Do you mean to set your cap at him?"

Amy gaped at her. She had meant to never set her cap at any man, but if she had a cap at all, she had to acknowledge it belonged squarely with one Henry Russell.

"I have been careful not to let my emotions lead me astray," she said slowly. "However, I do confess that I am falling in love with him."

Mrs Fortescue smiled, causing Amy to nearly fall off the seat. She had expected a telling off, a dressing down, a lecture. Instead, after a lengthy pause, the woman said, "I am delighted for you, my dear. I wondered if you might not have the courage to risk your heart again, but I should not have doubted you."

Amy was dumbfounded. That Mrs Fortescue was concerned about her heart was a shock. When she recovered her sense, a doubt lingered in her mind. "I think his family still disapprove of me."

It was Mrs Fortescue's turn to purse her lips. "Well! We shall see about that. But what of Mr Russell? It is quite obvious he has eyes for none but you, and he is to take over the lease of the farm so will at least have a measure of security in the future. I only hope he does not intend to string you along. Has he given you any sign of his intentions?"

Amy thought for a moment and then shook her head. "Not in so many words, but he has shared such personal things with me as to make me feel intimately connected with him. Indeed, I am glad he hasn't asked me to decide about a future with him yet. He has given me time to get used to the idea."

Mrs Fortescue nodded. "Yes, the last thing we want is undue pressure to be put on you. I am pleased he is being patient with you."

"Oh yes," Amy said with confidence. "Henry Russell is the most patient and kind man I know."

☙❧

Henry hurled himself at Stockton, smashing his fist across the scoundrel's face.

Stockton staggered back. Then he charged at Henry, but instead of hitting him, he grabbed him around his middle and tackled him to the ground.

Henry struggled, trying to roll over. "Hit me, you coward!"

Stockton pushed himself up to standing, and Henry followed suit. In his fury, he lunged at Stockton with both hands outstretched towards his neck.

Stockton struck out in defence and landed a lucky blow on Henry's cheekbone. Then he held his arms out in a placating gesture. "Now, Russell, calm down."

"Don't you tell me to calm down when you're molesting my sister!" Henry roared. "I'll knock your block off!"

Stockton dodged out of the way. "I don't *want* to hurt you, Russell," he said. "I'm not hurting Clara, either."

Henry eyed him warily, breathing hard. "I'll be damned," he said, panting, "if another woman I love gets ruined. She's an innocent, and you have no right!"

Stockton sighed and turned to Clara, which only infuriated Henry further. "I'll meet with you as soon as I can," Stockton said, reaching out a hand to her.

She extended her hand towards him, but Henry caught it. "Clara, you're coming home with me," he said, pulling her away. He turned back to Stockton. "And there'll be no meeting, either!"

Clara struggled in his grip as he led her away. "Stop it, Henry," she hissed. "This is humiliating."

He looked down into her pained face and let her go. "You should know better than to let a man take liberties," he said harshly. "You're not thinking of the consequences."

"I know him, Henry," she said, as they found their way back to the animal pens. "We love each other."

"What?" Henry stopped short and whirled around to face her. "Clara, don't you know a man will say anything to… to get what he wants?"

She rolled her eyes. "I'm not stupid, Henry. Mick has been courting me for months. He wants to marry me."

This was too much for Henry. He'd always had one grudge or another against Stockton. He certainly didn't trust him with his own flesh and blood. The man was a pompous prig… but clearly Clara had seen something in him to admire.

"Come on," he said gruffly. "Help me get the animals ready to go."

They worked in near silence for a quarter of an hour, while Henry's temper cooled and he attempted to come to terms with Clara's apparent relationship. After she said goodbye to her friends, they herded Henry's animals home together.

"You're just like Pa, Henry," Clara said, as she strode along beside him.

Henry frowned. "What do you mean?" He actively tried his best to *not* be like his father, to be kind and generous to others.

"Why, your temper, of course," she said with a laugh. "Doesn't take much, and you both fly off the handle."

Henry sighed. "Yes, I suppose you're right." He *was* just like his father. His throbbing cheek was the evidence. He hated himself.

"Mick makes me happy, Henry," she said, pulling his attention back. "I believe he really cares about me."

Henry glanced at her. "How long did you say this has been going on for? Why hasn't he come for dinner at the house, or visited?"

"He started paying me attentions not long after the new year," Clara said. "And he has come, Henry, but you've been busy."

Too busy to notice what was going on right under his nose? Too preoccupied with his own desires and ambitions to see that his little sister needed him?

He'd spent every spare second over the past several months working on the croft house or trying to contrive more time with Amy. What if Stockton's intentions hadn't been honourable, and he hadn't protected his sister from the same fate as... He shuddered. It didn't bear thinking about.

"How do you know he's willing to offer for you?" he asked.

"He already has," she replied. "He talked to Pa after he asked me to marry him, at the beginning of summer."

"And you kept it from me?"

She glared at him. "Can't you see why? I know how much you dislike Mick."

She had a point. He took a deep breath. "So there's already an understanding between you, then. Why haven't you got married?"

Clara sighed. "When he told his parents, they forbade him from marrying me."

Henry's mouth dropped open. "Why?"

"Because I don't have a dowry," she said, as if it were obvious. "And I'm not a gentleman's daughter. His mother and sisters look down their snooty little noses at me."

Anger flared again in Henry's gut. "My sister isn't good enough for them?"

She shrugged. "Obviously not."

"So, what will you do?"

She sighed again. "Mick doesn't want to give up. He hopes to convince his parents eventually. But without some money, I don't know what chance we have. They might find someone more suitable."

Money, status, and the privileged few – how these things ruled their lives. "And if they do?" he asked Clara gently.

"It will break my heart into a hundred pieces. I do love him, Henry. He makes me smile. He wants to look after me, and I want to be his wife."

"I understand," Henry said. He went around the other side of the herd in order to steer the animals down to the farm. "I want you to be well settled, too."

After saying goodnight to his sister a while later, he climbed into his bed, exhausted, and made a promise to them both. He would be a better brother. He would do whatever he could to help secure this union, if that would make her happy… if that would keep her safe.

Chapter Fourteen

The following morning, as his parents slept off the excesses of the previous night, Henry slipped out and headed to Amberley. After the highs and lows of the fair, he needed some wise counsel. When would he ever learn to rein in his temper? He headed to the parsonage. He knew William wouldn't judge him –at least not until he knew the whole story.

The gash on his cheek had flared up, rendering him a ruffian. He avoided the village and any condemning eyes, cutting across pastures instead.

The rhythm of his quick steps took him back to the thrill of dancing with Amy. He hoped he hadn't come on too strong, or scared her off by speaking so candidly. He sensed she had begun to open up to him, too, but something nagged at him. She was still far from his. She had relied on the gloves to keep herself protected from him. What would it take to have her trust him?

As he walked up to the Brooks' house, the front door opened and a lady stepped out.

"Thank you, vicar," he heard her say. "I shall finalise everything prior to the next vestry meeting."

Good Lord, it was Mrs Fortescue – of all the people to encounter this morning! He wanted her to think well of him, and here he had proved himself to be a hot-headed lout. Surely this would only confirm in her eyes that he wasn't at all suitable for her Amy.

He turned on his heel to dash down the garden path, intent on escaping her. He was too late.

"Oh, Mr Russell, is that you? What a jolly evening last night. I think Amelia was quite… oh my."

Henry had turned to face her, and there was no hiding his injury. "Mrs Fortescue," he said, nodding a bow. "It was certainly a memorable evening."

"Indeed." Her mouth quirked, and then she glanced over her shoulder at the house. "Going to seek forgiveness, are we?"

He smiled in spite of himself. "Something like that."

She continued towards him up the path. "For your sake, I hope your soul is still in good health." She gasped as she came up alongside him. "Dear me, that cheek will need to be stitched up. Get to Mr Lindsay as soon as you can."

Henry was completely taken aback; she seemed genuinely concerned for his welfare. This was far from the haughty curmudgeon he was used to. She was almost like… a mother. It was kind of her to suggest he see the physician, but of course he couldn't afford to pay the fees. He'd just have to ask his own mother to take a look at it. "Thank you," he said. "Good day." He tipped his hat to her and started for the door.

"Oh, Mr Russell," the lady called.

He turned around. "Yes, Mrs Fortescue?"

"I surmise you do not make a habit of seeing private physicians in time of need. Be assured Mr Lindsay is a friend of mine, and he will be happy to have me cover the bill next time I visit him."

Henry tried to follow this. "Are you offering to pay for him to stitch my face?"

She actually smiled. "I am."

There was kindness and there was pity. He did not accept pity. "I thank you, again, but I can't let you do that."

She waved a dismissive hand. "Nonsense. Go there now, and I will write to him. Consider it a special favour, for me. I should like to see your cheek heal properly."

Her domineering nature had returned, so he better knew where he stood. But did she mean she wanted him to mend his appearance for

Amy's sake? Surely not. He watched as she bustled off down to her waiting carriage. She gave him an imperious wave before setting off.

He could only stare at her. Perhaps he would see Mr Lindsay afterward, if time allowed before he had to return for the next feed at the farm. Perhaps.

࿇

Amy stabbed at her tapestry with her needle, not happy with the evenness of her stitches. She was still tired despite having a mid-morning nap. It had been a late night, and Ben had kept her busy in the early hours of the morning.

The main reason that she couldn't concentrate on her stitching, however, was because emotions were swirling around inside her. They endangered any sensible intentions she had been clinging to, to safeguard her heart and protect herself from being abused again.

Something was releasing within her, clearing the way for her to trust… and perhaps love. The very idea made her giddy, and anxious, and free, and frightened. But the fear was starting to be overtaken by hope in a potential future… with Henry. She could hardly bear to let herself believe that it might be possible, that she and Benjamin could be safe and loved, forever.

She glanced up at Mrs Fortescue, who was industriously completing a pattern with characteristic perfection. Did she see a slight curve at the edge of the lady's mouth?

She wanted to see Henry again, and she didn't want to wait for the next church service. As Amy started to think of ways she could engineer such a meeting, Mrs Fortescue spoke.

"I ran into Mr Henry Russell this morning," she said casually, not taking her eyes off her needle.

Amy nearly sprang from her seat. She took a breath to calm herself, unsure what this meant. "Oh, did you?" she asked as serenely as she could, also keeping her eyes down.

"Yes, indeed. It seems he may have stumbled on his way home after the harvest fête."

Amy's head jerked up. "Is he all right?"

Mrs Fortescue met her eyes and waved her hand flippantly. "Oh, he's perfectly fine. Just a few scrapes. However, I think perhaps it might be the neighbourly thing to do to check that he is fully recovered. I recommended he have Mr Lindsay look at his face in case he needed stitches."

Amy bolted up from her chair, her embroidery hitting the floor. "His face? Stitches? The doctor? I should go to see him right away."

"Sit down, dear," Mrs Fortescue said evenly. "He probably would not want you to see him with fresh bruising. And it is not the done thing for you to be visiting with him unattended. We shall go together tomorrow to call on the ladies. There is no guarantee he will be within the house at that time, but the ladies can pass on your regards."

Amy resumed her seat and considered this. Henry was hurt? Surely it had not been an accident. Had his father taken exception to his interest in her? Her heart ached to know. How would she endure a whole day in suspense?

Mrs Fortescue was probably right, though – they should not intrude on the household so soon. She sighed. "Very well. I would be much obliged if you would attend me there tomorrow."

❧❧

At the appointed hour, the Fortescue carriage rattled, rumbled and bounced its way down the lane to the Russells' farmhouse. The ladies were jostled around inside, with Mrs Fortescue vainly trying to keep her composure. Amy tried her best to not laugh. This vehicle was not made for farm roads.

"Have you, er, ever visited the Russells before?" she enquired docilely.

Mrs Fortescue shook her head and was bounced so high from her seat she almost hit the roof. Recovering, she said, "No, this is the first time I am paying them a call."

The carriage stopped moving, and both women fixed their hair and straightened their dresses before being assisted to the ground.

Amy followed Mrs Fortescue to the front door of the house. Movement in one of the downstairs windows caught her eye. It was the two Russell girls, clearly shouting. Their mother appeared, and her mouth dropped open. She pulled them away from the window just as Mrs Fortescue rapped on the door. It was several moments before the door was thrown open by Mrs Russell herself.

"Mrs Fortescue!" she cried, not quite managing a smile. "Come in!" She stepped aside and ushered the woman in, and then as Amy walked by her she said a curt, "Miss Miller."

"Good day, Mrs Russell," Amy greeted her, with pointed cheer. She bristled inwardly as they were shown into the little parlour. What did she have to do to make these people like her? She couldn't take back the past. She wished she didn't care what they thought of her, but she did.

Apparently did they care what the visitors thought of them – although perhaps only Mrs Fortescue – as the girls were hurriedly moving and hiding things in the room.

Clara picked up a bonnet from a chair and gestured for Amy to sit.

Mrs Russell shoved a pile of papers under a battered settee and perched on it next to Mrs Fortescue. "Good morning, ladies," she said, while retying the bun in her hair. "What brings you to see us today?"

Mrs Fortescue sat with admirable aplomb, her tall, broad figure a commanding presence in the small room. "Good morning," she said. "I thought it was high time we got to know each other a little better – we are neighbours, really."

Mrs Russell gaped at her and then exchanged glances with her daughters, who were standing awkwardly in front of the fireplace. "How kind of you," she finally said. "If I'd known you were coming, I would have prepared… something."

"On no account would I have put you to any trouble," Mrs Fortescue said, "which is why I thought we would just pop in."

Silence descended on the group, and Amy fingered the lace on her gloves.

There was a sudden crash, and the door to the parlour burst open. The two Mr Russells darted into the room.

At the sight of Henry, Amy almost leapt up towards him. He was indeed hurt, his cheek bruised and stitched together and his eye a little bloodshot. But he seemed otherwise in good health, and, to Amy's eye, quite the handsomest man in the world.

"We heard the carriage," Mr Russell said. "Thought we best say hello."

"Good day, gentlemen," Mrs Fortescue said with a nod.

Belatedly, they both dropped into awkward bows. "Ma'am," Henry said, and then turned to Amy. "Miss Miller." A grin crept across his face. "How are you today?"

She couldn't help but smile back at him. "I'm fine, thank you, but it seems I need to be checking how *you* are."

☙❧

His face. That damned fight with Stockton. The sweet concern in her eyes. "I'm quite all right, thank you, Miss Miller." He touched his cheek and then regretted it, holding back a wince. "It's nothing," he said, hoping his smile was convincing.

"I believe Amy likes to visit with your animals, Mr Russell," Mrs Fortescue said. "The pigs, especially."

He stared at her. "I think she does, Mrs Fortescue."

"Would you have leave to show them to her now?"

He did a double take. "Why, yes," he said, ignoring his father's grunt. "If that's your wish." Did she actually want them to spend time alone together?

Then her expression clouded. "Would there be a farmhand present in the, er, barn?"

She was looking out for Amy's safety and propriety, just as a mother should. "Aye, ma'am, there are a couple of lads in there mucking out the–"

"Thank you, I do not need the details." Mrs Fortescue looked to Amy. "What are you waiting for?"

"Oh!" Amy jumped up, and Henry stepped back to let her pass through the door ahead of him. He followed her out of the house.

They began to stroll towards the barn, and she said quietly, "What happened, Henry? Was it your father?"

"No, no." He coloured with shame. What would she think of him, knowing his temper was so unguarded? He took a deep breath. Now was not the time to tell falsehoods or evade the truth. If he was going to gain her trust, he had to be honest no matter what. "I found Clara with Mick Stockton," he said, "and I panicked."

He said nothing more, only looked over at her. She studied him for a moment and swiftly comprehended his meaning. "You needed to defend her honour?"

"That's what I did, yes. It turns out they're all but engaged, but still…"

"He should keep his distance until they are *married*," she said firmly.

"Exactly," he said, sharing a look of understanding with her.

Amy appeared to be lost in her thoughts. "That must be what Clara meant when… But why does he not just propose?"

Henry explained what Clara had told him about Stockton's family's reluctance.

"Poor thing," Amy muttered. "I know how it feels to be disapproved of. At least an honourable gentleman wants to marry her. Here's hoping he *remains* honourable."

They had reached the barn, but Henry didn't open the door for Amy. Another idea had started in his mind.

Amy's guardian had encouraged them to go outside together. And even though she had checked there would be others present, the walk over to the barn would be enough time to… He would not squander this chance. It was time to let her into his private world.

"Amy," he said, "there's somewhere else I want to take you."

"Oh yes?" Her brows rose.

"Yes. I should drive you there if we are not to be away too long." He gestured she precede him to the stables.

She acquiesced, but not before throwing him a quizzical look. "Just where are you taking me, Mr Russell?"

He quickly got a mare ready and hitched the reins to his little gig before jumping onto it. "Somewhere dear to my heart… that I would like to share with you."

She let him help her up into the gig, the hand she gave him gloved in lace. "Will we be chaperoned?"

He looked into her playful eyes, and his heart soared. "No, we shall not." Then he studied her seriously and took up the reins. "Do you trust me, Amy Miller?"

Her expression lost its mirth. "Yes, Henry Russell, I do."

He smiled at her fondly and flicked the reins. They pulled away from the stables and down a bridle path towards his future home.

The day was clear and cool, and the huge oak trees lining one side of the path were rich in autumn colours. Henry drank in the crisp air. A bundle of nerves, excitement and anticipation, he had never felt more alive. Was this the day he would ask her to marry him, and dare he hope she would say yes?

They rode in a comfortable silence, and he stole frequent glances at his beloved. Was it possible she was even more beautiful now than she had been at the fair? Memories of holding her in his arms danced in his mind, and he found himself smiling.

"What are you thinking of, Henry?" Amy asked, a curious smile playing about her own lips.

He took a breath to answer, but before he could speak, she leaned her head over to rest on his shoulder, as if it were the most natural thing in the world.

His heart began to thud so loudly he was sure she would be able to feel it. It was such a small gesture, and yet it was the whole world to him. She trusted him, felt secure with him. Did she know he was hers for the taking?

"I was remembering our dance the other night," he said finally. "And I was noticing how pretty you look today."

"Oh!" Her head bobbed off his shoulder, but then she tucked it in closer. "Thank you."

Henry breathed a sigh of relief, feeling his boldness had been rewarded. Something in his heart confirmed that now was the time to be completely open with her.

Before long they rounded a bend, and the little house came into view. "There it is."

She sat up straight again. "The cottage?"

"Yes." Would she like it? He began to sweat. It was a far cry from Briarwood. "My father acquired the lease a short time ago. There's a small acreage attached." He took a deep breath. "It is to be my home while my father is still living."

They drew up in front of the building, and Henry jumped down.

"Really?" Amy examined the house while he tied the reins to a post. She waited for him to come beside her, and let him lift her to the ground. He didn't immediately let go, and she didn't remove her hands from where they rested on his chest. She held his eyes with a sincerity that suggested she knew the meaning of such a moment. Then she said softly, "Will you show it to me?"

He nodded, and reluctantly released her. He unlocked the front door and pushed it open for her to enter. After closing it behind himself, he followed her through the little foyer and into the kitchen diner.

Light slanted through the windows, bouncing off the polished tiles of the floor. It created a warm glow, but it couldn't outshine Amy's radiance as she turned to face him. "It's lovely, Henry! You can see the garden."

He beamed. "I built the cabinets, and I made this table." He touched the smooth surface of the table top.

"It's beautiful," she said, also running her hand over it. "I think perhaps your talents are wasted on the farm."

Pensive, she moved through to the parlour. He showed her the work he'd done on the beams, the floor, and the walls. She went over to the fireplace. "It would be so cosy in here in the winter," she said. "It reminds me of my family home."

Encouraged, Henry asked, "Can I show you upstairs?"

She nodded, a little timidly, before leaving the room and ascending the staircase. He showed her the two smaller rooms first and then the main bedroom. She went to the window and took in the view out over the pastures.

With her back to him she asked, "Why do you not live here now, Henry? Is it just that you've needed to do this work to make it habitable?"

He came to within a few paces of her. "Yes, that, and... I can't afford to have help to look after it. What I need is... a wife." He cringed. How mercenary that sounded, as if he thought a servant and a life companion were interchangeable.

She turned around, her eyes wide, and he was unsure if she'd taken offence. He ploughed on regardless. "What I mean is, I wouldn't want to be here alone. I want to have a family, I want to have... you."

She gasped, and her hand flew to her mouth. "Oh, Henry," she breathed.

As she took tentative steps towards him, words tumbled out of his mouth. "The income from the land will be modest, and our life would be more simple than you're used to. But I'd look after you, Amy, and little Benjamin, of course... if you were mine."

She was inches away from him now, her eyes locked on his. "Don't you mind, Henry? That Benjamin isn't yours?"

"I don't mind at all," he said, smiling down at her and fighting the urge to embrace her, close as she was.

"But your eyes, Henry!" she whispered.

"What of them?"

"Ben's eyes are so dark," She gulped. "Even perfect strangers will know he isn't yours."

He shook his head. "Perhaps people may be unkind every now and then," he said, "but that's nothing compared to the boy having a father to look after him... to *love* him." He looked deep into her eyes. "Don't you see? When I look at him I only see you."

"Really?" Tears filled her eyes as she gazed up at him.

He shrugged helplessly, feeling his own emotions close to breaking the surface. "I just want to make you happy, Amy," he said, his voice cracking. "I care about you more than anything."

With a tremulous smile on her lips, she replied, "I care about you, too. I only wish that I may make you as happy as you're making me."

He laughed lightly. She really had no idea. "You're my reason to live."

She closed the gap between them, so close they were almost sharing the same breath. She searched his face, and he closed his eyes for a moment, willing himself to stay still, overcome by the joy of her so near.

She reached up with a shaking hand, and brushed her gloved fingers lightly across the wound on his cheek. Then she ran one finger down the length of his jaw and rested it on his chin, just below his lips.

He shivered. The feeling of the lace against his skin was almost more tantalising than her bare fingers would have been. Still he did not move. He would not. To frighten her now would break this wonderful spell, this tender connection between them.

At last, she tilted her head up towards him, her eyes intent on his mouth. Henry held his breath as she shifted her hand behind his neck and pulled herself up to him. He closed his eyes and resisted the urge to drop his head to meet her.

Her lips touched his, and his world was forever changed. The softness of her mouth, coupled with her sweet intensity, set off a spark inside him that would never die. A long-held hunger began to be satiated. He placed his hand on her back, gently caressing her with his thumb. And he kissed her back.

Chapter Fifteen

Amy was in a foreign world. Love, security and pleasure overwhelmed her senses in equal measure. She drank them in, drank *him* in. She hadn't realised she was thirsty for him until this moment.

Her body pulsed with delight as she felt the tender pressure of his response to her kiss. Happiness, now such an unfamiliar emotion, began to consume her.

He wanted to be with her. She could belong with him, could belong in this place. He would be a father to Benjamin. He would be hers.

She threw her other arm around his waist, pulling him tight against her. He responded, encircling her waist with his arms, and their kisses deepened.

A bolt of desire shot through her, and with it, a flash of panic. With rising passion came rising anxiety, and she suddenly wrenched herself free, stumbling backwards. The room became a blur as agonising memories blurred her vision.

Henry's eyes flew open, and he reached out to her. "Don't be afraid, Amy," he said. "I won't hurt you."

She shook her head and pressed the heels of her hands against her temples, trying to rid herself of the images tormenting her – shock, agony, betrayal, and a horrible sordidness that would always linger.

"I'm sorry, Henry," she said. "I can't do this."

She darted past him and ran from the room, then down the stairs. She burst through the door and to the cool air outside, where she doubled over and sucked in desperate breaths.

What was she doing, alone with a man in the middle of nowhere? Far from help and those who would protect her? What was she doing, allowing herself to trust a male who had the power to defeat and destroy her? How could she have let herself become so vulnerable, so weak?

Henry joined her but kept his distance. "Will you tell me what happened?" he asked.

She looked at him, taking in the anguish in his expression. It was too much to bear. "Please take me back."

He stiffened. "Of course."

She stepped up into the gig clumsily, before he had the chance to offer her any assistance. She sat as far to the left side as she could, and after he had untethered the reins, he mirrored her on the right.

"I'm sorry if I rushed you," he said slowly. "I have tried my best not to. Please tell me I still have a chance of being with you."

She couldn't even contemplate the possibility; any thought of being possessed by another human being was repugnant to her. "I don't think *I* have a chance," she said, sadness dripping from her voice. "I am forever ruined."

"You were never ruined in my eyes," he said, and her heart wept.

He sighed, and proceeded to drive away. The journey was in stark contrast to the one they had taken only a short time ago. Then she had been content and hopeful. Now she felt depressed and hopeless, with a shadow over her despite the bright sunshine.

When they arrived at the main house, she staggered down from the buggy, tears streaming down her face.

She pushed her way back into the parlour, where Mrs Fortescue now sat with only Mr and Mrs Russell.

Mrs Fortescue was on her feet in an instant. "Amy, what's wrong? What happened?" Henry arrived, and she turned on him. "What did you do?"

Amy shook her head. "We must go."

"Of course, my dear." She turned back to the Russells. "My thanks for your hospitality."

They fled the house and re-entered the carriage. Still weeping, Amy would not look Mrs Fortescue in the eye.

The carriage began its precarious drive back down to the road.

"Amy," Mrs Fortescue said, "you must tell me what happened. Are you... hurt?"

Amy began crying harder but shook her head and managed to squeak, "No."

Mrs Fortescue moved from across the carriage to sit next to Amy. She put a tentative hand on Amy's shoulder while she waited for her cries to subside into shaky breaths. "There, now." She gave Amy's shoulder a gentle squeeze before releasing her. "I thought he would declare himself," she said softly. "Did he not?"

Amy sighed. "Yes, I think he did. He told me he wants to look after me and Benjamin, to make us happy."

"And then?"

"Then I got scared," Amy said, still shaking with the overwhelming emotion of it.

"I see. Did he touch you? Did he try to kiss you?"

Amy shook her head. "No, I kissed him. And then it made me remember... the past, and I couldn't be with him anymore."

Mrs Fortescue nodded. "Perfectly understandable. You mustn't be too hard on yourself."

These words, though sympathetic, were enough to start another torrent of tears.

Amy had seen a perfect picture of what she wanted her life to be. But she couldn't have it. She had reached for it, but it was beyond her grasp. "I'll never be able to love anyone," she said with a sob.

Mrs Fortescue placed a hand on her knee. "Give it time, child. The best things in life are worth waiting for. And sometimes, our most beautiful moments are born out of pain."

Amy thought of her precious child, who was the most wonderful thing in her life but certainly born out of pain on many levels.

She took a deep breath in and out. "I hope I haven't hurt Henry too badly. I told him I couldn't be with him."

She looked into Mrs Fortescue's eyes and didn't find reassurance, but there was understanding, tinged with sadness. "Try not to worry," she finally said. "It must be hard on you both."

❧❧

"May I buy you a drink?"

Henry looked up from his near-empty pint of ale, startled. Mick Stockton stood before him at the counter of the pub.

"If it pleases you," Henry said with a shrug. He doubted anything the man had to say could make him feel any worse. He eyed Stockton warily as he sat on the stool next to his and ordered two pints.

Granville poured the ales and put them in front of the men. Stockton waited for the barman to walk away before he began speaking.

"You look like a man who is down on his luck."

Was it that obvious? The fact that he hadn't slept in three days, could barely stomach any food… could hardly breathe.

He drained the last of his first drink and forced himself to inhale. "Have you ever been so close to getting what you yearn for that you can almost smell it, only to have it snatched from your grasp?"

"Aye," Stockton replied. "More than once."

Henry picked up the next pint. "There is a lady who I would die for, but she isn't willing to take a risk on me."

Stockton nodded. "I saw you together at the fair. You seemed the picture of happiness, but one cannot wonder at her reluctance." He took a sip of his drink. "*I* have a lady who is willing, but I will be disinherited if I proceed."

Henry took a large swig of ale, remembering how eager Clara was, how heartbroken she seemed. Despite his history with Stockton, Henry had no reason to doubt the man's ability to be a good husband to his sister. In the many years he'd known Stockton, the worst sins he'd known him to commit were provocation and snobbery.

"Is it just that she wasn't born a lady?" Henry asked.

Stockton swallowed a mouthful. "I do not think they question her manners or moral character, really. It is simply a matter of the dowry."

Henry sighed. "Money." Money would stop Clara from marrying her beloved, was stopping him from being his own man, and had stopped him from proposing to Amy a year ago.

He did want Clara to be contented. At least one of them should be.

129

Somewhere in the increasing haziness of his brain, the seed of an idea started growing. He didn't have enough funds to keep his own staff or lease his own property, but what he did have saved could be put to a higher purpose.

He turned to Stockton. "If Clara had a dowry, what then?"

The man looked at him askance. "Why, I would marry her immediately and set up house with her in my cottage." The familiar pang of jealousy churned in Henry's gut. Stockton was already settled in a house with a housekeeper and manservant installed.

"And why do you want to marry her?"

Stockton paused with his glass halfway to his mouth and then set it down. "She is simply the most enchanting creature I have ever known."

Henry raised an eyebrow. "And?"

Stockton smiled. "And she is of good humour, with a quick mind, kind disposition and even temper. She is in my every thought."

Henry nodded, satisfied. "In that case, I will do what I can to make her your bride."

Stockton chuckled. "I only wish you could help."

Henry looked back at his glass. "If only there were someone who could help me."

Long after Stockton had finished his drink and taken his leave, Henry sat at the bar going over and over the events at the croft house in his mind.

Everything had seemed to be going so well, almost better than he ever could have imagined. Amy appeared to genuinely like the house, and the improvements he had made. Her presence in the rooms seemed natural, and he felt more at home there with her than he ever had by himself.

When she told him that she cared, when she stretched up to meet him and initiated that most heavenly kiss… he let himself go, surrendered himself to the sensation – and to her. And then, just at that vital moment when his future was beginning, she suddenly fell into some kind of darkness that she couldn't see her way out of.

He should never have let his guard down. He shouldn't have given in to his urges. Dammit, he'd taken her fully in his arms and kissed her with the eagerness of someone drinking a life-saving elixir. No wonder she'd been afraid. If he'd just remained stoic and still, she might not have pulled away. He was a damned fool.

"You awright, mate?"

Henry jerked his head towards the sound. It was Granville, clearly wanting to close up the pub. Henry hadn't realised he was the last patron there.

He forced a smile. "Right as rain," he said, pushing himself onto his feet.

As he stumbled into the night, the crisp autumn air confronted his lungs and cleared some of the fog in his brain.

The situation with Amy was beyond him. But with Clara, he had a fair idea of what he could do. He couldn't fix her birth – she would never be the daughter of a gentleman. But she could become a lady by marriage, if he stopped being so selfish and gave her everything he had to give.

With the way things were, he wouldn't need to live in the croft house any time soon, so he might as well give his life savings to Clara. He'd already spent some of them on the cottage, but he hoped what was left wouldn't be an embarrassment as a dowry.

The decision to give up on his dream of independence, and of love, was gut-wrenching. As he shuffled home, the finality of it became too much.

Before he gave up his nest egg, he needed to know for sure that Amy would never want him.

He wouldn't seek her out – she mustn't feel in the least as if he was harassing her. Indeed, the pain of the rebuff was so raw, he probably wouldn't be able to face her for a while. But at some point he had to know whether he had done something to cause her to run away, and if there was any likelihood of her coming back to him.

Chapter Sixteen

Amy poured the tea, her hands hardly shaking at all. She managed to make all five cups without incident, and she beamed as she handed each one out in turn to Mr and Mrs Fortescue, and Mr and Mrs Brook. The vicar and Cecilia were paying a visit, quite possibly the last one Cecilia would make before it became too uncomfortable for her to travel far beyond her house.

It had been three weeks since the disastrous episode at the Russell farm, and Amy was attempting to go on as best she could without dwelling on it. Mercifully, Benjamin occupied most of her time. It was only in the quiet hours that she thought back to losing the possibility of the life she craved, and the love she longed for. When she lay in bed at night, the memory of Henry's embrace haunted her.

She knew he deserved an explanation. She hadn't seen him at church in the weeks since that day – either he hadn't been present, or he had gone out of his way to conceal himself from her. She was secretly glad for the reprieve. She didn't want to see any evidence of his hurt, or have to explain why she would draw him to her one minute, and push him away the next. She would rather not have to delve into those feelings again.

She hoped he wouldn't hurt for long. Distance would do them both some good. In time he would stop loving her, and they would be friends again. And maybe, eventually, she would stop hoping for his love and all that it promised.

He needs a wife to share the smallholding with, she remembered. He would have to find another. The thought was like a knife through her heart. The idea of him settling down with another woman was excruciating.

"What do you say, Amy?" Mr Brook asked, and then four pairs of eyes were upon her.

"Oh!" She flushed scarlet. "Pardon me?"

"We were discussing the merits of educating girls in mathematics, dearest," Cecilia said gently. "William has suggested it for the local school, but the headmaster won't hear of it!"

Amy cleared her throat. "As it happens that the lady of the house often has to manage the household expenses, I think counting numbers is a valuable skill for girls," she said. "Not at all unfeminine." She picked up the plate of biscuits in front of her. "Would you like more, Mr Brook?"

Amy offered the treats to each person, and breathed a sigh of relief when Mr Fortescue began speaking to the vicar, shifting the attention away from her.

Conversation turned to matters that had arisen during the last meeting of the parish vestry, which both the Fortescues had attended. When the health of the church bell became the topic, Amy caught Cecilia's eye and indicated they should move to another part of the room.

Cecilia let Amy help her to the window seat.

"You must have the patience of a saint," Amy said to Cecilia with a grin. "Most of these parish visits are likely very tedious. And in your condition, you must be wanting quiet rest."

Cecilia smiled back. "On the contrary, I usually enjoy joining William on his rounds. But you are right, I cannot be on my feet for long periods or help as I used to. I ache all over these days."

Amy took her hand. "It will soon be over, Cici, and then you will have other trials to endure! As well as many wonderful things."

Cecilia nodded. "I am so tired, I fall asleep just after sundown most evenings. Poor William!" She giggled, and when Amy realised her meaning she joined in. The others turned around to stare at them.

Amy tried to assume a serious expression, until they were no longer being observed. "I confess I do not understand how you can bear to continue with… the marital act," she whispered. "Even when you weren't pregnant. It seems to me it is all about the gentleman's pleasure."

A blush took over Cecilia, right to the roots of her hair. "Oh my dear…" she murmured, studying her hands. At length, she spoke. "While the *act* is certainly uncomfortable at first, it soon becomes quite bearable." A smile spread across her mouth. "In fact, once one is accustomed to being so close and unguarded with the one she shares her heart with, it can actually be quite lovely. And not at all just for the gentleman." She giggled again.

Amy shook her head. "How fortunate you are able to enjoy it, dearest. I don't think I will ever get the chance."

Cecilia squeezed her hand. "Oh but I am quite certain you will, Amy. You have such a capacity to love – all it will take is the right man to recognise it. Are you sure you want to give up on Henry? He appeared genuine in his affections."

"I think he is – or was." Sadness enveloped Amy as she considered the prospect of letting him go. "But I am afraid to yield to my feelings, to be vulnerable. It's too much of a risk. I can't enjoy that intimacy with him, or anyone."

"You deserve to be loved completely, Amy," Cecilia said, looking deep into her eyes. "The only way to do that is by giving all of yourself, and having faith in the other person. Trusting someone else is a conscious effort, and this will be so much harder for you. But I believe you can do it. You are such a brave, strong woman. When you do, the rewards will be greater than you can imagine. The right time will come."

"How good you are to me," Amy said, squeezing her friend's hand in return. "You have always seen the best in me and pictured the brightest things for my future. I only wish I could share your optimism. Perhaps once I could have."

Shortly thereafter Agnes came in with Benjamin and announced she was leaving for her afternoon off. Amy moved to a secluded chair to feed him, and then she and Cecilia played with him on a rug until it was time for the Brooks to take their leave. They accepted the proffered carriage for the short journey home and were farewelled on the front doorstep. As the carriage pulled away, Benjamin suddenly vomited all down his dress and then rubbed the milky substance through his hair.

"Oh!" Amy cried. "I shall have to bathe you." She rushed inside with the Fortescues close behind. "And Agnes has left," she said, to no one in particular. "Oh well, I'm sure I'll be able to do it on my own now."

"May I assist you?"

Amy stopped in her tracks and spun back to Mrs Fortescue, unable to hide her shock. "What do you mean?"

The lady stood in front of her, shifting her weight. "I should like to help you bathe the child, if you have no objections."

Her eyes were clear and earnest. Amy couldn't think what ulterior motive the woman could possibly have. This would not help her cause of schooling Amy in the ways of becoming a lady. She had never volunteered to help with Benjamin before. Her behaviour was baffling in the extreme.

"Certainly, you may assist," Amy said.

Mr Fortescue disappeared into his library, and a tub of warm water was ordered. The ladies ascended to the nursery, and Amy used a cloth to clean the worst of the mess. She then removed Benjamin's dress and handed it to Mrs Fortescue. When Amy took the pilcher off, a little gasp escaped from Mrs Fortescue.

Amy threw her a questioning look.

The lady's eyes had filled with some sort of emotion, a kind of wonder. "His little legs," she whispered. "They are so small, and yet so rounded. I had forgotten… that is, I do not have experience with infants. How delightful."

Amy caressed each chubby thigh. "Why yes, I think he is quite delicious!" She gently tickled his tummy, eliciting a smile and a gurgle. A wonderful wave of motherly satisfaction washed over her.

"Only look at that lovely belly," Mrs Fortescue cooed. "Those tiny little arms…"

Amy smiled at her. Then she removed Benjamin's napkin and slowly lowered him into the water, holding him under his shoulder. She splashed a little water over him and then glanced at Mrs Fortescue. "Will you pass me that cloth, please?"

"Certainly." The item was quickly produced.

Amy took it, then hesitated. Mrs Fortescue was so eager. Amy couldn't explain it, but she was brimming with motherly pride and she ached to share her joy. Whatever the woman's reasons were, whether they were kindly or underhanded, she felt compelled to accept this offering. She passed the cloth back to Mrs Fortescue. "Would you like to bathe him?"

Mrs Fortescue's eyes searched her own as she took it. "Are you sure?"

Amy smiled and nodded. "I'll guide you." She cradled Benjamin in both hands and moved to the side a bit to let the other woman closer.

Mrs Fortescue submerged the cloth. "Hello, little Benjamin," she said. "How cosy you look in there." At the sound of the woman's voice the baby looked at her, and as she slowly rung out the cloth over his stomach and let the water trickle onto him, he smiled up at her.

"Oh, my." Mrs Fortescue smiled back at him, her complexion colouring. She ran the cloth over his torso and then down his arms.

Amy watched in awe, the woman's tenderness as surprising as it was welcome. Benjamin's little body relaxed as she bathed him, and Amy began to wash his wisps of hair.

"His hands are clenched," Mrs Fortescue said, as she washed the crease that was his wrist.

"They only seem to relax when he is asleep," Amy said. "Try using your finger instead of the cloth." She demonstrated how gently rubbing the bottom of his palm made his fingers flex slightly.

Mrs Fortescue hesitated before putting the cloth to one side. She tentatively reached out her finger and copied what Amy had done. "Oh," she said with a gasp. "His skin is so soft!"

She trailed her fingers down his round belly. "He is a perfect creation, Amelia." She turned to look Amy in the eye. "You should be very proud of him. I can comprehend why you would never wish to leave his side."

"Thank you." Amy swallowed, flummoxed by the lump in her throat.

❧

It was the last week of October, and Henry scrunched through fallen leaves as he helped his sisters unload vegetables to sell at the village market. There were calls of greeting from around the village green as they made their way to the family's stall in the bright morning sunshine.

Henry hefted a large basket onto the counter and began unloading pumpkins. He spent the morning behind the counter serving customers, and ignoring Clara and Tilly's protests when he lent his tone-deaf vocals to the songs they sang.

Henry had just finished putting some coins away in a tin under the counter when he looked up to find Amy standing in front of him, her maid in tow.

"Amy!" he cried, knocking the tin over. "Bother!" Coins spilled out all over the ground, and he bent to pick them up while also trying to talk to her. "How have… you been?"

"Hello, Henry," she said, the sound of her voice penetrating his heart. "I'm well, thank you. How are you?"

He finished tidying the money and straightened up to face her. How was he? In a dark, miserable hole, wondering if everything he had ever worked for in his life was for naught. "I get on tolerably," he said.

She met his eyes, and then her expression darkened with sadness. How much had he revealed with just one look?

Clara came to stand beside him and exchanged greetings with Amy and her maid. Then she turned to Henry. "I think we can manage here now, if you'd like to take a look around the market." She eyeballed him meaningfully, letting him know she expected him to take up the offer without any argument.

"If you're sure, Clara, I'll see if Miss Miller needs any help with her shopping." He attempted to smile at Amy, and she nodded, moving to the side to let him exit the stall.

"Jenny," – Clara beckoned to the girl – "why don't you stay here and tell Tilly and me all you've heard lately."

Jenny nodded, approaching the other girls eagerly.

Henry mouthed "Thank you" to Clara and she flashed him a grin before turning back to absorb the flow of gossip pouring forth from Jenny.

"May I walk with you?" Henry asked Amy.

"Please," she replied, and they exchanged shy smiles.

The market bustled with village folk going about their business. Henry and Amy meandered up and down the aisles without speaking. It reminded Henry of their time at the fair after the dance, when Amy had taken his arm. Today, he sensed there was no point in offering it.

He cleared this throat as they stopped by a stand of preserves. "I hope things at home are still getting better?"

She nodded. "Indeed, I think we are making good ground. Mrs Fortescue even seems to be taking a liking to little Ben."

"Is that so?" He smiled. "That's great to hear."

"How are you getting on with the croft house?"

"Slowly but surely," he replied. "I'm trying to make some chairs for the kitchen table at the moment."

Amy picked up a jar of marmalade and then put it down again, staring out to the fields beyond. It was as if she wanted to look anywhere but at him. It stung. But he could also sense she did want to speak with him. Why else would she have approached his stall? He must be forthright. When would he get the chance to talk openly with her again?

"Amy," he said, "would you like to talk somewhere more quiet? Perhaps in the meadow behind Jones's?" It was just out of sight of the market, which would give them privacy but hopefully wouldn't make her feel uneasy.

"Yes, I would," she said, and he breathed a sigh of relief. With all the activity in the market, he hoped their departure wouldn't be noticed.

Amy led the way through a gate at the end of the green and then along a path. They sat on a bench under a large tree, and as a cool breeze rustled the leaves, Amy drew her shawl tighter. She turned to him, her face a study in anxiety. He wished he could scoop her up into his arms and tell her he would make everything all right.

"Henry, I feel I owe you an explanation for what happened last month."

He stared at her. He hadn't expected her to be so direct. "You don't owe me anything," he said. "Though it would help to know what I did wrong." It was basically all he'd thought about since then.

"It's not that I don't want to be with you," she said, pleading with her eyes. "I want to trust you… I thought I did. But when I let myself… give into my feelings…" She blushed and drew a hand over her eyes. "At first I was so happy, and then I began to panic. I suppose it's because it reminds me of… things." She looked at him helplessly, and he nodded. Her pain was unbearable.

"I understand. Please don't think about – that," he said. "I only want to know how I can help you. I know I shouldn't have given into my own feelings. I'm very sorry for it." His voice wavered at the end of his speech, and he swallowed hard.

"Don't blame yourself," she said, reaching a hand out towards his knee but then withdrawing it. "It's lovely to be wanted. In fact, it's what I crave more than anything. And I feel so terrible. You offered yourself to me, and I ran from you. You don't deserve that."

He glanced at her at the exact moment a tear fell from one of her eyes. His heart constricted.

"I don't want you to worry about me," he said, after a time. "I just want you to know that my offer and my... hopes, they haven't changed."

She frowned. "I can't have you hoping, Henry," she said. "I cannot bear it. I'm very sorry if I led you on, if I made you believe I am capable of making some sort of commitment. But I simply can't go through with it. Not now, not ever."

His mouth dropped open.

"Not ever?" he repeated. "Are you sure? I thought you'd like Benjamin to be raised with a father. I want to look after you both, and I won't demand anything from you. Perhaps one day, you might become more at ease with me..."

"No, Henry," she said. "I can't ask that of you. When you marry, you should enjoy your... marital rights. It's not fair of me to ask that you go without a proper union."

His breathing quickened, as the horrible finality of what she was saying began to penetrate his mind. Of course she would assume that he would claim what she referred to as his marital rights. While he might have hopes that she would eventually feel comfortable with him, he would never presume...

"Amy," he began desperately, "I want to be with you. I would want you even if we *never* touched. Don't think I want to... take... anything from you. Will you let me be your friend? Please?"

More tears ran down her cheeks. "I do want to be your friend, Henry, but I don't think I can."

"Why not?"

"Because when I'm with you, the temptation is too great."

He gasped, finally understanding. She was attracted to him, but she was so haunted by the past that she couldn't give into her feelings.

She went on while he continued grappling with the truth. "Henry, I don't think I could ever be with you – or anyone – that way."

"I don't care," he said, his own eyes welling up. "Don't you know I would do anything for you?"

She shook her head. "As I said, it wouldn't be fair of me to deny either of us. Besides, you will want children of your own."

"There's no rush for that. We would have one child already."

She got to her feet. "Henry, please forget about me. I want you to be happy, to find someone to share that lovely property with."

He stood face-to-face with her, not ready to give up. "Forget you? I love you."

"Henry." She gulped, her hand over her mouth. "Please don't."

He reached for her. "I'll wait for you," he said firmly. "As long as you need."

She observed his hand but did not accept it. "No, you shouldn't wait for me. You deserve someone else, someone better. I can't stand the thought of denying you everything you've worked so hard for."

He sighed, sensing his efforts were in fact pushing her away. "There is no one else," he said. "But I can see you've made up your mind. Don't worry, I won't ask you again. But I want you to know I'm not giving up on you. You can always to come to me." He took one last, long look deep into her wounded, beautiful eyes. "Even if you just need a friend, you know where to find me."

He turned and walked away from her. He could hear her sobbing, but he didn't look back. What point was there, when there was no way he could comfort her without scaring her. He stepped up his pace and swiped away angry tears. Damn and blast that Barrington. He'd ruined both their lives.

He was almost running by the time he reached Clara and Tilly, who were now packing up the market stall.

"How did you – oh." Clara saw his face and then closed her mouth on the question. "Come on, Tilly," she said. "I'm starving. Let's get home as fast as we can."

Henry nodded his thanks and helped them move the remaining items to their cart. On the journey home, the girls chatted away as Henry silently drove the horses, his mind a cacophony.

Amy had essentially said she wished she could marry him. It was just that she was too scared of completely committing herself to another person. And she wanted him to move on. Well, maybe he would. His heart would always be hers, but he needed to stop hoping for that new and beautiful life and just focus on what he had.

When they got back to the house, he pulled Clara aside in the parlour.

"What is it, Henry?" she asked. "Are you all right?"

He shook his head. "No, I'm not, but I've made a decision."

"Oh yes?"

"I have something I want to give you. I have some funds saved up. I was going to use them for the smallholding, for animals, plants, furniture and other supplies… but there is little hope I'll be able to set up house there any time soon."

She regarded him sombrely. "Are things that bad with Amy?"

He nodded. "It looks like I've ruined any chance I might have had. So I want to give everything I have to you instead. So you can marry Stockton."

"What?" Her eyes widened in disbelief. "Would you really do that for me?"

"I'd like to, yes."

"But I would feel horrible, taking all your money from you."

He shrugged. "I want you to have it. It will do me good to see you happy."

She smiled at him. "I'm very lucky to have such a brother. But I can see you're upset. Please think about this for a few days, and if you still feel the same way then let's talk to Pa. If he thinks your capital is enough to tempt the Stocktons, he can go and make the offer."

"I'll do that," he said, giving her a quick hug. But his mind was made up. If he didn't focus his energies on helping his sister, the pain of losing his love would drive him mad.

Chapter Seventeen

A few weeks later, Amy sat playing with Benjamin on the floor in the drawing room, while Mrs Fortescue was at the desk writing correspondence.

Amy waved a rattle in front of the baby and then marched a finely crafted toy soldier along the rug beside him. But Benjamin just held out his chubby hands for the sheep Henry had made. She sighed and handed it over. It was nigh on impossible to keep the man from her thoughts.

There was some relief in having shared her feelings and fears with Henry, but she had not been entirely successful in her mission to have him give up hope.

Something in her rejoiced at his steadfastness, that despite her best efforts he would not be persuaded against her. He would still choose her, even after she had done her best to reject him. Surely that said a lot for the strength of his affections. Even if she was not brave enough to be with him, her admiration for him only grew with the knowledge of his determination to be with her.

When she was at a low ebb, the memory of his declaration of love lifted her heart. Perhaps, one day, she might heal from her trauma enough to find solace in his arms... if he didn't find another first. For now, she must make the best of things, and she was growing more and more comfortable with the Fortescues.

Mrs Fortescue stood, a pile of folded letters in front of her. She crossed the room and took up her sewing box. Then she sat with it on the sofa nearest to Amy and Benjamin.

"I heard some news today which might interest you," she said, as she picked up a thread and scissors.

"Did you?" Amy asked.

"Yes, indeed." Mrs Fortescue threaded her needle. "Clara Russell is to be married. They are to start reading the banns this Sunday."

"Oh! To Mick Stockton?"

"You knew?" The lady's disappointment was palpable, so used was she to being first with any intelligence.

Amy shook her head. "Not about the engagement. That should mean Henry's face will be safe from harm now."

Mrs Fortescue's needle fell into her lap. "I beg your pardon?"

"Nothing." Amy smiled to herself and resumed making Benjamin's sheep leap back and forth over his tummy.

The wooden toy was a stark reminder of Henry's thoughtfulness, of how he cared for them both. How ungrateful she was. She had thrown everything he'd given her back in his face. He must think their friendship extremely one-sided.

Perhaps she should make him something, to show him she appreciated his faith in her. She eyed the items in Mrs Fortescue's sewing kit, and thought back to their last conversation. A seed of an idea dropped into her head.

She turned to Mrs Fortescue. "I am in mind of a project. It will be a gift."

"Excellent," the lady said. "You know how much I approve of using one's talents to help those less fortunate."

Amy held back a smile. She wasn't sure how much the local poor appreciated the intricately embroidered handkerchiefs Mrs Fortescue bestowed upon them, but she knew they were crafted with the best of intentions.

"It is not for the poor," Amy was compelled to explain, "but for… a friend."

"Oh." Mrs Fortescue's eyebrows shot up. "*Oh*. I see." An indulgent little smile settled on her lips.

"May I borrow some paper and a pencil?"

"Certainly you may." Mrs Fortescue fetched the items from the desk and gave Amy a book to press on.

Amy thanked her and began drawing various designs on the paper. She moved her pencil almost absentmindedly as she watched Benjamin try to pass the sheep from one hand to another.

When she looked down at her paper again, she gave a start. What had she done? It would be like stitching her very heart into fabric.

If everything went wrong, no one would ever see what she'd done. But perhaps, if her dreams fell into place, eventually…

"If I am to proceed with this," she said, "I shall need help to purchase fabric and other supplies."

Mrs Fortescue nodded. "I would be only too happy to help. It will be wonderful to see you applying yourself to something."

The words may have been kindly meant, but they made Amy's blood run cold.

"I know I have failed to please you in my efforts to become more like a lady," she said. "I hope you know it is not for lack of trying. I have done my best to acclimatise, to avoid embarrassing you. I know at times you must have been ashamed of me, and I assure you, I have felt it keenly."

"Ashamed?" Mrs Fortescue whispered the word, her eyes wide. She opened her mouth again but then closed it, covering her face with one hand.

Amy could sense she had crossed a line, and as someone who was essentially a charity case, she could be skating on thin ice. But after months of trying to appease this woman, it appeared nothing had been good enough.

"Amelia," Mrs Fortescue began, but Amy cut her off.

"That's not my name!" She sprang up from the floor. "I'm Amy. This Amelia person you are trying to make me into is not who I am."

"But you were given the name Amelia when you were born," Mrs Fortescue said. "I think it a most lovely name."

Amy planted her hands on her hips. "How do *you* know what name I was given?"

"Because…" Mrs Fortescue stood and came face-to-face with Amy. "I gave it to you."

Amy's arms fell to her sides. "What?"

Benjamin started babbling, and Amy resumed her position next to him on the floor, a deep frown on her face. Whatever could the woman be about?

Mrs Fortescue sat on the other side of Benjamin. "Can you not see?" she asked, her eyes beseeching. "Have you not guessed?"

As Amy's locked her gaze with Mrs Fortescue's, realisation slapped her in the face. Her eyes, the gloves, her tenderness with Benjamin... She gasped. "You are my..."

"Mother," Mrs Fortescue confirmed, with a tentative smile. "I had to give you up, all those years ago."

As Amy's mind reeled, the lady's eyes misted over. "I held you in my arms," she said softly, "and my heart was full. And then... you were taken from me, and my arms were empty. And my heart... it would never be the same again."

Amy swallowed, a multitude of questions tumbling in her mind. One begged to be answered first.

"Why didn't you want me?" she whispered.

"Oh, my dear..." A tear fell from Mrs Fortescue's eye and she wiped it with the back of her hand. "I had no choice! The decisions were made for me. Put yourself in my place. But I loved you, more than I can say. That is why I stayed in Amberley, so I could be near you. I contributed to your clothing and education. I did everything I could, without undermining the Millers." She became increasingly fraught as this speech went on, and it was too much for Amy.

She scooped up Benjamin and blinked back her own tears. "I very much appreciate your kindness to me now, but you abandoned me as a babe. I've lived with the hurt of that rejection all my life. And now, knowing you were there the whole time... that I've been *here* this whole time without knowing the truth... I feel as if I've been duped." She went to leave the room, but Mrs Fortescue caught her shoulder.

"Please," she said, her voice breaking. "You must believe it was never my intention to hurt you. I have always done what I thought was best."

Amy turned back to her. "What do you mean?"

Mrs Fortescue let go of Amy and took a few breaths before replying. "Why do you think you were able to become a lady's maid? Do you think Lady Ashworth would have looked to the daughter of a farmer for her own daughter's companion?"

A darkness began to swirl around Amy's heart. "Speak plainly. What do you mean by this?"

Mrs Fortescue touched her fingertips to her temples as if in pain, her eyes closed. "Lady Ashworth is a dear friend. She knew… she knows how dear you are to me. After your parents died, I was sick with worry over what would become of you. I knew you could not be expected to take over the lease on your own, and would soon be evicted. I begged Lady Ashworth to consider taking you in as staff. I thought she might have you work in the kitchen or as a parlour maid, and I was simply delighted when she decided Catherine was of an age to have her own maid."

Her smiled faded, and she hung her head. "Despite the good fortune of having you placed so well, of course I now wish things had turned out differently, that you had not fallen victim to… Well." She brushed her hands together briskly. "We cannot help the past now, can we."

It was as if the bricks in Amy's fragile foundation were being dismantled one by one. Here she had thought that the Barringtons had seen some potential in her, some worth. Instead, they had employed her out of guilt, as a favour.

"I wish you would have left well alone!" Amy hissed between clenched teeth. "I would rather have looked after the farm on my own, in the knowledge that its success or failure was in my own power! Instead I became nothing more than a pawn in a rich man's game. And I did not even achieve my position on my own merits – I had to have you beg on my behalf! How insulting that I could not be judged capable without such persuasion! A poor farmer's daughter indeed. Perhaps you knew all along that I would fail. I thought I had found my place, somewhere to belong. A part of me had died along with my parents, but John Barrington's affections, and Catherine's kindness, helped pull me from my sorrow. Did they know of your subterfuge?"

Mrs Fortescue gasped. "My *what*? Everything I did was in your very best interests! I cannot speak for Lady Ashworth, but as she is my friend, I do not think she would repeat any conversation we had in confidence. You may be assured your relationships in that house were purely of your own forming. My influence ended once your placement was secured."

Amy shook her head, dragging one hand across her face. She fixed

Mrs Fortescue with a weary stare. "Lady Ashworth knows I am your daughter. Who else knows?"

"Why, Mr Fortescue, of course. And I did tell Mr Brook after we decided to take you in."

Mr Brook... Did Cecilia know? Had Lady Ashworth told all her family? Had any other villagers put two and two together, and were they all laughing at her?

Completely overwhelmed, she backed out of the room without another word. Still carrying Benjamin, she retrieved her shawl from the cloakroom and marched to the front door. She had to be somewhere else. This house and its secrets could be her undoing. She needed to talk to someone she could trust.

Was it possible that Cecilia could have kept this from her? In her panic and paranoia, she couldn't be sure.

As she set off down the lane, Amy remembered Henry's promise. He said he would be a friend if she needed one.

Where else could she turn?

❧

Henry glanced up at the grey clouds scudding across the sky and then resumed spreading hay for the cows. The wind was picking up, and it tossed about the lighter pieces of hay. Some flicked up at Henry's face. "There's a storm coming in," he muttered to himself.

Straightening, he stretched his back, which ached from a long day in the fields. As he gazed towards the farmhouse, movement caught his eye. Was that someone coming down the lane? Was that *Amy*?

He uttered an oath, threw his fork aside and dashed off down the hill. In his haste he tripped on uneven ground, but he recovered himself and continued running all the way down. Amy paused several feet away from the house and she whirled around to face him as he sprinted up to her.

"Henry! I'm so glad you saw me."

The wind had blown nearly all of her hair free of its bun, and it whipped around her face. She looked pale, with a new kind of strain in her eyes. Her baby was tucked up inside a shawl, but Amy was wearing only a dress without any kind of overcoat. She must be freezing.

He reached out to her before he knew what he was doing, and when she glanced at his hand, he dropped it hastily.

"Is everything all right?" he asked, panting. "Why did you come here on your own?"

She took a moment before replying. "Can we speak privately?"

What could be the meaning of this? Nodding, he said, "The barn?"

She nodded as well, and began to walk in that direction. Once they were safely inside, she brushed the hair from her face and kissed Benjamin. Then she looked up at Henry.

"I have just made a discovery," she said to him, her eyes large and solemn.

He held his breath. "What is it?"

"I can still hardly believe it, although I can see how it must be true." She blew out a long breath.

Henry waited.

"I found out just now that Mrs Fortescue is the one who gave me up when I was a baby. She is my mother!"

Henry's mouth fell open, and his heart froze over. All words left his brain, and he stared at her.

Amy frowned, her eyes narrowing. "You know?"

Damnation. "What?" Henry panicked. "Why – why would you say that?"

"I can see it in your eyes. You're not surprised."

He swallowed hard and then took a deep breath. Now, of all times, he had to be truthful with her. "Yes," he said, his voice shaking. "Yes, I know. That is to say–"

Amy advanced on him. "You knew and you never thought to tell me?"

Henry shook his head helplessly. "I put two and two together, but I didn't know for sure. I thought there must be a good reason for you not to know. I thought it wasn't my place to tell you."

She stepped back again, a scowl darkening her features. "But I trusted you. I thought you were looking out for me."

"I was," he said desperately. "I am."

"What else are you keeping from me?" she asked, her eyes flashing with accusation.

"Nothing!" He took a step towards her, but she thrust out her palm to keep him at bay.

"How can I believe you? How can I ever trust you again? You lied to me!"

It was a knife through Henry's spirit. He'd been more open with her than anyone he'd ever known. He'd put his very heart on the line. "I didn't lie, Amy!" he told her, breathing hard. "I would never lie to you!"

"You knew all this while and you kept it from me. You deceived me." Her voice had become cold, her expression detached. "How long have you known?"

He sighed and looked at the floor. "I guessed it when I saw you at Jones's, after you sneaked Ben away to the farm."

She gasped. "But that was months ago! That was before…"

"I wanted to tell you, Amy, honestly I did," he said, trying to penetrate that coldness in her eyes. "I thought it might upset things if you knew. And I didn't even know if I was right!" He could feel her slipping further away with every word he spoke. "I did try to tell you – that day after the haymaking. Do you remember?"

Her eyebrows knitted together. "Here, in the barn?"

He nodded.

"You only asked me about why the Fortescues had taken me in."

"I wanted to see if you had already guessed at the truth. But then I worried that if you confronted Mrs Fortescue, it would make things very awkward for you – especially if I was wrong."

"But we've spent so much time together since then, Henry. I can't believe you would keep such an important thing hidden that entire time."

"You must know I thought I was doing the right thing." He sighed. "I've done my best to be honest with you, Amy. Everything I've shared with you is true."

She shook her head sadly. "I was letting my guard down. I thought there could still be a future for us one day. Now… I just don't know…"

He took a small step towards her, looking deep into her eyes. "Please, Amy. Don't give up on me."

She didn't move away, but as she looked up at him, a tear ran down one cheek. "I did have hope for us," she said, her chin wobbling. "But if I can't trust you then I can't see a way forward. I can't open myself up to the risk of being betrayed again."

"But Amy," he said, appalled, "I would never betray you – not like that!"

A tear escaped from her other eye. "I know you wouldn't do anything that bad, Henry," she said, her breath coming in fits and starts. "But I would always wonder if you were hiding something from me. And I can't live like that."

Her words crushed his soul. He couldn't live without her in his life. "Can't we return to how things were before?" he asked. "Please!"

She shook her head. "No, not now. Don't make this harder than it needs to be. Being around you puts my feelings at risk, and I hope you understand there's too much risk in loving you. Disappointment would be the end of me."

As more tears fell, she turned to leave.

"Don't go!" His words came out as a sob.

She glanced back at him and said "Goodbye, Henry" before rushing out of the barn.

He caught up with her outside. "Let me drive you back home. I don't want you walking alone in this state."

"Leave me be!" she shouted, and she scurried off down the lane.

He stared at her retreating form.

She had still been hoping… But now there was no hope.

How cruel, and how tragic, that something he had realised quite by accident had been his downfall. That all his efforts to be honest with her, and to allow her to come to him in her own time, had been for naught. He had known all along this might happen. He'd sensed that withholding this information would ruin them. But he'd put it to one side of his mind while enjoying the wonderful prospect of winning her and loving her as his wife.

Her trust, so fragile, had been his for but fleeting moments. Now, it was impossible that he could earn it back again. He would have to watch her and her child going about their lives, knowing that he would never be a part of them.

Chapter Eighteen

Amy slept late after a fitful night. The twin shocks with Mrs Fortescue and Henry were too much to bear. Everything she'd thought she had known was a lie.

During the darkest hours, as a storm raged outside, she thought back over her life. How must her parents have felt, having such an intimidating presence dwelling so near? All the little things which had seemed to Amy like good luck or happy blessings were actually the machinations of her secret guardian. Knowing who her birth mother was had given rise to more questions than answers, and they ricocheted around her mind for hours.

Eventually Jenny came in with a breakfast tray, but Amy could only nibble at her toast.

"Are you feeling unwell, miss?" Jenny asked, peering at Amy in the gloom, the curtains still drawn.

Amy took a breath to reply, but her feelings threatened to overflow. "No," she managed to croak. "I am well, only tired."

"Shall I come back in a few minutes to dress you, then, miss?"

Amy shook her head. She could not endure seeing the Fortescues today. She had gone directly to the nursery on returning from the farm, spending the evening there before stealing down to her room. "I will remain in bed to rest," she said. "Please ask Agnes to bring Benjamin here when he needs me."

"As you please, miss," Jenny said, bobbing a curtsey and turning to go.

When she was only half-way towards the door, the maid swivelled around again. "If you don't mind me saying so, miss…"

Amy sighed. "Yes, Jenny?"

"Don't worry, he'll come around."

Amy was momentarily dumbfounded and then collected her wits. "Who?"

"The farmer's son, Mister Russell. Everyone knows he's been courting you. I can't think of any other reason for you to be feeling down in the dumps – must be a lover's spat. I've a sense about these things."

"Do you now?" Amy sputtered.

Jenny nodded. "And my ma says that if a man's dead keen on you, he'll come crawling back with his tail between his legs every time, so don't you worry. It'll all blow over before you know it."

Amy blinked hard and drew in a deep breath before replying. "Did you ever love someone, Jenny?"

It was Jenny's turn to hesitate. "Do you mean was I ever courted, miss?"

"Yes, or did you wish someone would court you?"

"Well… I have to admit I've fancied one of the footmen here for months, but don't you go repeating that, miss!"

A laugh nearly erupted from Amy's throat. "Your secret will stay safe with me, Jenny. And thank you for the advice. You may go."

It was clear the maid had never been in love, had never felt so deeply entwined with another person's soul that she hardly knew where hers ended and theirs began. She had never known that profound longing for her beloved's presence, the thrill of hearing them speak her name, the timeless pleasure of drinking in their eyes. And the deeper knowledge, only present once infatuation had given way to something more meaningful, that she would give anything for the other person's sake.

Henry's eyes as she'd seen them last came unbidden to her mind: two tortured orbs, seething with intensity as he'd begged her not to give up on him. Even though she had in that moment decided to give him up, now she still craved nothing more than to be in the comfort of his company. She wanted to know the security his arms would provide, if only she could let herself accept it.

That's when it hit her. She did love Henry. The strength of her regard for him made his betrayal all the more hurtful.

Now there was no way she could trust him with her heart.

❧⚜❧

The next day, Amy sat on her windowsill gazing out over the gardens with some mending in her lap. The storm was passing, a ray of sunshine piercing through the charcoal clouds. Amy's mind was still in turmoil.

There was a knock at her door, and it was not Jenny's hesitant rapping. It must be Mrs Fortescue; Amy knew she would have to face her sooner or later. But she no longer knew how to act around this woman, who had been in equal measure a cold enigma and a trusted confidante. Now Amy wondered what she had divulged to this person – little details which would have meant so much more if she had known she was in fact speaking with her own mother.

"Come in!" she called. She sat up straighter and steeled herself.

The door opened, but it was not Mrs Fortescue who crossed the threshold – it was her husband. "Good morning, Amy," he greeted her, in his quiet way.

"Mr Fortescue!" She leapt to her feet. "Uh, good morning, sir."

He smiled. "I come in peace, dear girl. Sit down." He went over to her dressing table and picked up the chair. He brought it over to the window as she sat down again.

"What… can I do for you?" Amy asked. She'd never talked to this man on her own before.

He took a breath and made eye contact with her. "I know you have had a shock," he said, "and I cannot possibly begin to imagine how you must feel. My wife, on the other hand… I know only too well the depth of her feelings, and she has been in great distress these past two days."

Amy lifted her eyebrows. "*She* has been in distress?"

He nodded. "To be sure. She is terrified of what you might think, and of the possibility of losing you."

Amy could only stare at him. It was beyond her capability at the present moment to put herself in Mrs Fortescue's shoes. Her own feelings were confusing enough.

"She does not know I have come to see you," Mr Fortescue went on.

153

"Indeed, she would be mortified if she knew. But as the man who has been by her side since almost the beginning of this, I had to speak on her behalf. She insists she will wait for you to come to her, but we have no idea if or when that will happen. In the meantime, I cannot do nothing."

Amy swallowed. Once again, the quality of the love this man had for his wife was obvious. His sincerity humbled her. "I will hear whatever it is you have to say."

Mr Fortescue shifted in his chair. "I want you to understand that your mother's intentions have always been admirable. I know this state of affairs puts you in an odd position, and Lord knows she can be cantankerous sometimes, but she only wants the best for you. If circumstances had been different, she would absolutely have kept you as her own."

Amy frowned. "How do you know that? I believe you did not know her at the time I was born?"

"You are right, I did not, but in all the years I have known her, there has been no doubt of her loving you. After we married, all she wanted to do was come and claim you, but she knew it was not fair to the Millers. Do you know how hard it was for her all those years, to stand by and watch someone else raise her child?"

"She could have visited me," Amy insisted. "Made some sort of connection."

"She didn't want to interfere," Mr Fortescue said gently. "And there was no logical reason why she would have anything to do with the Millers. So she would only write to them and send funds, clothing or whatever else you might have needed."

Amy sighed, trying to absorb all this information. "Did you ever consider leaving Amberley, if it was so painful for her?"

Mr Fortescue nodded. "Aye, we did – well, I did. I thought starting a new life away from the memories might be good for us. But she would not be persuaded. She wanted to be near you, to watch you grow. Only imagine how heartbroken she was when the very situation she thought would secure your future ended up failing you so appallingly."

"The situation was fine," Amy rasped, her emotions starting to get the better of her. She could not tolerate Mrs Fortescue assuming any guilt for that misfortune. "I did thrive, but I also indulged my fancies, and that was mostly my own doing."

To her surprise, Mr Fortescue reached out and lightly touched her knee. "I see so much of her in you, the same strength, resilience and compassion. I have faith you two will work something out between you."

He stood, gave her an encouraging smile, and left the room.

☙❧

William sat opposite Henry in the vicarage parlour, his fingers pressed together at the tips at his chin. "I do hope, my dear fellow, that I did not put you wrong with my advice."

Henry shook his head. "I followed my own conscience, and I just couldn't go through with telling her my hunch."

William nodded. "It is unfortunate this whole business has muddled your relationship with her. You seemed to be getting along so well."

Henry shrugged. "It's all water under the bridge now. She's made it quite clear she won't have me. I've broken her trust, and that's the end of it."

There was a silence, and when Henry raised his eyes to meet William's, he was met with such compassion and sympathy that he immediately looked away again, lest his feelings get the better of him.

"She will need time, to be sure," William said. "But I think she will need you now more than ever. Everything she knew about herself has changed. You must remain steadfast, and put your hurt aside if she needs comfort."

"I don't think she needs me," Henry mumbled. "She has Cecilia, and you… and her mother, of course."

William smiled. "You and she are of the same ilk – that is very clear. You know the way of life she is most comfortable with, and you can relate to her on a level we cannot. From what I have observed, she seems at ease with you. Moreover, Cecilia is about to be a lot less available!"

Henry sighed. "Yes, I suppose that's true."

"There is another thing, of course," William said. "No one can provide solace quite like someone in love. And you do love her, do you not?"

Henry cleared his throat. "Yes, I do, and I told her that."

"Well done, old chap! Was that before she found out about…"

Henry nodded miserably. "But even then, she pushed me away."

"Well, it is hardly surprising she would be reticent, though I know this would be hard on you. Has she given you any sense of her feelings towards you?"

Painfully, Henry dredged through his memories. "Yes," he said at last. "She said she cared, and wanted to be with me. But that was before our last meeting. Now, everything is lost."

William reached out and grasped Henry's shoulder. "Do not lose heart. Things do not always work out the way we planned, but in many cases, they turn out better than we could have dreamed." He sat back in his seat.

Henry didn't know how to reply. He'd already lost his heart, and now he had lost all hope as well. He kept his eyes on the pattern of the rug on the floor.

A few moments later, William spoke again. "I was very pleased to receive your father's letter with the news of Clara and young Stockton. It will be my privilege to marry them."

Henry managed a smile. "Aye, I hope he won't disappoint her. When I realised how serious she was about him, I made a decision to give up my own plans for the sake of hers."

"Oh?"

Henry explained that he had given his life savings to Clara for her dowry, and that this would set back his plans for the smallholding for years.

"That was a very noble thing to do, Henry," William said. "I am proud of you."

Henry shrugged again. "I wanted to ensure her happiness. I felt terrible for not seeing what was right under my nose. Until the fair, I had no idea he'd been courting her. Besides, I won't be needing to marry any time soon."

"Hmm," William murmured, rubbing his chin.

"William!" It was a shriek, piercing through the house from upstairs.

In an instant William was out of his chair and sprinting from the room. A few moments later Henry heard his muffled exclamations from above, and a chill ran down his spine.

Something was very wrong.

Chapter Nineteen

Tears blurred Amy's vision as she fed Benjamin. It had been a day since her talk with Mr Fortescue, and although she hadn't yet found the courage to seek out his wife, her heart had moved considerably in the past four-and-twenty hours.

She smiled down at her baby. She loved this tiny person more every day. She imagined how painful it would have been to give him up. How lucky she was to have been rescued by the Fortescues. Without them, she would have sunk into poverty and desperation. And now, she knew it wasn't just luck that had landed her here.

She tried to put herself in Mrs Fortescue's position, who had tried her best not to interfere while watching her daughter grow up. She'd had to love her child from a distance so as to not reveal her position. She would have known the deep connection only a mother can feel, but would not have been able to act on it openly. How tragic and terrible, and, in a way, heroic.

It was only now, with a mother's heart, that Amy could begin to understand and truly appreciate Mrs Fortescue's actions. How much had she sacrificed for her daughter's sake? How much hurt had she suffered, even at Amy's own hands as of late? How had she borne everything and still maintained her outward composure and sense of duty?

What a fine example she had set, of bravery, altruism and devotion. What an excellent model for Amy to follow in being a selfless parent.

Amy *could* feel that same strength running through her veins, and she was grateful for it.

However, her mind still swarmed with questions. There were things she had wished to know her whole life, and now she would finally get the chance to uncover them. But did she have the courage to face what could be uncomfortable truths? She could only but begin a journey to discovery, and see where the answers might take her. It was time to face her past, present and future – and the one woman who could hold the key to them all.

Amy left Benjamin in Agnes's care and made her way down the hallway. It was shortly before Mrs Fortescue's regular breakfast hour. Amy hoped to have some time alone with her before she descended to the public part of the house.

She knocked on the door to her chamber: three hesitant taps.

When the door opened, it was Mr Fortescue who appeared. "Good morning, Amy," he said with a smile. There was a muffled sound from behind him, and he half-turned towards it. "Yes, my dear, your Amelia is here. Will you see her now?"

Amy's heart skipped a beat at being referred to as "hers". The answer must have been affirmative, for Mr Fortescue beckoned her in.

Amy followed him into the room, which was lavishly decorated in tones of blue. It was the first time she'd set foot in it. A large four poster bed stood in the centre of the back wall, and Mrs Fortescue sat on the end of it. She was still in her dressing gown, and her hair hung loose around her shoulders.

Amy stopped a few feet in front of her, and Mr Fortescue murmured an excuse. He left, closing the door behind him.

Mrs Fortescue smiled at her, but there was a new hesitance in her eyes.

"Good morning," she said, a squeak of strain in her voice. "Will you pull that chair over?" She indicated one in the corner of the room.

Amy approached and sat on the bed with her instead.

Mrs Fortescue's eyes widened, and she stared at Amy open-mouthed.

Amy rushed to fill the silence before she lost her nerve. "I hope you will forgive my rudeness these past few days. Confining myself to my room was in no way meant to be an affront to you. I just needed some time to start to get my thoughts together."

Mrs Fortescue nodded. "I am not offended, my dear, only worried for your sake. I know this must have been a considerable surprise."

Amy took a deep breath. "Why didn't you tell me earlier, then? How could you have lived with me all this time, and not think I had a right to know?"

Mrs Fortescue sighed. "I was afraid you would reject me. I know how much you despise me. I am clearly not the mothering type."

"I do not *despise* you," Amy said. "In fact, I have grown to quite depend upon you. You are not at all who I first thought you were." It was incredible that a woman like Mrs Fortescue, who seemed so in command of herself and others, could be afraid of *her*.

Mrs Fortescue blinked rapidly. "That is a relief. Thank you."

Amy ploughed on. "I have some questions."

"That is understandable. What would you like to know?"

"Well…" Amy looked down at her hands. "Who is my father?"

There was a slight pause before Mrs Fortescue replied. "That is a reasonable question, and you have a right to know." She sighed. "He was a gentleman… by birth, if not by his behaviour. He was in the militia, and his regiment was stationed at Shrewsbury that summer. I was instantly taken with him, and he with me. So infatuated was I, there was nothing I would not do for him. And in my innocence… I let him take advantage of me. Shortly thereafter, his regiment moved on, and I never saw him or heard from him again. We had known each other two short months. My grief over his absence was soon eclipsed by the knowledge I was with child. I was but sixteen."

Three years younger than I was. "What was his name?"

"Thomas Hewitt."

Amy nodded, meeting her mother's eyes again. "And what was *your* name?"

"Shirley Lane."

"What of your parents? Are they still alive?"

Mrs Fortescue regarded her lap. "I… *believe* my mother is still living. However, my parents wanted nothing to do with me after I fell pregnant. They arranged for my safe convalescence and then washed their hands of me. I boarded with the Jones's after you were born, working in the shop.

It was there that Mr Fortescue first saw me."

Amy took this in. So she would never know her grandparents, let alone her real father. She let go of a breath, thinking about what Mr Fortescue had told her. "What sort of help did you give my parents – the Millers?"

Mrs Fortescue rubbed her eyes with one hand. "A lot of things," she said. "Your education, for example."

Amy nodded, a puzzle piece falling into place. She'd attended the school for three years, until she was ten years old and big enough to help around the farm. It was rare for a farmer's daughter to be sent out to a day school, and Amy had always believed she'd qualified for some sort of scholarship. It was where she had befriended Cecilia and learned to read, write and speak properly. Without that experience, there would have been no chance of her getting the position at Ashworth Hall.

"It was very hard for me," Mrs Fortescue went on, a tremor in her voice, "to not reach out to you all these years, especially after the Millers died. It was torture knowing what happened to you last year and not immediately removing you from your situation and trying to make everything better. I only intervened when the time seemed right, when it was reasonable that someone who had no apparent relation to you should help you." She held Amy's eyes, her expression a mix of regret and sorrow. "I was so afraid that when we took you in, you would grow to hate me. Loving you from afar was safer, somehow."

Amy recognised this speech as some sort of apology, but she was too overwhelmed to decipher her own emotions. The sincerity emanating from this woman, her mirror image in many ways, pierced her heart. When Mrs Fortescue reached out a hand, it was the most natural thing in the world to take it – to accept it.

"Do you not know how proud I am of you?" Mrs Fortescue whispered. "How happy you have made me as I have watched you grow? How I wished I was the one who shared your achievements, and wiped your tears? I knew I had done the right thing in leaving you be with the Millers when I saw the wonderful woman you had become. And now–"

The bedroom door burst open and Henry Russell came running in, with Mr Fortescue and the butler close behind.

"Amy, you must come quick!" Henry said, panting. He took in the sight of them on the bed, his eyes wild.

Amy had never seen him in such a state. She let go of Mrs Fortescue's hand and pushed herself off the bed. "What is it?"

"It's Mrs Brook – Cecilia. The baby. You need to come. Now!"

Mr Fortescue helped his wife rise, and she addressed the butler. "Send for the carriage."

"There's no time to get your horses and coachman ready," Henry shouted. "Amy must come back with me on foot, right away. I've already fetched the Grants and Mr Lindsay."

Something about the look in his eyes terrified Amy. Was Cecilia in trouble? She turned to Mrs Fortescue. "Will you let Agnes know I will be gone for the rest of the day?"

"Certainly, my dear." She turned to Henry. "You will look after her?"

He nodded and extended his hand towards Amy. "Of course I will. Let's go, Amy."

She rushed past him, out the door and along to the main staircase. They ran from the house together, and down the lane towards the village.

⁊❧

By the time Amy and Henry reached the village, they had slowed to a brisk walk, and both were flushed and puffing hard. They drew curious looks from passers-by as they rushed to the vicarage.

Not a word had been spoken since their departure from the house. A terrible foreboding hung between them.

When Henry had charged into Mrs Fortescue's bedroom, it looked like he had interrupted a tender moment between the two ladies. His present dread was slightly tempered by the hope that Amy would enjoy a warm relationship with her mother. Would he ever get the chance to ask her about it?

"Henry," Amy said, between gasping breaths.

He met her frightened eyes.

"Why the panic? Is it just because… the baby is coming earlier… than expected?"

"No," Henry replied. "William said there was a lot… of blood."

Amy winced and then increased her pace, muttering something to herself.

When they reached the Brooks', Mr and Mrs Grant had just arrived. Amy embraced Mrs Grant, and together they went up the stairs. The maid, Emma, came running into the vestibule carrying a pitcher and a bundle of linen, and she also hurried up to the bedrooms.

Henry took a deep breath and went into the parlour. William was pacing about the room. Mr Grant had perched on the edge of the sofa and was studying his hands.

Henry began to back out of the room. He had no place in this family emergency. He could be of no use to anyone.

"Henry, will you stay?" William approached him with pleading eyes. "For the time being, at least? I should like Mr Grant to have some company if... if I am needed."

Henry nodded and clutched the doorframe. "Whatever you need, William."

A scream rang out from above, and William stumbled. Henry caught his shoulder, steadying him. "Be strong," Henry urged. "She's in good hands."

William did not reply, only holding Henry's eyes with a look of desolation. Despite his encouragement, Henry knew that it was a very risky business. There was nothing to be done to save mother or baby – they would just have to wait and let things run their course.

Henry also worried for Amy's sake. What kind of dreadfulness might she be witness to? Had her own feelings healed enough to prepare her to comfort another woman through such an ordeal?

The waiting seemed interminable, with hours of intermittent silence and cries. Emma came in with bread and tea, and Henry returned to the kitchen with her to help build a fire over which to cook a stew. He chatted with her about ridiculously trivial things in an attempt to keep their minds from the tribulation playing out above them.

It was after dark when Cecilia's cries became almost unbroken. Mr Grant lay sprawled on the sofa with a newspaper, his hands shaking as he gripped the pages.

William and Henry were on their feet, and sweat dripped from the vicar's brow.

A scream erupted which seemed to shake the house. William squeezed his eyes shut and buried his head in his hands. "I must go to her!"

"Yes," Henry said hoarsely. "Go!" He squeezed William's shoulder and looked into his bloodshot eyes. "God be with you all."

William nodded his thanks and ran from the room.

❧

"Keep breathing!" Amy tried to encourage Cecilia in between her cries. She was sitting behind her on the bed, her arms under Cecilia's, supporting her as much as she could. The contractions were ripping through Cecilia's body almost constantly now. The bed was soaked with blood.

Mrs Grant sat weeping in a chair in the corner while Mr Lindsay examined his patient.

He straightened. "You need to push, Mrs Brook."

"I can't," sobbed Cecilia. "I don't know how."

She turned her head and looked up into Amy's eyes. "I'm scared," she whispered.

Amy smoothed back her hair and smiled. "You can do it," she said. "It won't be long now, and it will all be over." Her smile faded, and she swallowed hard. She could not bring herself to promise Cecilia that shortly she would be holding her child in her arms. Cecilia was so pale and weak, Amy was desperately afraid she was about to lose her friend forever.

As if reading Amy's thoughts, Cecilia said, "Will you tell William I love him?"

Amy gasped, and blinked away tears.

Suddenly the door to the bedroom opened, and William strode in.

"You can tell him yourself," Amy said.

Cecilia took in the sight of her husband, and managed a little smile.

"Mr Brook," Mr Lindsay said, frowning. "This is no place for–"

William held up his hand. "No, you shall not stop me." He walked around the physician and lay gently on the bed, wrapping his arms around Cecilia. "If my wife is to die, she will know I loved her to the end."

Amy shuffled away and off the bed. Cecilia lay gazing up at her husband, and a sort of peace came over her countenance. Then, agony distorted her features, and she wailed in pain.

"It's another contraction," Mr Lindsay said. "You must push now! Miss Miller, come here and help me."

As William coached his wife, Amy helped Mr Lindsay hold Cecilia's legs. When the contraction was over, Cecilia collapsed back into her husband's arms. "I don't think I can do it," she said, panting. A minute or so later, William coaxed her into action once again, but his eyes were wide with fear. Wave upon wave crashed over Cecilia, and each time she grew weaker. After what seemed like hours, Mr Lindsay went to his bag and withdrew an instrument.

"What is that?" Amy asked.

"Forceps," Mr Lindsay told her. "A device from France. It will help me get the baby out."

Through the next contraction, Amy maintained her position while the physician tried to pull the baby from its mother with the instrument. It was not until the next contraction that the head finally came into view. The rest of the body slipped out a few moments later.

There were no cries. The room was silent. Cecilia lay back on William, her eyes closed. William stared at Mr Lindsay as the physician inspected the tiny being, listening to its chest and touching various parts of its anatomy.

"It's a girl," Mr Lindsay croaked, "but she is no longer with us. I am so very sorry, William."

A cry sounded from Mrs Grant, who staggered to Cecilia's other side.

Amy regarded the rigid baby, and tears rolled down her cheeks. She pressed her hand to her mouth and looked to William. He was gently stroking his wife's face, talking to her softly.

Mr Lindsay handed the baby to Amy, and she accepted it automatically, though horrified. The physician then dealt with the cord which attached the baby to her mother, who still lay lifeless.

"Clean the child," Mr Lindsay instructed her quietly. "Wrap her up and give her to Mr Brook, then ensure we get Cecilia some food and drink. We need to give her some strength. Then you may go – the family must grieve privately."

Amy nodded, transfixed on the little purple body she held in her arms. "Will Cecilia recover?"

"I do not know." Mr Lindsay took a deep breath and mopped his brow with a handkerchief. "I will help with the afterbirth, and then we need to let her rest. I will check on her in the morning."

Numb with shock, Amy took the baby to the washstand and cleaned her up the best she could. Then she wrapped her in a muslin cloth and took her to William. He carefully transferred Cecilia's weight to her mother, and then cradled the little girl in his arms.

"She's beautiful," Amy whispered.

As William bent to kiss the baby, Amy took one last look at Cecilia and then turned away.

She stumbled down the stairs, and then found Emma in the kitchen. She asked the maid to take the Brooks some simple provisions, and then nearly collided with Henry in the hallway. What was he still doing here?

"Amy!" he said. "I thought I heard your voice." He took in her expression. "Oh, dear Lord, what's happened?"

She shook her head, tears pouring down her cheeks. "The baby…"

Henry squeezed his eyes shut for a moment. "And Cecilia?"

"She's still with us, but it's not certain if she'll survive."

"Oh, Amy…" Henry reached out to her, as if inviting her into a sympathetic embrace, but before she could decide whether to accept it he dropped his arms and stepped back. Still, he held her eyes as he spoke. "I'm so sorry you had to–"

He was interrupted by the sound of a throat clearing from behind them in the parlour. Amy started in dismay. "Is that Mr Grant?" And would she have to tell him the tragic news?

"Yes, it is," Henry said. "Here's what we'll do. I'll let Mr Grant know what has happened, and see he looks after his wife. Then I'll take you home. Go into William's study and wait for me – I'll only be a few minutes."

"All right." True to his word, Henry collected Amy from the study a short time later. As they exited the vicarage, Henry picked up a flaming torch just outside the door and proceeded to guide her through the darkness.

Amy's feet were leaden. As they plodded through the cobbles in the village, she tripped and fell.

Henry's caught her around the waist with one arm. She was so tired, she didn't have the presence of mind to free herself from his hold.

She regained her balance and allowed him to keep a hand on her shoulder while they continued their journey. He wasn't touching her skin, after all, so she could bear it.

The supportive touch did have an effect on her feelings, though she was not frightened. Instead, it made her all the more aware of the awfulness of the day, and the terrible uncertainty of what lay ahead. She began to weep again.

"Amy?" She did not look at Henry but she could hear the distress in his voice.

"What if she dies? She is so drained, it's as if there is none of her left."

He tightened his grip on her. "All we can do is pray. She may yet live."

They arrived at Briarwood, and not long after the front door thudded closed, Mrs Fortescue came running down the stairs with a candle, dressed only in her night-rail.

"My dear," she said. "How is…"

Amy lifted her eyes, and the candlelight illuminated her face. She did not speak, only shaking her head in sorrow.

Mrs Fortescue laid the candle on a side table, closed the distance between them, and wrapped her arms around Amy.

Amy yielded to the comfort and began to sob. "Cecilia's baby is dead!" she managed to choke out. "How devastating for her and William!"

She was vaguely conscious of the front door opening and closing, and of being led to the staircase, whereupon Mrs Fortescue sat them both down.

Amy wept uncontrollably for several minutes, and Mrs Fortescue offered silent sympathy, holding her firm and lightly stroking her hair. It was the first time Amy had consciously received comfort from her mother, and she was exceedingly thankful for it.

When Amy's breathing had slowed enough to allow her to talk again, she blurted out, "Cecilia has lost so much blood. I think the labour may have finished her off. I might never see her again!"

"We must hope for the best," Mrs Fortescue said, through Amy's new flood of tears. "But if we do lose her, she would have known your strength and kindness to the very last. You must console yourself with that knowledge."

She pulled back, and in the dim light Amy could just make out her face. "I know how worried I was for you, when it was time for you to have your baby. You cannot know how relieved I was to learn that both of you were healthy afterwards."

Amy nodded solemnly. She now had some insight into how her mother might have felt during that time. "Ben," she said, pushing herself to standing. "I must go to Benjamin."

Mrs Fortescue helped her up the stairs and urged Amy to come to her if she needed anything. Then she left Amy to see her son in peace.

Amy took her sleeping child into her arms and crept back to her room with him. She lay awake with him all night: feeding, cuddling, caressing, telling him how much she loved him. She had never been more aware of how much she not only wanted him but needed him. She could now not imagine her world without him. The idea that he could have been snatched from her before his life had even begun was too painful to consider. Her heart bled for Cecilia, and for William, and for the poor little creature they had treasured for all these months who would never know their love.

Chapter Twenty

Henry could think of nothing but the Brooks and Amy in the days that followed. It was not until church three days later that he found out any news. Everyone affected by the tragedy was of course absent, but the vicar performing the service told the parish about the baby's demise. Cecilia was weak, but it was believed she would survive. A collective sigh of relief went up from those gathered.

It was a great weight lifted from Henry, as losing Cecilia would have shattered Amy and William. At least things weren't as bad as they could have been.

Still, the haunted look in Amy's eyes after that dreadful incident remained with him. The thought of her having to witness such a difficult birthing, and then seeing the dead child, was enough to make him feel ill. Would she withdraw further from the world, and from him, as a result of sharing in this trauma?

Hopefully she wasn't suffering too much. It was all so soon after the shock of finding out about her mother. He wished he could visit her and provide a measure of diversion, but he knew he wasn't welcome. She had allowed him to accompany her in those exceptional circumstances, but he was certain there would be no further contact. His life would continue as it always had – without the independence he wanted or the love he needed.

At least Clara was content. His sister hummed a happy tune as she helped their mother serve the family's lunch of roasted pork and stewed vegetables. She set a plate in front of Henry with a grin, but her smile faded as she looked at him.

"Is everything all right, Henry?"

"Oh…" He shrugged. "It was an eventful week, that's all." He attempted a smile.

She eyeballed him for a moment and then turned back to the hearth. He picked up his fork.

He was still toying with his food when the girls finished their lunch and left the room.

Mrs Russell put her down knife and fork and smiled at Henry. "She's ever so grateful, you know."

He glanced up at her. "I know. I'm glad."

"Shame about Amy Miller."

Henry dropped his fork. "What?"

His parents exchanged a glance. "It's a shame things didn't work out between you. The terms were very good."

Henry frowned. "What terms?"

His father spoke up. "When you were off showing Amy the pigs or chickens or whatever it was that day, that woman Fortescue offered a dowry for the girl. A generous dowry."

"But that would mean…" Henry's mind spun. "You could have given the money to Clara, so she could marry Mick."

"Aye. We could have set something aside for Tilly as well."

"And I would still have had funds to set up my farm."

His mother nodded. "Just so. Such a pity."

Anger ignited in Henry's gut. "But you told me you'd never consider her for a daughter-in-law. Why do you now act as if you always wanted it?"

"Well…" His mother stood and began clearing the plates. "Considering the circumstances…"

Henry shook his head, appalled. "Considering the *money*, you mean."

Mr Russell looked him straight in the eye. "Practical things must come first in life, boy. When will you learn?"

Henry ignored this and pushed his chair out, moving to help his mother carry the large pot from the table. "Does Amy know about her dowry?" he asked her, as he set the pot down by the hearth.

"You'll have to ask her."

He sighed. "I won't be doing that. I may have had a chance with her once, but I wrecked it."

His mother nodded, though her eyes were sympathetic. "She left in such an upset that day, we didn't think there was any point telling you about the dowry."

Little did they know, it had got even worse after that. "Does Clara know about it?"

Mrs Russell moved back to the table to clear more dishes. "No, the girls were out of the room when we discussed it, and we didn't want her getting her hopes up."

"I see." For nearly two months, his parents had been hoping he would offer for Amy. It was such a reversal of their previous stance. "If Amy had agreed to marry me," he said to them both, "would you have accepted her child?"

"If *you* wanted to accept it as your own," said Mr Russell, "that's your decision. We just wouldn't have you bringing it into this house."

Henry smiled wryly to himself as he left the kitchen and headed for the stairs. Not much had changed, then; it was only that money held sway over pride.

Knowledge of the dowry wouldn't have changed his actions. He couldn't have loved her or wanted her any more as it was. But knowing the impact the funds would have had on his family made losing her all the more regrettable.

If he were to marry Amy, he could guarantee the material happiness of them all... but mostly, he wanted to secure *her* happiness. It was indeed a pity that he'd lost her trust for good.

❧❧

Amy fell into a new routine wherein she shared the care of Cecilia with William and Mrs Grant. She spent a couple of hours every morning and afternoon by Cecilia's side, feeding her, reading to her, or just holding her hand while she slept. She tried to time her visits to coincide with Benjamin's naps, so she wouldn't have to take him with her and add insult to injury.

With every day that passed, her friend gained more strength. It was William's wish that his wife would soon be able to make the short walk to the churchyard, where they would hold a burial service for their baby.

A week or so passed, and Amy was ready to continue working on her embroidery project. She tried to distance herself from what it was, and whom it was for, and just focus on the manual task of creating it. It was good to have something to keep her mind occupied.

She soon needed more supplies, and she walked into the village with Benjamin in his pram and Jenny as her companion. Mrs Fortescue had taken a trip to Milton with Mrs Lindsay for the day, and it was Agnes's afternoon off.

They reached Jones's shop, and Amy appraised the pram.

"It's far too big to push around the aisles in there," she said to Jenny. "Will you stay here and mind him? I'll only be a couple of minutes."

"Of course, miss."

Amy bent to drop a light kiss on Benjamin's cheek and then went into the shop. She consulted her list and proceeded to put various items in her basket.

As she was paying Mr Jones for the goods, the bell above the door jangled, and Mrs Russell came in with Clara.

Amy put her change in her reticule and waved to Clara. She met her halfway down an aisle, by the stationery supplies.

"Hello, Amy," Clara said cheerfully.

"Hello, and congratulations!" Amy said, pulling her into an embrace. "How long until you will be married?"

Clara hugged her affectionately. "In ten days," she replied, as she pulled back. "Ma is helping me make a new dress for the wedding, and we're here to pick up the material."

Amy smiled at her, even as envy squeezed her stomach. Would she ever make such a dress for herself? "I'm so happy for you."

Clara studied her, and Amy hoped she hadn't betrayed her true emotions.

"Amy," Clara said softly, after a moment, "are you sure you don't want to marry my brother?"

Amy's heart skipped a beat. Where had that come from? "Why do you ask?"

Clara looked about, as if checking no one was in earshot. "He's given me everything he has, for my dowry, so I can marry Mick."

Amy frowned. "You mean, funds?"

Clara nodded. "All his savings. It means now he can't afford to get his house set up… or be married. I'd hate to think I'm depriving you both by accepting his gift."

Amy stared at her, taking in the gravity of what Henry had done.

"If there's any chance you do want to be with him," Clara went on, "you must tell me."

Guilt hit Amy hard. Her refusal of Henry had caused him to abandon hope of any alliance at all, and give up his material security as a result. He could still offer for a woman with her own funds, but that could not be relied upon. Clearly he had decided helping his sister was a better use of his money than using it for his own future. The fact that his choice made it impossible for him to set up the croft house made her sadder than what was reasonable.

"It is right that you should honour your brother's decision and be married," she finally said. "As for me, marriage is an impossibility."

Something moved outside the shop window, catching Amy's eye. "I should go," she said, gathering up her basket. "I shall look forward to seeing you in your wedding attire!"

She pushed her way through the shop door and stopped dead. Her basket fell to the ground.

John Barrington was leaning over the pram, and as she watched in horror, he reached out towards Benjamin.

He's going to take my baby! Amy's heart jumped into her mouth. "Get back!" she screamed.

Barrington jerked upright, his head whipping around towards her.

"Get away from my child!" In three quick steps she was upon him, and she pushed him away from the pram as hard as she could.

He staggered back into the street, his expression cloudy. "He's my son," he murmured, frowning at her.

"No!" she shrieked. "He's not yours, and he never will be!"

Jenny was standing in the street a few yards away, with Tilly Russell. She came running over as other people began to gather and stare. "I'm sorry, miss!" she said. "I was only chatting for a minute!"

"You should be sorry!" Amy hissed at her, before advancing on Barrington again.

Barrington held his hands up in a gesture of surrender. "Enough," he said gruffly. "Enough." He turned on his heel and stalked off down the road.

Amy glared at his retreating figure, her emotions in an explosive whirl. The whispers around her escalated into curious chatter.

She stumbled back to the pram, pushing past Jenny to gather Benjamin into her arms. She cuddled him close, whispering a string of broken assurances into his ear. She had to get him home. She had to get him safe.

Someone broke through the crowd.

"Amy!" It was Henry, suddenly at her side. She couldn't look at him. "I thought I heard your voice. What's the matter?"

She shook her head, suddenly dizzy. She must have swayed, for Henry took hold of her elbow for a moment to steady her. She closed her eyes, attempting to gather her thoughts. "It was him."

"Who?"

She shivered, forcing herself to look up at Henry. "*Him.*"

His gaze narrowed. "Barrington?"

She flinched.

"Barrington," he growled. "Where is he?"

Jenny pointed. "He went that way."

"Look after her, will you?" Henry said to Jenny. "Take her home and to bed."

He sprinted off down the street without another word.

Chapter Twenty-One

Henry barely felt the ground beneath his feet as he dashed through the village, his eyes roving left and right in search of his quarry. He should have been with his mother and the girls at the shop. He'd driven them to the village and then left them to go to Jones's while he saw to some repairs at the blacksmith's.

He should have been there to defend Amy from that bastard. If Barrington had hurt her or the child, Henry couldn't be held responsible for his actions.

He had been too afraid to defend her honour in the past, but he wouldn't let anything stop him now. He might be risking his family's livelihood, but in that moment his blood ran so hot he couldn't think straight.

Amy couldn't be expected to confront Barrington; doing so might destroy her. It would be up to him to take revenge for her. The rogue needed to know what he'd done, and that people mattered, no matter what their station in life.

He spotted Barrington outside the public house, in the process of untethering his horse. Henry slowed his pace, approaching from behind.

He took some deep breaths, in and out. This time, he wouldn't let his fists do the talking. His words would be his weapons. This man needed to know what he was.

He marched up to Barrington, and at the same time, the man turned around. His gaze ran over Henry, and then he resumed focus on his horse, reaching for his saddle.

His indifference did nothing to improve Henry's opinion of him. It only reinforced the fact he was an arrogant brute who thought himself superior and above judgement.

"I'll have a word," Henry spat out.

Barrington looked at him again, with one eyebrow raised. "Who are you? I know I've seen your face."

Henry sighed. "I'm Henry Russell. The son of–"

"Oh yes, the farmer. I remember. What can you have to say to me?"

Henry stepped forward and squared his shoulders. "It's about Amy Miller."

Barrington's eyes flashed with sudden interest. "Oh?"

"Yes. You scared her half to death just now. And I for one am not going to let you get away without you knowing how much you've hurt her."

Barrington gaped at him. He'd probably never had anyone speak to him like that in his life. Henry expected him to mount his horse in that instant and gallop away home. But the man stood his ground, shifting his weight but looking Henry straight in the eye.

That was enough encouragement for Henry to go on. "Do you realise what you did to her? You took her innocence. You made her unable to trust or love anyone again. She'll never be happy because of you!"

Barrington blinked hard and ran one hand over his face. "I admit I was surprised to see her still in the village," he muttered, almost to himself. "And the child…"

"Surprised? Inconvenient for you, is it? I'll have you know you left her destitute, on the verge of life in the workhouse. She was taken in by good people, but that's no thanks to you. You used her and then deserted her." He swallowed, regrouping. "I know what you people think. Those of the lower classes don't deserve your pity or your help. We exist simply to serve you. Well, you have to know that we hurt just as much as any lord or lady – we have feelings and rights. And what you did to Amy is just plain evil."

Barrington's eyebrows rose again. "Are you finished, sir?"

Henry blew out a breath. "Yes, I suppose I am." Had he secured an eviction notice for the Russell family? It was worth it, for Amy's sake. "What do you have to say for yourself?"

Barrington continued staring at him, and at length shook his head. "I was a fool. I was the bloody devil." He looked directly into Henry's eyes, but there seemed to be no soul there. "I wish it could be undone."

With this admission, Henry's vengeance became impossible. It appeared as if the man standing in front of him was not the same one who'd left Amberley a year ago. A new feeling crept into Henry's psyche – pity. He tried to shrug it away. He didn't want to feel anything like sympathy for this monster, and yet there it was. Henry believed Barrington was sorry for what he had done. He hadn't thought it possible. All words promptly left his head, and he could only stand there, frowning at his contrite nemesis.

"Are you going to look after her?" Barrington asked suddenly.

"What?"

"A man does not challenge another man unless there is a significant degree of feeling in the case. You love her, do you not?"

Henry nodded, more emotions clouding his vision.

"And you intend to do the decent thing by her?"

"I hope to, if she will have me."

"You are a better man than I am," Barrington said. "My good wishes to you both. I will try to stay out of the way."

At that, he sprang up onto the saddle, and rode away.

His mouth falling open, Henry watched him disappear from view. What, or who, could have provoked such a change in the man?

అporకు

"Bed? Don't be ridiculous!" Despite Jenny's best efforts to calm her down, Amy was in a state of severe agitation. She paced about her bedroom and Jenny followed, attempting to extract her hair pins.

It had been several hours since Amy's clash with Barrington. She had struggled to eat luncheon before feeding Benjamin and putting him to bed. Now her maid was trying to convince her she should likewise rest.

"Leave me be!" she finally cried, and Jenny dipped into a startled curtsey before hastening from the room.

Amy was immediately remorseful for snapping at the poor girl, but she was at her wit's end. She had known John would return sooner or later, but the shock of seeing him had been like a physical blow. It brought back the ghastliness of what he had done to her, and it made her feel helpless and exploited once again.

The image of him reaching for her precious child summoned her nightmares and struck terror into her heart. Had he intended to steal her baby? Was having a reminder of his folly this close to home so repugnant that he wanted to make it disappear? She could not even think about what means he could use to get rid of her baby.

She paced back across her room and then remembered his words: "my son". Did he want to take Benjamin as his own, turn him into a Barrington and see that the child forgot all about her?

No matter what the man's intentions were, she needed to protect Benjamin. What could she do to keep him safe?

Her blood pulsed loudly in her ears as her panic escalated. Through the throbbing, she thought she could hear the sound of horse's hooves. Was it her imagination?

There was an unmistakable knocking, someone pounding on the main door. That was *not* her imagination. Her anxiety accelerated. She felt she was under attack.

She ran to the bedroom door, threw it open, and then tiptoed down the hall and across the landing. Peeking around the corner and down the staircase, she saw the butler crossing the entrance hall to open the door. He greeted the visitor and then stood aside.

In walked John Barrington.

Amy gasped and reeled backwards as she clamped a hand over her mouth. *He knows where I live. He knows where Benjamin is.* Had he come to claim him so soon?

She dashed back to her room as quietly as she could and closed the door behind her. She leaned back against it, struggling for breath. She could see only one course of action.

"I must get him out of here."

She began to charge about the room, grabbing a shawl and a travelling bag from the wardrobe, and then changing her slippers for boots. She took long strides down to the nursery, hearing footsteps downstairs and the butler's voice.

"…see you to the drawing room…"

Once in Benjamin's room, Amy threw various supplies into the bag and made a sling out of a napkin. Then she crept up to the cradle, picked up her sleeping infant and nestled him into the sling. A memory flitted across her thoughts of the last time she had taken flight with Benjamin, about six months earlier. At the time, she'd hardly known her own mind. Now, she was assured in her role as a mother, she'd become a daughter all over again, and she'd even enjoyed the attentions of a man, if briefly. She was not going to give up all she had gained.

When she emerged from the nursery, she heard footsteps moving up the stairs. She ran down to the end of the hallway to the servants' staircase. The narrow spiral took her all the way down to the ground floor, and she found her way to the back door.

Once outside, the December chill stung her lungs. The sun was low in the sky, casting an amber glow on the gardens. She pulled Benjamin closer and wrapped her shawl around them both before edging down the side of the house and ducking behind a hedge.

She paused to catch her breath. If no one had seen her by now, she would leave undetected. But where could she go?

Of course she couldn't trouble the Brooks. There was no way she could go to Ashworth Hall and seek Catherine's protection, not with her brother living under the same roof. As for Henry Russell, well, he'd breached her trust once…

The sound of voices from the house spurred her into action. She began running again, still not sure where she was going. She needed to find a place to hide while she figured out what to do. She headed away from the village, keeping off the road. As the daylight began to dim, her instincts took her towards a place which had become a kind of home in her mind.

She had begun to feel a measure of security, if not exactly belonging, with the Fortescues. Now, within the space of minutes, that had been shattered.

In the hurt and confusion which followed her violation, she hadn't allowed herself to consider the gravity of John Barrington's deception. Once, she had looked upon him as a sort of saviour; now, he was a curse upon both her and Benjamin. Of course he would take exception to her living right under his nose. She was a fool to ever think she would have some stability, some relief. It was as if there were a target on her back, and little Benjamin himself was in the firing line. There was no one who could help her.

❧❦

Henry's axe slammed into a log, splitting it in half. His aim when chopping wood was always dead on, but in matters of the heart he'd failed to hit the mark once again.

Barrington's puzzling response to his verbal assault several hours earlier still dominated his thoughts. Just when Henry thought his chance had come to confront the horrible bully whose deeds hung over him like an evil shadow, the damned man hadn't risen to fight his challenge. Instead, he'd capitulated almost immediately, denying Henry the satisfaction of being the one to make him see how much hurt he'd caused.

Still, he'd said his piece, and if nothing else he'd spoken for Amy as a father or brother might.

As Henry picked up another log, his mind tumbled over everything that had happened to Amy in the last few weeks. She'd endured so much, and what would she still have to suffer through?

The look on her face when he'd seen her outside Jones's had been ghastly, her eyes like two moons and her skin whiter than a sheet. It was as if the distress of her encounter with that villain was as fresh now as it had been then.

His axe cut clean through to the ground, splitting both the wood he'd intended to halve and the stump he was using as a base. He had a sudden undeniable feeling that she needed him. He couldn't shake it off.

He stretched his arms behind his back and examined the sky. The sun had dipped almost to the horizon, barely shining through a thick veil of hazy clouds. In the north, thicker clouds were gathering, and the nip in the air told him snow was on its way.

Given the lateness of the hour, a visit was insensible, even inconsiderate. But he didn't care about propriety at this moment. He only cared about her.

He threw his axe into another nearby tree stump and set off at a brisk pace. By the time he'd left the farm's borders, he was running as fast as he could.

Yes, she didn't want to see him. After today's confrontation, she was probably even more resistant to male company. But he couldn't rest until he knew she was well and safe.

She needed him, he was certain of it. And this time, he was *not* going to let her down. Nor would he ever again.

When he arrived at the Fortescues' door, his courage faltered for a moment. He was in his dirty working clothes, and he'd run himself into a sweat. Perhaps they wouldn't even grant him admittance... and he wouldn't blame them. Amy had probably branded him a liar and a fraud.

He looked up at the house. There was something strangely still about it today. He beat on the door and held his breath.

When the butler eventually opened it, the man appeared surprised, and then alarmed, and then repulsed. "Yes?" he said at last.

"I'm here to see Miss Miller," Henry said, with as much dignity as he could muster.

The butler sniffed, arching one eyebrow. He opened his mouth to speak but then turned to look over his shoulder.

"Why, Mr Russell!" Mrs Fortescue appeared at the door. "Whatever are you doing here? Come in, come in! You'll catch your death out there."

He smiled his thanks and followed them both inside.

"You'll join me in the drawing room, Mr Russell," Mrs Fortescue called, as she sailed across the vestibule.

"Yes, ma'am," Henry muttered, as he almost jogged to keep up with her.

Once in the grandly furnished room, the lady closed the door behind them and paused before indicating a chair.

"Oh, no," Henry said. "I wouldn't risk staining it. I'll stand, if it's all the same to you. Is Miss Miller about?"

Mrs Fortescue took a seat on a couch and frowned at him. "Why do you want to see her, at this hour?"

He swallowed. "Given what happened today, I had to check on her."

"What happened?" she asked. "I am lately home from Milton and am yet to see Amelia myself."

His eyebrows knotted together until he realised she meant Amy. "I don't know the details of what was said, but Amy saw Mr Barrington today."

Mrs Fortescue gave a start and almost fell off her chair. "Barrington?" she whispered. "John Barrington?"

He nodded.

She immediately reached for the bell pull and tugged on it several times.

Henry didn't try to fill the silence in the moments while they waited, but he glanced at her awkwardly several times.

A maid came rushing in.

"Oh good, Jenny," Mrs Fortescue said to her. "Will you fetch Amy for me?"

"Certainly, ma'am." The maid curtsied and left the room.

Henry blew out a breath. Soon he would see her, and everything would be all right.

Mrs Fortescue turned to him. "I must thank you for looking after my – after Amy, that terrible day when Mrs Brook lost her baby."

He guessed at what she had been about to say. "Mrs Fortescue, Amy told me. I know you are her mother."

The lady's eyebrows shot up. "Oh, she did, did she? I wonder who else knows."

"I haven't told anyone," he said. "I actually suspected the truth for many months before she found it out."

"How long have you known?"

"Since the first time I saw you two side by side."

She nodded. "I cannot be surprised that you saw the similarities, given how strongly you feel about my daughter."

It was his turn to be taken aback. He reminded himself that the whole village had seen him dancing with Amy; it wasn't as if it was a secret. He blushed all the same.

She studied him keenly. "Yet," she went on, "even as your relationship deepened and you had ample opportunity to share the facts with her, you did not."

"I couldn't be sure," he croaked. "And I assumed you had your reasons."

She nodded again. "I did. I wanted her to like me before she found out. That you would handle this in such a sensitive way tells me far more about your character than you could know."

He dropped his gaze. "When she realised I knew, she took it as a betrayal. Now she thinks she can't trust me ever again."

"Oh dear," Mrs Fortescue said. She was silent for a moment. "Give her time, Henry. I believe her feelings for you are deeper than the scars of her past."

He shook his head. "I think this secret was my undoing."

"I can see your heart was in the right place. Do not fret – I think she will learn to trust you again if you remain steadfast. I will help if I can."

He blinked. "You will?"

She smiled. "Have you not seen that I have been encouraging your suit?"

"Yes, I suppose I have," he said, as the puzzle pieces came together in his mind. "But why? I would've thought you wouldn't want her to be with any man, or at least not a man like me."

"I would rather keep her protected, that much is true. But I can see in your eyes a love which transcends anything else she might have." She sighed. "I know she belongs back in the life she grew up in. I cannot hold on to her forever. You will inherit the farm lease; at least that gives her security for the future. The main things I need for her are love and trust. I can see how you have treated her with gentle kindness. I have observed your patience and your frustration. And you have borne it all with love."

Henry was dumbfounded. Had she really seen all that in him?

"Tell me," she continued, after a moment, "why did you not offer for her before the babe came?"

He hung his head. "I was to be disinherited if I did."

Mrs Fortescue gasped. "And now?"

"Now... the situation has improved." Henry was trying to think of how to elaborate on that when the door burst open and Jenny came running in with the butler on her heels.

"We can't find her anywhere!" Jenny cried.

Chapter Twenty-Two

"W hat?" Mrs Fortescue leapt to her feet.

The butler cleared his throat, his brow set in a deep line. "She was not in her room earlier either, when Mr Barrington asked to see her."

"Barrington was here?" The blood seemed to drain from Mrs Fortescue's face. "Oh, dear Lord."

"I thought she must be busy in the nursery," the butler went on. "And I did not like to disturb her."

"We've searched the house from top to bottom, and there's no sign of her! The baby's gone too," Jenny said, wringing her hands. "I haven't seen her since she dismissed me, before that gentleman called. She was ever so upset about seeing him in Amberley."

"Good God!" Mrs Fortescue covered her face in her hands.

"I knew it!" Henry said, mainly to himself.

Mrs Fortescue looked at him. "What did you know?"

"That she was in trouble," he said. "That she needed my help."

Mr Fortescue came striding into the room. "What is the matter?"

His wife apprised him of the situation.

"Surely she would have gone to see her friend Mrs Brook?"

Jenny shook her head. "She's taken the babe, sir. She doesn't take him to the Brooks' anymore, on account of them losing their own child."

"Maybe she went to Milton," Henry suggested.

The butler shook his head. "None of the horses are gone, so unless she has borrowed someone else's carriage…"

"I see," Henry said. "We wouldn't be able to track her down there tonight in any case."

Mrs Fortescue had begun to weep quietly, and Mr Fortescue rubbed her shoulders. "Now, Russell, we need a plan," he said. "Night is falling. We must make haste."

Henry nodded as the lady moaned. "If you can spare one of your horses, sir, I'll ask at the Brooks', and find out if she was seen by anyone at the pub."

"Aye, and I shall go to Ashworth Hall and make enquiries there. Perhaps she wanted to see Lady Catherine."

Mrs Fortescue shook her head miserably. "It is unlikely she would dare go there, with the lady's brother back in residence. And it is too far for her to walk!"

"I cannot think of any other places she would be, my love," he said gently. "Can you, Russell?"

Everyone turned to him expectantly. He shrugged sadly. "No, I can't. But I'll check the outbuildings on our farm, just in case."

"Right-o. Let us meet back here in an hour."

Mr Fortescue gave the butler instructions with regards to horses and asked Jenny to fetch Mrs Fortescue a cup of tea and some biscuits.

Before long, both men had set off at a gallop into the descending night, carrying torches. A horrible weight had settled at the bottom of Henry's stomach. Amy was in danger, he was sure of it. He could only hope they would find her before it was too late.

ॐ◌

Dashing through the woods, Amy tripped on a tree root, causing Benjamin to whimper. "Hold on, my love," she said, panting. She knew she had to cross the road at some point, but in the seeping darkness, she found it hard to know exactly how far she had come. She darted out into the open and across the muddy lane, nearly slipping on a particularly slick patch.

When she recognised nothing on the other side, a different kind of panic began to gnaw at her. "If I just continue in that direction, I will surely come across it sooner or later," she said to herself. "I will surely come across *something*…"

She walked on, the initial burst of anxious energy leaving her and nervous exhaustion setting in. She had to sit amongst the woods to feed Benjamin, and by the time he had finished it was pitch black. She walked slowly with her arms outstretched to avoid banging into trees. Her own hunger started to make itself known.

When she finally reached a clearing, she didn't see the signs of life she had expected. Deflated, she brushed away the tears gathering in her eyes.

With the night came a penetrating cold. Now that she was hardly moving, its bitterness encircled her like an icy cloak. She tucked Benjamin down lower into her dress and drew in a breath of the frigid air. She had to keep moving.

She decided on a direction and set off at a renewed pace. Pain suddenly shot up her leg as her ankle twisted on an unknown obstacle, and she tumbled over into some sort of ditch.

With one arm around Benjamin, she tried to break her fall with the other. Her wrist buckled under their weight and she screamed as her arm bent under her body when they landed.

She lay there, unmoving, shock holding her in its grip. Her baby's sudden cries brought her back to reality. She pushed herself to sitting with her uninjured arm and then caressed him with it. "Are you all right, my darling?" she said, her voice quaking. It took some minutes to settle him, and then she tried to calm herself down, but it was no good.

Her whole arm was in agony, and the pain radiated through her body. When she tried to push herself up, her ankle collapsed. Finally yielding to sobs, she gave up. She would have to stay where she was for now, and could only hope she would have the strength to find help in the morning light.

The temperature seemed to drop with every passing minute. And then, something began pricking at her face like frozen needles. Snow.

What if poor Benjamin froze to death before the morning? She curled up on the ground, trying to cover him with as much of her body as possible without smothering him.

If only her parents were still here – then none of this would have happened. She missed them terribly, now more than ever.

She had made such a mess of things. Just weeks before, she had been hopeful of a life anew, and of a deep love to heal her aching heart. Now, all was lost. Her burgeoning sense of security with the Fortescues had been compromised in one moment. And she might die out here alone, without anyone to care that she was gone... And what would become of her poor little boy?

She'd been a fool to believe, even for a moment, that she was worthy of love, and a safe future for herself and Benjamin. Barrington had known what she was – a stupid girl, good only for using and casting aside. Well, she wouldn't be used again. She would have to find a way to survive on her own. Trusting anyone was too risky. She couldn't even trust herself.

There were many hours before dawn, and she was in pain and so cold. So very, very cold...

৵৵৽

"No, I am afraid we have not seen her since her visit this morning," William said, standing on his doorstep, his face illuminated by a candle.

"Oh." Henry had told himself it was unlikely he'd find her here, but it appeared he'd still been harbouring some optimism. The disappointment was crushing. "Could you ask Cecilia if Amy mentioned going somewhere this afternoon, or if she knows anywhere else she might go?"

William nodded. "Of course, though I do not want her to worry. Come in."

Henry waited in the parlour with only the light of one candle. His confidence in finding Amy alive and well that night was also like a small flame, getting less bright by the minute.

William came back some ten minutes later. "Cecilia thinks Amy might have taken Benjamin to see Mr Lindsay, if he was poorly?"

Henry nodded, seeing the pain in his friend's eyes. Of course Cecilia would think of the child first.

"She also suggested trying at Harcourt Lodge. Amy is reasonably familiar with Cecilia's parents."

It was worth a try, although Henry didn't think Amy had ever mentioned them.

William walked him back to the front door. "My only other

suggestion would be to check the church and surrounds – many people end up there if they are lost or afraid. I am very sorry I cannot help with the search. I still do not want to leave my wife."

Henry shook his hand in thanks. "I understand, William. I know what it is to want to protect another person with your life, even if you can't."

William grasped his shoulder. "I pray you find them soon," he said, his eyes earnest in the candle's light. "I pray they are safe."

As Henry rode the short distance to the church, little flakes of snow began to swirl lightly about him. He nestled down into the scarf Mr Fortescue had lent him. He'd also borrowed a greatcoat and hat. How pleasant it must be to own such nice clothes, which felt so fine against his skin. His shirts were all starched to within an inch of their lives, rendered coarse and stiff. If Amy did ever learn to trust him again, could she really give up the luxuries she now knew? The question seemed crazy, given his current concern for her welfare, but it passed through his mind all the same.

He searched all around the church building, amongst the graveyard and through the surrounding trees, calling Amy's name all the while. There was no response, but she was in his memories. He coughed back tears as he recalled that day when she had introduced him to Benjamin properly for the first time. It had been the beginning of his desire to not only take Amy as his wife, but also to take her baby as his son. Would he ever see them again?

As he was about to re-mount the horse, he heard a carriage approaching, and he waved his torch to get the driver's attention. It was, as he'd hoped, Mr Fortescue returning from Ashworth Hall.

The man stepped down from the carriage, raising his collar against the snow and wind. "Any luck?" Henry shouted.

"I am afraid not," he replied. "She has not been there for a couple of months at least, and never on her own. Lady Catherine did not know of anywhere else she might be."

Henry mentioned the Lindsays and Grants, and Mr Fortescue agreed to visit both, as they were on his way home.

"The snow's getting thick, lad," he said. "I need to get home to my wife before long, else we have more missing people to account for!"

"Aye," Henry agreed, sheltering his eyes as he peered into the gloom.

"I still need to check at the pub, and then if you don't mind I'll ride your horse home and search around the farm before… stopping." Giving up? On her? It was unthinkable, but it was true – there was no sense in trying to look for her when he could barely see the ground in front of him. As if to illustrate the point, the snow snuffed out his torch.

"Bloody hell," he muttered under his breath. He re-lit the torch with one on the corner of the carriage. He waved as Mr Fortescue set off again and then mounted his horse and galloped off towards the pub. His efforts there were in vain – no one had seen her since that scene in the village.

He headed towards home, now moving slowly, and calling out for Amy every few yards. By the time he had finally turned the mare into the Russell stables, he was hoarse, and the tears that had coursed down his cheeks were nearly frozen. He checked the empty stalls before going to the house.

Henry burst in on his family, all gathered around the fire in the parlour. "Has anyone seen Amy?" he rasped. "Has she been here?"

Clara and Tilly stared at him open-mouthed, and his parents exchanged a glance. "No, Henry," Mrs Russell said. "Were you expecting her?"

"She's gone missing!" Henry fled from the room and marched straight back out into the snowstorm. He ran over to the barn, picked up the lantern burning outside the door and charged in, screaming her name. He peered into every nook and cranny. At last acknowledging it was fruitless, he fell to his knees in the middle of the barn.

If it weren't for the events of the day, he wouldn't have worried as much. He would have told himself she was out visiting, perhaps some sort of charity call, and had chosen to remain where she was when the weather started closing in.

But it was no ordinary day. She had faced the shock of seeing her baby's father without warning, in such a public place, and then the scoundrel had had the gall to hunt her down at her home. It was little wonder she had fled. If only she had come to him. If only he hadn't let her down.

He had a horrible tormenting feeling she was slipping away not just from him, but also from life.

ॐ

Henry lay awake all night, desperate for the dawn to arrive. There had been no word from the Fortescues. They were none the wiser as to her whereabouts.

He bolted upright with a gasp as an idea hit him with almost physical force.

Would Amy have gone to the croft house? It had been weeks since he was there – there was little point in continuing to make it fit for habitation when he had no wife or money. But maybe Amy had thought of it as a safe haven. Would she? It was unlikely, given she had made it clear they had no future, and the last time she was there with him she had scarpered.

It was worth a chance. He jumped out of bed and went to the window. The first rays of the dawn were glowing in a clear sky to the east, allowing just enough light for him to see the carpet of snow over the farm.

He washed himself hurriedly, the shock of the cold water reviving him despite his lack of sleep.

He dressed in several layers, including the greatcoat and scarf given to him by Mr Fortescue. Pulling on his boots, he tiptoed his way down to the front door and out into the hushed world.

He drew in a lungful of frosty air and began to run.

If she had made it to his cottage, she would have found it locked… but she could have found shelter in the barn. It would have provided almost no respite from the cold, though. For the hundredth time he hoped with all his might that she would somehow find her way back to the Fortescues this morning.

As he sprinted along the snow-white road to the croft house, he began calling her name and scanning the landscape.

What was that?

A few hundred yards from the cottage, just beyond the thicket which marked the holding's boundary, something was protruding through the snow. Could it be… He changed course and raced across the field, stumbling over the uneven ground. It had lain unproductive for some time now, and there were deep ruts where a plough had been drawn. Whatever the mystery object was, it was partially buried in a particularly deep furrow, three or four feet deep, and obscured by the snow. He couldn't make it out until he was within a yard or two.

He cried out, a raw sound of anguish and relief and horror. It was her! She was curled up in the ditch, covered in snow, her arms wrapped around the baby. The top of her head was above the ground. Her eyes were closed. She was pale and still. Had she been like that all night?

"Amy!" he shouted, throwing himself down on his knees beside her. He brushed as much snow off her as he could.

He reached out a shaking hand to touch her cheek, and gasped. She was frozen. And little wonder – she was wearing only a dress and shawl.

Breathing hard, he leaned down and laid his head against her chest, willing her heart to beat. He listened as hard as he could above the roaring of his blood in his ears.

"Please, Amy…"

It was there. A faint heartbeat. He could just make it out.

"Oh, thank God!" he murmured, raising his head. He reached down to the infant and discovered warmth. With the movement the child stirred and began crying softly.

Tears also began to flow from Henry's eyes. "I'll do my best to help your ma!"

He pulled Amy up to a near sitting position and shrugged out of the greatcoat, wrapping it around her. Then he wound the scarf around her neck and tucked it around the baby.

He had to get her in front of a fire with warm food and bedding. He'd take her home to the farm and then send word to the Fortescues.

But first he had to get her out of this wretched hole. He came around behind her and put his arms under hers, trying to haul her up. The angle made it nearly impossible, and before he could try again, she moved her head and groaned a little.

"Amy!" He came back around to face her, and gently shook her shoulders. "It's me, Henry. I found you. I must get you out of there."

Her eyelids fluttered, and then she blinked up at him, her eyes glassy.

"We need to get you warm," he said, breaking into a smile. He was so relieved to see her awake, even though she was clearly ill. He decided pulling her out forward would be easier. "Take my hands, Amy, and we'll get you up."

She frowned and regarded his hands in terror, shaking her head.

He took a deep breath, reminded of that first day she had refused to touch him. Now, time was of the essence.

"Amy," he said firmly, reaching out and leaning as far into the ditch as he dared, "take my hands."

She hesitated and then reached towards him, but a moment later she flinched and sank back even further into the hollow. Her eyes were filled with fear. "I can't!"

The shadow over Henry's heart darkened. Did she really trust him so little that she would rather stay in the cold and risk her life?

He focussed intently on her eyes, trying to show her the depth of his love. He would never give up on her. "You *must*."

Chapter Twenty-Three

There was the sound of a man's voice, and her baby crying. Amy was so cold she could hardly think. All she knew was Barrington was after them.

She tried to drift back into nothing, the sweet oblivion she had dwelt in just now, where hurt and fear didn't exist.

But he kept talking; he wouldn't let her sleep. What did he want from her? Was he going to take Benjamin?

She forced her eyes open. The world was too bright.

It was Henry Russell above her, not John Barrington, but his hands were stretching down towards them.

She tightened her arms around her baby and shook her head. He would not take Benjamin from her.

Pain besieged her senses, burning in her arm and up her leg. With the throbbing came an awareness of her surroundings, and the indistinct memory of falling.

She was in a hole, and Henry was reaching down to her. Did she want him to bring her up?

"Amy." His voice cut into her anxious thoughts. "Take my hands."

His voice was strong, and she knew she was weak. For Benjamin's sake, she had to get them out, and this might be the only help she would get. She had no idea where they were.

She lifted her arms towards the light, and her right arm shot needles of agony through her. It was then that she noticed Henry's hands were bare, despite the snow. In her haste to leave the house, she had also forgotten her gloves, and this meant she would have to touch his skin with her own. All her fears came back with overwhelming force and focussed into that one point: his hands.

"I can't!" she cried, wrenching herself back as far as she could. She gasped as her ankle buckled beneath her.

"You *must*," he insisted, and something about his voice pulled her eyes up to his. His gaze was filled with kindness, and safety… and love. It was pure emotion she couldn't deny. In the midst of so much warmth, the ice at the core of her frozen heart began to melt.

"I won't hurt you," he said, and she believed him. She didn't know why, but it was enough to allow her to take a breath, push off from the ground and grasp his hand with her good one.

His hand was rough and calloused, but its raw strength gave her courage. She cried out in pain as he brought her over the precipice.

Henry hauled her up and brought her to her feet as if she weighed no more than a sparrow. He gently released her hand.

"Can you walk?" he asked.

She tried putting weight on her bad leg, and it crumpled. She grabbed at his shoulder for support and shook her head. "No," she said. "I hurt my ankle. My arm, too. How far is it to… oh!"

Henry scooped her and Benjamin up into his arms in one smooth motion and began to march forward.

"Is that really…" She gave up her objection, seeing how ridiculous it was. Any dignity she might have had had long since gone by the wayside. They would all get dry and warm much more quickly if she let him carry her.

She coughed violently and then spoke soothing words to Benjamin. Beneath her sling she directed the baby to her breast, praying there was still some sustenance to be found there. Once Benjamin was drinking, she let herself relax into Henry's arms, her head bobbing on his shoulder. As Henry trudged through the snow, Amy closed her eyes and felt the sun's rays on her face. She let the motion of the journey lull her into a kind of weightless calm.

She didn't remember arriving at their destination, and didn't know where it was, but she knew Henry had put her down. She was undressed and re-dressed, and protested feebly when Benjamin was removed from her arms to be attended to.

There was warm milk and buttered bread and the dancing flames of a fire. Later – how much later she couldn't say; was it hours or days? – there was a carriage ride, and she was carried up some stairs. More changes of clothes and into a nice, soft bed, although the ensuing slumber wasn't sweet. She drifted in and out of feverish sleep and nightmares, sometimes feeling as if she were floating above herself and other times as if she were trapped at the bottom of a deep, dark pit from which she would never escape.

She was aware that Henry was there, and then he was not. Mrs Fortescue – her mother? – was a continuing presence. In her delirium Amy wondered if she had dreamed the woman's confession.

There was another man coming and going; in time she recognised him as Mr Lindsay. Was there something wrong with Benjamin? She called out for her son repeatedly, and sobbed when she was told he couldn't be brought to her at that moment. She never wanted him out of her sight again – ever.

She dreaded falling asleep, for her dreams were mad visions of her worst fears.

Finally, her mind took her to another place – somewhere she could rest and be happy. Benjamin was sitting at her feet, playing contentedly. There was a cosy fire burning in the grate, and when she looked down, she saw her stomach was swollen with child. This knowledge brought her gladness, not angst. It would be different this time; it would be right. She looked around the room, trying to identify where she was. Ah, of course, it was the parlour in Henry's little cottage. And then, with a joyful sort of nervous energy, she turned to look beside her on the couch, and there was Henry himself, smiling down at her.

She opened her eyes. The weight of the fever had left her. She turned her head, and Henry was there, his eyes clearly swollen and red in the candlelight.

"Amy," he whispered. "Are you all right?"

She smiled up at him. "Hello, Henry. I think I am."

As Henry watched Amy's blood dripping into the bowl beneath her elbow, it felt as if it were his heart that was bleeding. She was so ill, Mr Lindsay said. There was no guarantee of the fever breaking. She had been too cold for too long. The deep creases on the physician's brow were a bad sign. They were very close to losing her. Henry would lose the only woman he'd ever loved. He had never been more scared in his life.

He cursed himself for not finding her earlier. When he'd set off for the Fortescues that day, had she already been lying injured in that ditch, only hundreds of yards away from the woodblock?

He'd felt so helpless on bringing her to his family. He'd collapsed onto the couch in the parlour, completely out of breath from carrying her through the snow, while his womenfolk found her warm clothes and tended to the child.

On her being brought to sit with him by the fire, the fever was already taking hold. He fed her, and she did eat and drink a little, but her eyes were glazed and wild.

The Fortescues were duly notified and arrived to claim her. For the next three days, Henry had kept vigil at her bedside in tandem with her mother. She showed no signs of recognising either of them.

As Amy lay there in the grip of the fever, Henry renewed his commitment to her and Benjamin. If she lived, and if she wanted him, he was hers. Whether in marriage or not, he would always watch over them. He may not be able to provide all the little luxuries she had become used to, but if she needed a friend, an ally, and someone who wanted her just as she was – a farmer's daughter, a mother, a brave heroine – he would be there for her. But he hoped one day it would be in marriage, for he loved her with everything he was.

On the evening of the third day, Henry bathed Amy's forehead with a cool cloth and then resumed his position in a chair by the bedside. He didn't dare touch her skin to check how warm she was, but perhaps she looked a little less flushed?

His breath caught in his throat as her eyes opened. And then, she turned to him. His heart pounded mercilessly. "Amy, are you all right?"

Her lips curved into a smile, and her eyes were clear and bright.

"Hello, Henry. I think I am." Her voice croaked, but she sounded like his Amy again.

He grinned back at her and felt the blood flow in his veins once more. "I thought I'd lost you!"

He wiped a tear away and reached for a glass of water. He slid his hand under her pillow to support her head so she could sip from it.

She frowned suddenly. "Is Benjamin well?"

Henry nodded. "They've been taking good care of him. He's right as rain."

Amy relaxed back into the pillow.

"We'll have him brought to you, and I should let the others know you're feeling better. Where's the uh…"

She pointed to a plaited rope on the other side of the bed, next to her injured arm, which was tied up in a sling. "Pull that," she said, smiling, "and they'll come."

"Right-o." He leaned across her as he took the rope, and his face came within inches of hers. Something sparked inside him. He paused, and then sat beside her on the bed. "I hope you don't mind me being here, Amy," he said. "I know you would rather I keep my distance."

"Mind?" Her eyes danced. "Are you not the one who found me and brought me to safety?"

He nodded. "Er… yes. But if I'd taken action sooner…"

"Hush." She put a finger to his lips, and her expression mirrored his own surprise.

It was the first time she'd initiated touch between them, save for that unfortunate kiss. While she withdrew her finger, she held his eyes.

"I will always be grateful for what you did," she whispered, "and I'm sorry for the trouble I put you all through."

"Don't be sorry," he said huskily. "I'm just glad you'll get better. Although," he gestured to her foot, propped up on a pillow, "you'll be off your feet for a while."

She sighed. "I'll miss your sister's wedding, and I won't be able to visit with Cecilia. Still, it could be much worse, I suppose."

He nodded seriously. "Much worse."

"But when I am recovered, Henry," she said, peeking at him from beneath her lashes, "I hope we can–"

"Oh, Amelia, you're awake!" Mrs Fortescue burst into the room, followed by her husband and two maids.

Henry sprang off the bed and backed away. He exchanged a brief smile with Amy and then quietly left the room.

As he descended the staircase, he let out a frustrated breath. It was unlikely that he would get any more time unchaperoned with Amy. Would he ever find out what she had been about to tell him? He doubted anything had changed. She had expressed simple gratitude to him, nothing more.

❧

Amy still harboured the fear of John Barrington coming to steal his child. Each time she heard someone arrive at the house, her heartbeat accelerated and she held her breath.

On this particular morning, as she sat up in bed with a book, she heard knocking on the front door and the murmuring of voices. She tried to tell herself it was just morning visitors for Mrs Fortescue, but her temples began to throb. Benjamin was in the nursery sleeping. Why hadn't she insisted his cradle be brought to her room? With her ankle still dreadfully sore, she wasn't able to go to him without assistance.

There were footsteps in the hallway and then a rapping on her door.

"Miss Miller," the butler intoned. "Lady Catherine Barrington to see you. Shall I admit her?"

"Lady *Catherine*?" Not John? She began to breathe again. Fixing her hair hurriedly, she nodded. "Yes, please."

A few moments later, Catherine rushed through the door laden with packages. "Oh, my dear!" she cried, laying her bundles at the foot of the bed. "How I have worried for you!" She dropped kisses onto Amy's cheeks and seated herself on the bed.

"Hello, Lady Catherine," Amy greeted her warmly. "How good of you to come."

"Of course I would come to see you, and it would have been sooner except Louisa and I went to stay with a cousin near Shrewsbury. When my mother wrote to me and told me you were gravely ill, I asked to return home immediately." She grinned. "But not before a visit to the high street to procure some things to cheer you up!"

Amy shook her head, smiling. How funny it was that the aristocracy found comfort in material things. She already had everything she needed to get well. "I assure you your presence is enough."

"Nonsense!"

Catherine began opening up the various parcels containing biscuits, a pretty shawl, tea, a ladies' periodical, candied fruit and a lovely but tiny and therefore impractical reticule.

"My lady, you've outdone yourself!" Amy blushed. "I cannot accept all this."

"Oh, but I insist that you do." Catherine pushed her purchases to one side and her countenance became solemn. "Now, I do have something else to give you, and not without trepidation."

Amy frowned. "Yes?"

Catherine drew the strings on her own reticule and took out a letter. "This is from John," she said, and Amy gasped. "He begged me to give it to you, and I only do so because he assured me it will not upset you."

Amy stared at the missive. "Do you know the contents?"

Catherine shook her head. "No. John said it concerns private matters."

She handed it to Amy, and after a moment's hesitation, Amy took it from her. She tucked it under her pillow. "I shall read it later."

"Of course."

There was a pause, and Amy took a deep breath. "I hope you will not think me impertinent if I ask you something…"

"I am sure I will not."

"It is only that… it would have made things easier if I had known your brother was coming back to Amberley. It was a great shock for me to see him in the village that day. I gather he'd been away for the year his father stipulated, but a little warning would have been nice."

Catherine nodded and wrung her hands. "I am sorry. I wish I could have written to you before we departed Hampshire, but there was no time! John wanted to set off so suddenly, I was barely able to pack my things before the carriage left."

"Really? Why was he in such a hurry?"

Catherine paused. "I have an inkling," she said finally. "It was nothing to do with you or the child. Once we arrived back in Amberley, I was

198

busy unpacking my things and had no idea he had gone into the village. I did not know he came to see you at Briarwood either, until Mr Fortescue rode over that evening."

Amy nodded. "I was afraid for Benjamin," she explained. "When I saw John in the village he looked as if he wanted to take him." She met Catherine's eyes without masking her fear.

"Oh, my dear." Catherine took her hand. "I am sure he wishes only good things for the child, and the best thing for him is clearly his mother. I hope the letter goes some way towards giving you assurance in that regard. You will come to me, if you have any worries?"

Amy took a shuddering breath. "I will," she promised.

"I know he can never make it right," Catherine went on gently, "but I hope in time you might come to forgive him. I think he genuinely does regret it."

Amy couldn't respond to that; it was too much. She could only squeeze the lady's hand and swallow back tears.

Catherine brightened. "Now, shall I tell you all the news?"

Amy blinked. "If you like."

The lady launched into a detailed dissertation of the local goings-on, and various pieces of gossip from her extended family.

Amy pretended to listen, but all she could think of was that folded piece of paper underneath her pillow. Did she have the courage to read it? What could he ask of her, when he had already taken so much?

It wasn't until much later that evening, when the rest of the household had gone to bed, that Amy picked up the candle from her bedside and reached under her pillow.

With trembling hands, she opened the letter.

Chapter Twenty-Four

Dear Miss Miller,

I hope you will honour me by reading this letter. I did want to explain myself in person, but I understand your reluctance to see me.

I am only recently cognisant of the depth of the injury I have caused you. An apology will not suffice, but I beg of you to acknowledge I am truly and deeply sorry for what I have done.

I want to do what I can to support the boy. I am aware you will be disinclined to receive anything from me, and that money is no recompense for the hurt I have inflicted upon you. I ask not that you accept this for my sake, but rather for his. He need never know the identity of his benefactor.

I believe you know I am in possession of a small estate in Hampshire, Mulberry Manor. My father has written to our lawyer to have the ownership transferred to your son. All you must do is name him and sign the deeds on his behalf. You will be called upon to do this in a month or two.

Any profits from Mulberry Manor from that point onward will be kept in a trust, which will be available to the child when he comes of age, and can presumably be used to fund his university education. Thenceforth, he will receive all regular income from the property, whether he chooses to live there or not. I hope you will accept this.

I intend to return to Hampshire forthwith to tidy up my affairs and take my leave of the place. The steward there will resume overseeing matters and will be at your bidding. I will then be away from Amberley as much as I can – I do not intend to make you uncomfortable if I can possibly avoid it.

I thank you for reading this letter and considering my offer. I wish you and the child the very best in life. You will never hear from me again.

Yours,
John Barrington

Amy reread the letter twice and then put it back under her pillow. She didn't know what she had expected it to contain, but she certainly hadn't expected that. It would take her some time to absorb the man's sentiments, and understand the implications of his proposal.

His remorse was surprising; his generosity reminded her of the man she had thought she knew. But still, memories of that horrible night haunted her daily and would impact her for the rest of her life. Nothing would change that.

The enormity of it all caused her to shed fresh tears, and she lay awake for most of the night, attempting to piece together her feelings.

Benjamin cried out just before dawn, and she waited impatiently for Agnes to bring him to her. As she held him in her arms, the prospect of having his future well-secured was a comfort to her. Surely she couldn't deny him the chance to better himself, even though it would mean a painful connection to the past.

At the very least, it seemed as if she could lay her worries to rest regarding Barrington's intentions towards Benjamin. Perhaps her taking flight when he visited that day had been foolish, but how was she to know the man would have such a change of heart?

She pushed the thoughts from her mind and chose to focus on the way Ben's long, curved eyelashes rested on his plump cheeks. "My little angel," she whispered.

⇠⇢

Later that morning, a different visitor was shown in, and this one was most welcome. It was Cecilia, and it was the first time Amy had seen her out of bed since that terrible day.

When her friend entered the room, Benjamin was feeding from Amy's breast, and she cradled him with her good arm. As Cecilia reached around the child to embrace her, Amy cringed. How unfair of her to rub salt into the wound by performing this motherly task in front of a woman who had lost her child.

"I shall ring for the nurse," she said, attempting to unlatch him.

Cecilia smiled. "No, dearest, you keep him with you," she said softly. "I would not deprive you for the world."

"It is so good to see you well again," Amy said, as Cecilia sat on the bed next to her. Her friend's colour was much improved, but there were new creases around her eyes, and they would likely never fade. "How do you get on?"

"Tolerably," Cecilia replied. "We had a small burial ceremony for the baby yesterday, and it is good to have done that. I feel as though I may try to occupy myself with some tasks again, and be useful to William."

"Oh, Cici, I wish you would not worry about being useful. Everyone understands you need to grieve."

"But I also need to do something," Cecilia persisted. "If I relive that tragedy over and over again, I shall go mad. Besides, I was anxious to see you, knowing you have been through such an ordeal." She indicated Amy's injured arm. "It must be frightfully inconvenient, having the use of only one hand."

Amy shrugged. "It is not forever," she said sombrely.

Shame weighed heavily upon her for having ever felt resentment towards Cecilia. Amy had endured a difficult pregnancy, to be sure, and a baby born in less than ideal circumstances – but she had ended up with a healthy child.

Cecilia picked up on her meaning. "It is true, we really mustn't take things for granted, especially when it concerns people we love. I know you have been through hell, dearest, but I do hope you can be happy with little Benjamin. From my perspective, you are lucky to have been blessed with such a treasure. I envy you, you know."

Amy nodded, tears pricking her eyes. "Yes, I am fortunate indeed. I must confess, dear Cici, I have been jealous of *you*. But we all have our struggles, do we not? How can we ever think our own are greater or more difficult to bear? I have suffered, but out of that pain has come fulfilment beyond measure."

Cecilia smiled at her. "You are a remarkable woman, and I am very proud to call you my friend."

At this Amy's tears would not be contained. "And I you," she managed to say.

Cecilia produced a handkerchief and blotted Amy's face before speaking again. "What about Henry?"

"Well… he was there for me when I needed someone the most," Amy said, and then sighed. "But he lied to me, Cici."

"Oh, really?" Cecilia frowned. "How so? From what I know of him, I thought he would be incapable of deceit."

"He discerned that Mrs Fortescue was my mother and he did not tell me."

"Ah." Cecilia considered this. "Did he give you a reason why he withheld the information?"

Amy remembered that ghastly moment when her blossoming feelings had been crushed. "He said he was afraid it would make things difficult for me."

"I see. And how do you think you would have reacted, dearest, should he have told you what he supposed?"

For the first time, Amy pushed her hurt aside to look realistically at the situation. "I really cannot say," she said finally, "but my temper being what it is, I suppose I would not have been very rational!"

They both laughed, and then Cecilia became serious again. "Had I known the truth," she said, "I would also have struggled with whether to tell you."

"Honestly?" This Amy had not expected.

Cecilia nodded. "The news was of such a magnitude that it would have been only fair for the lady herself to tell you of it."

"Oh." Amy frowned, realising at last that building up this issue to be so insurmountable was really just a means to hide behind her fears. "I am so dreadfully afraid of trusting someone again," she admitted.

"I understand, my dear Amy," Cecilia said, leaning over and gently grasping her shoulders. "But if you have a chance of loving someone, you must not give it up. You must cling to it with everything you have. You never know when that chance will be stolen from you. It is better to have made the most of it. Sometimes, loving someone means enduring the greatest grief you will know."

Amy could see that the relentless optimism her friend had possessed all her life was waning. How could she refuse to take her advice now?

"Thank you, my dear," Amy whispered, another tear escaping. "I cannot believe I almost lost you."

Cecilia pulled back and dabbed at her own eyes with the handkerchief. "I do hope I will always be here for you," she said. She cleared her throat. "How is your relationship with Mrs Fortescue now?"

While the lady had been attentive during her recovery, she had not broached the subject of their connection again.

"The long hours abed have given me plenty of time to get used to the idea," Amy said slowly, "though I do wonder how true a bond we can ever have. There is still a fair degree of awkwardness."

"I suppose that is to be expected," Cecilia said. "The only thing I would say is to give her a reasonable chance. This must be very hard for her. She knows she cannot replace the woman who brought you up. But this is another chance for you to know a mother's love… and there are other benefits besides."

Amy arched an eyebrow. "Such as?"

"Such as assistance with your baby." Cecilia's eyes sparkled. "And future babies."

Amy gasped. "Cecilia Brook, what a rascal you are!"

The friends enjoyed each other's company for a while longer, and then Cecilia stood to leave.

"Are you going back home?" Amy asked.

Cecilia shook her head. "No, I am going to help decorate the church for Mick and Clara's wedding tomorrow."

"Oh, of course. Do give them my best wishes, if you get a chance."

"So I shall."

Thinking again about her friend's advice, Amy sat up straighter and called out before Cecilia left the room. "Cici, would you fetch me my sewing kit from the wardrobe please? There is something I need to finish."

❧

"I do."

As Clara spoke the words which bound her to Mick Stockton in matrimony, her face alight with pure joy, Henry couldn't stop himself from smiling. His little sister was grown, and a wife, no doubt soon a mother. And she wouldn't have to toil away in the fields or milk any more cows, being a gentleman farmer's wife. It was right; it was good. He hoped his contribution would mean real and lasting happiness for her.

Still, he couldn't resist a quiet word with Stockton at the wedding breakfast. "I hope she brings you wedded bliss, brother, but if I ever hear of you mistreating her, I'll make you regret it."

"I have no doubt of it," Stockton said with a grin, clapping him on the back. "I would expect no less."

Henry had been attempting a menacing look, but he broke into a grin, too.

Clara joined them. "Have you made your peace, then?"

Henry shrugged. "For now."

She laughed at him. "Oh, Henry. I know I can depend on you to be my protector. But I have a new guardian now." She looped her arm through her husband's and smiled up at him.

"And I shall guard you with my life, my love," he answered.

Henry made his excuses as they stared lovingly into each other's eyes.

After the wedding celebrations had drawn to a close and the remaining Russell family had returned to the farm, Henry readied the horse and gig.

"Going somewhere?"

Henry whipped around to face his father. "Yes, I was going to my, er, the croft house, Pa."

"Mind if I join you? I'm keen to see what you've done to the place."

He took a steadying breath. "If you like."

Until now, the cottage had been his alone. He wasn't ready to have his father trample all over his labours with criticism and mockery. But the smallholding was still technically his father's until Henry married, so he could do little to prevent him from visiting it.

The journey to the property passed mainly in silence, with the odd perfunctory remark about the wedding. On arriving at the house, Henry opened the door and let his father go before him. He joined him in the parlour.

"By Jove, it's like a different house." Mr Russell inspected the walls, the window frames, the ceiling, and the fireplace before moving through to the kitchen. He let out a low whistle as he surveyed the cupboards, and slapped an appreciative hand on the table.

Mr Russell glanced up. "Some of those windows needed replacing?"

Henry nodded. "Aye."

He left his father to go upstairs while he made some adjustments to the hearth. He'd wanted to come to the cottage today to remind himself of what his own future could be like, if he was able to secure the hand of his lady. Today was a day for dreaming. Tomorrow he could go back to the mundane destiny that awaited him.

He sat at one of the dining chairs he'd made. He shifted on the hard wood. It wasn't the most comfortable furniture in the world, but at least he'd fashioned it with his own hands. He closed his eyes and imagined bouncing baby Benjamin on his lap in this chair while Amy served up supper. The image was so clear, so true.

Creaking on the stairs alerted him to his father's return. He stood and met the man in the entryway and then led him back outside. They had a look around the stables, which Henry hadn't had a chance to fix up yet. He showed his father the various improvements he would make, and, back outside, outlined his plans for animals and vegetables. They were plans which were unlikely to come to fruition now that he'd given up his life savings.

They jumped back up on the gig, but Henry hesitated before starting the return journey.

"What do you think, Pa?"

"Well." Mr Russell drew in a breath, and Henry braced himself, waiting for the inevitable condemnation. Why had he invited it? He knew his father would always find him wanting, but for some stupid reason he still found himself craving his approval.

"I think you've done well, boy."

"What?" Henry stared at him.

"This place was a mess, and I didn't think you'd have the gumption to even take it on. I thought the lands would just be a useful addition to what we have, but you've proved me wrong. You've worked hard, and what you've done is bloody good. You really want to make a go of it, don't you?"

"Yes," he sputtered, overcome.

He spurred the horse into action before he could make a fool of himself. His father had stopped short of saying he was proud of him, but the praise was more than enough. Henry had waited twenty-six long years to hear such words.

"You've been spending a lot of time with the Miller girl again, haven't you?"

Henry glanced at his father. "I was helping care for her through the fever, but now she's getting better I don't think I have a place with her. Though I would like to."

"Well, in any case, given what I've seen today, I think you've earned the right to choose your partner in life, no matter who it is. Your mother and I will support whatever decision you make – and we'll help you if we can."

Henry coughed to hide his surprise at this remark. An offer of help... of independence. He stopped short of asking his father if he'd been on the whisky. Perhaps the emotions of the day and seeing his daughter so content had produced this change of heart.

"Thank you, Pa," he said. "And if I do manage to marry Amy Miller one day, will you acknowledge her child?"

Now Mr Russell coughed. Henry had crossed a line, but it was one worthy of such trespassing.

He leapt into the silence. "Amy has proven herself to be a good worker, even as a new mother – can you forget how she helped us this summer? And we always had a friendship with the Millers. I don't think Amy would ever ask anything of you. She's far too proud. But it would be a great favour to me if you would accept Benjamin into our family along with his mother. He's a fine little fellow. Please."

Henry turned to his father and they met eyes – a rare occurrence. In that moment, something transmitted between them... something visceral, powerful, and important. It felt as if some kind of mantle were passing.

"Aye," his father said, "I can see she's a good woman. If it means that much to you, I'll speak to your mother about it. She's the one who really can't stomach the idea of accepting the child."

"Thank you," Henry said, and they spoke no more about it. He knew his mother, for all her blustering, would respect his father's wishes... Eventually.

Chapter Twenty-Five

Amy laboured over her embroidery in the drawing room, thrilled to be finally up and about and using both hands. She savoured the winter sun streaming through the windows.

So engrossed was she that she hardly noticed Mrs Fortescue enter the room. She jumped when the lady spoke.

"Why, that's beautiful, Amy!"

"Oh!" *She finally called me Amy.* She looked up into her mother's admiring face. "Thank you."

"Is it your own design?"

Amy nodded shyly.

Mrs Fortescue examined her stitching more closely. "Any lady would be proud of such work. Well done."

Amy beamed; she couldn't help herself. She still had no aspirations to be a lady, but pleasing her guardian after all these months was reward in itself – more satisfying than she would have dreamed, given her reluctance to master all the ladylike pursuits which had been thrust upon her.

Then Mrs Fortescue gasped, comprehension dawning in her eyes. "Is this for…?"

Amy blushed and nodded again. Why not put her heart on the table? This lady – now her nearest relation – had seen her at her most vulnerable. She had nothing to lose. "I intend to accept him if he offers again."

Mrs Fortescue inhaled in delight, clasping her hands together. "What wonderful news." She sat next to Amy on the couch. "You are confident you have conquered your qualms, then?"

"I think so. Lately I have come face-to-face with my fears – and I can separate them from what I have with Henry."

"I am very glad to hear it," Mrs Fortescue said with a smile. "And proud of you for having such courage."

Amy held the lady's eyes, drinking in the encouragement and praise. "Thank you," she said, swallowing back emotion. She turned back to her work. "It would be a long engagement, so I would need to encroach on your kindness for some time yet. He has given all the funds he had for setting up his own house to his sister, to enable her marriage. Clara told me of it herself."

"How selfless of him," Mrs Fortescue said. "I will be able to help with that."

Amy glanced at her. "What do you mean?"

"I have long intended to provide you with a dowry to ensure you and Benjamin will have some security when you marry. There is no reason why it could not be used on the provisions you would need at Henry's little property."

Amy stared at her, open-mouthed. She had said it so casually, as if granting a sum to someone which would be the enablement of their dreams was an easy, everyday occurrence. "You would give me a dowry?"

Unexpectedly, Mrs Fortescue took her hand, and surprisingly, the act made Amy feel a bond between them. "I see it as my privilege as your mother. It would be the last gift I could give you before you leave this house and my protection. Then, someone else will be looking after you." Her chin wobbled.

Amy could only imagine giving her child away, and was compelled to embrace her mother. "I wouldn't be going far," she said softly, on her shoulder. "I still want you to be in our lives."

A sob escaped from Mrs Fortescue. "That would mean the world to me," she whispered.

There was a tap on the door, and Agnes came in with Benjamin.

Amy took him and covered his face with kisses. When it was just the three of them again, she turned to her mother. "Would you like to take him?" It occurred to her the lady had never held her grandchild.

Mrs Fortescue nodded, her eyes shining. "If it pleases you."

Amy transferred Benjamin to his grandmother's arms, and her heart warmed at the pure joy on the lady's face.

"Well, hello there, Benjamin," she said. "You are a very loved little boy." She looked up at Amy. "You are both well loved, and always will be."

Her spirit now overflowing, Amy smiled back tremulously. "I am so very grateful for everything you have done for me. For us."

Mrs Fortescue shook her head as she gazed back down at Benjamin, who gurgled contentedly. "It is I who is grateful. This year has been the best of my life."

Amy relaxed back on the couch and took a moment to really see the love her mother had for her child. She swelled with pride.

The circumstances in which her sweet boy had been conceived were now irrelevant, inconsequential. He was her reason for living, and must also be her reason for being brave in choosing a life for them both.

Mrs Fortescue could never take the place in her heart belonging to the woman who had raised her as her very own child. But in this moment, Amy received the affection of a mother, and she felt herself finally letting go, allowing this woman to love her. Shirley Fortescue had been there for her when no one else had, and the idea that she had actually been looking out for her throughout her life was finally reassuring.

She was part of a family again. She belonged at last. She knew though that she could not stay here, that she must make her own way, but it was this very foundation of love and support that would give her the confidence to strike out and risk her heart. She knew what she must do.

She could not ignore Henry's devotion and selfless service. Her heart had discerned that he was honourable. He had shown her his love in the way that he had cared for her, and in not asking anything of her in return. It was the exact opposite of what John had done: taking all and giving nothing.

She had thought she loved John. Now she realised she hadn't known then what real love was. She certainly knew now what it wasn't.

She had never known John's true motivations, his fears or his heart's desires. He hadn't let her see beyond his veneer of charm and easy-going humour. Only after his betrayal had she witnessed the true extent of his ruthlessness, his callousness. How could she have loved him, when she never really knew who he was?

That was in her past, and she could now dare to aspire to a better future. A year ago she had felt broken, conquered, unworthy, lost. Now she knew who she was and she knew what she wanted. And she wanted Henry Russell: as a partner for her life, a father to her son, an equal to her mind and a sanctuary for her heart.

Henry had slowly but surely built a safe and secure place in her heart, mirroring his dedicated crafting of the furniture and fittings in the lovely little cottage. Every join was perfect, every hole filled. It was beautiful yet simple and innocent in its perfection, much like her love for him. She knew, like she had never known anything before, that she could trust him with her whole heart, and that he would love and care for her precious child.

This was no small miracle; why, only six months earlier she had thought she would remain alone for the rest of her life. And now, her heart was brimming over with the love of a good man, the devotion of a mother, and an unbreakable bond with a baby boy. She could not help but wish the tragic events of the previous year could be undone, of course, but without the painful learnings she had endured, she would not know how to appreciate what love could be.

How Henry loved her – so completely she knew he would always put the needs of her and Benjamin ahead of his own, and she would do the same for him.

❧

Amberley's quaint stone church was coated in snow. The Russell family shuffled through the slush in the churchyard to attend the Sunday service. As was his habit, Henry looked to the front pews before taking his place near the back.

His heart leapt. There she was: his love, his light, his world. It was the first time she'd attended church since her illness. He tried to focus on William's sermon, but his mind was consumed with Amy. Unable to contain his joy, he sang the hymns with gusto, prompting questioning looks from his family. He didn't care if the smile never left his face – in fact, he hoped it wouldn't.

After the service, his parents and sister were eager to get home and out of the cold. This time, he wouldn't delay them with subterfuge. "I want to talk to Amy."

"Be quick about it," his father said.

When the Fortescues emerged from the church, Henry started towards them. Mrs Fortescue caught his eye, and she leaned towards Amy, saying something in her ear. Then the woman marched straight up to him, blocking his path.

"Good day, Mr Russell," she said, and he wondered how a simple greeting could sound so overbearing.

"Good day," he replied, and he looked over her shoulder at Amy. She sent him a sympathetic smile.

"If your family can spare you, I should like to invite you to take luncheon with us today," Mrs Fortescue said.

"You – you would?" Henry gaped at her.

She only looked at him and raised her eyebrows.

He cleared his throat. "I'm sure my family doesn't need me – I mean, I would love to come, Mrs Fortescue. Thank you for inviting me."

She nodded. "Join us in the carriage, will you?"

"I, uh–"

She had already walked away, before he could shame himself with further stammering.

Henry had never been in a fancy carriage in his life. He rushed back to his family and explained the summons. When he found the Fortescues' carriage, the footman winked at him before he stepped up into it.

The other three occupants were already seated inside, and they each acknowledged him. He took the seat next to Mr Fortescue, across from Amy, facing backwards.

"Mr Russell," Amy said, nodding at him in what he hoped was a friendly manner.

"You look very well, Miss Miller," he said, and though he was trying to sound gentlemanlike, he really meant it. Once again she had colour in her cheeks and life in her eyes. He wanted to tell her how beautiful she was. Instead, he lurched forward ridiculously as the carriage set off.

If luncheon was a trial, he was sure to be found wanting. Even though he was clothed in his Sunday best, he felt shabby sitting at the finely dressed table in the elegant dining room. He wished he'd at least tried to comb his hair properly. He didn't know which fork was which, and accepting food from a platter offered by servants was downright embarrassing. The other three made conversation about the church service, the weather, the militia stationed in Milton, and the latest styles of dress the Barrington ladies were wearing.

They did attempt to engage with him, but he couldn't think of anything more than one-word answers. He shared glances with Amy from time to time, but perhaps they were looks of pity?

"Are you enjoying your food, Mr Russell?" Mrs Fortescue enquired.

Henry looked down at his plate. On it was some sort of pastry concoction filled with foreign fruits. He hadn't figured out which utensil was appropriate to use yet. "I am, thank you," he replied. "It's very, er, good."

Amy smiled at him in a way that suggested she was laughing at him. He wanted to dive under the table. He'd never felt more out of place.

If he was lucky, there would be more of these occasions in his future. He'd have to ask Amy for lessons... Or perhaps this experiment had simply taught him that she was beyond his reach.

At last the meal was over, and he expected to be dismissed.

"Let us take tea in the drawing room," Mrs Fortescue said, standing.

Henry clamped his lips together to avoid swearing under his breath. He followed the others to the room and waited for Mrs Fortescue to sit. At least he knew enough about manners to know he shouldn't just plonk himself down first.

But she didn't sit. Instead, she turned to her husband. "Mr Fortescue?"

He was on his way to reclining in a leather chair, but he pushed off the arms to stand again. "Yes, my dear?"

"I should like to discuss that matter with you now, if you please."

He frowned. "That matter? Which matter?"

She glared at him. "That important thing we need to discuss. In your library." She raised her eyebrows and looked over to Amy and Henry.

He stared at her, and then at the other two, and then a grin stole across his face. "Ah, right you are. Certainly."

Mrs Fortescue turned to Henry. "We shall be back in about a quarter of an hour."

He regarded her in confusion, and then the penny dropped and he nodded meaningfully. "Thank you."

It was now quite plain to him that the whole lunch had been engineered to give him the time he needed alone with Amy. That explained the forced invitation, the awkward small talk, and now, the hasty exit of their chaperones. He wouldn't waste this opportunity. He was more than ready... But was she?

He turned to Amy, and she smiled at him timidly.

"Would you like to sit down?" she asked, indicating the small couch. He did so, and she sat next to him, only inches away.

He took a deep breath. There was so much to say, and a limited time in which to say it. He owed it to Amy to tell her everything, properly, as a gentleman would. What if he scared her off again at the very last hurdle?

"How are you feeling?" he asked, trying to make eye contact. "Your arm, your ankle?"

She kept her eyes downcast. Her neck seemed to be flushed. "Much better, thank you. Just some achiness every now and then. How are you? Missing Clara, I collect?"

He shrugged. "Yes, of course, but she's where she belongs." He began to sweat. There was no time to waste. "Amy, I–"

"I have a Christmas present for you, Henry." She spoke over him, perhaps not hearing his attempt to start a speech of sorts.

His mouth dropped open. "A what? Oh, Christmas?"

She nodded. "I know it's still several days away, but I've made something I want to give you, and I think now is the right time."

"But I have nothing to give you."

She was already on her feet and retrieving a basket from a table on the opposite wall. She came back to sit with him, placing it on her lap. "Here it is," she said, still not looking at him. "I hope you like it."

Mystified, he watched her remove a pincushion and several spools of thread, before taking out her embroidery frame. Underneath was a vibrant design on white cloth, and as she pulled it out of the basket, he saw it had been sewn onto a scarlet backing fabric.

She handed it to him.

"Thank you," he said automatically, although he had no idea why she would give him some sewing as a present.

"Look at the pattern."

He did... and the breath left his body. It was his cottage – their cottage? – so lovingly rendered there was no mistaking it. And above it in red script were three letters: a bold *H*, a bold *A*, and a smaller *B* intertwined with them.

"Amy," he said, his voice shaking. "Does this mean...?"

She nodded, finally meeting his eyes. "They're cushions for the dining chairs you made, Henry. I hope you don't mind my presumption..."

"Mind? How could I mind..." He ached to take her hand, to pull her into his arms, to kiss her softly and tell her she would make his dreams come true. But he swallowed hard and resisted the urge to touch her, lovely as she was.

"I want nothing so much as to bring you and Benjamin home to the cottage with me," he said. "These are beautiful, Amy, and just the homely touch it needs. And now we will be able to sit on the chairs I made without crippling ourselves."

She giggled. "I wanted to show you it's my dream, too."

He shared a smile with her, his heart bursting. "Is it your dream to be with me, Amy? I know you've had your doubts, your worries..."

She nodded, her eyes shining. "Yes, Henry. I do want to be with you, with all my heart. I've seen your goodness in the way you sacrificed everything for your sister, in how you wouldn't give up on searching for me, and in the way you looked after me. I know you'll be by my side through times good and bad."

He tried to take this in. She knew about Clara's dowry? It hadn't been his intention for it to aid his suit with her, but he was pleased it had all the same. And she did want to be with him, heaven be thanked. He would spend his days proving he was worthy of her.

He looked deep into her beautiful emerald eyes. "Amy Miller, I want you to be my wife, and I want Benjamin to be my son."

Her lips quivered, and a tear ran down one cheek. "Are you quite sure, Henry? I still need you to be patient with me, to take things slowly..."

It took everything he had not to wipe away her tear, not to stroke her cheek and show her how gentle he could be. But she had to be the one to make the first move.

"I understand," he said, "and it makes no difference to my feelings. You don't have to worry."

She nodded, and smiled through her tears.

"Oh, Amy, please let me take care of you both. I do love you so."

"And I love you," she said, and she reached over to him with one trembling hand.

He held his breath and held her eyes, willing her to know she was safe with him.

Her fingers grazed his ginger curls, and then she ran her hand through his hair and down to the nape of his neck. He closed his eyes. It was a heavenly sensation which sent shivers down his spine.

He heard the rustle of her moving, and when he opened his eyes her face was dangerously close to his.

"I will marry you, Henry," she whispered, her eyes on his lips. "Kiss me."

He gulped; this was when things had gone so wrong last time. "Are you sure?" He took a tendril of her hair from where it rested beside her neck, and twirled it around his fingers, tentatively mirroring what she had done without actually touching her skin.

"I'm sure," she said, and she closed her eyes as she leaned towards him.

His defences faltered. He was powerless to resist even if he should. As her lips met his, he took her head gently in his hands and kissed her back with all the love and tenderness of a man finally united with his destiny.

She sighed contentedly and then nestled her head into his shoulder.

He exhaled slowly, overcome with relief that she had not run from him again. She also didn't flinch when he put his arm around her and drew her closer. They remained this way for a minute or two, until the Fortescues returned to share in the happy news.

Chapter Twenty-Six

One month later

"Oh miss, they look so pretty." Jenny finished winding a strand of Mrs Fortescue's pearls through Amy's hair, and the effect was indeed quite stunning.

"Thank you, Jenny," Amy said, staring at herself in wonder. "I can't believe this day is here."

Until recently, she'd assumed she would never marry. And now here she was, in a beautiful dress with her late mother's blue ribbon stitched inside of the hem. Lady Catherine had given her a pair of fine silk stockings and Cecilia had tied together the most beautiful winter bouquet of forget-me-not, daphne, stock, and heather in shades of pink, purple and white.

She swivelled on the chair to take her shoes from Jenny, slipping them on her feet. It was unlikely she'd be wearing fancy footwear from now on, given she would be a working farmer's wife. But she wouldn't have it any other way.

She pulled on a creamy white glove and held out her arm so Jenny could fasten all the tiny buttons, which stretched up her forearm. Once the other glove was likewise secured, she embraced her maid.

"Thank you for everything," she said. "I'll miss you."

As Jenny pulled back, she swiped at her eyes. "I hope you'll be happy, miss."

Amy checked her reflection one final time before making her way to the nursery.

There, Agnes held a sleeping Benjamin, dressed in his best gown. Amy took him carefully and kissed him. "How I love you, little one," she whispered. "We have a bright future ahead of us."

The following week, Amy would meet a representative for the Barringtons at an office in Milton, to sign the deeds to Mulberry Manor on behalf of her son. The name she would put on the property title would be Benjamin Russell.

She gave the baby back to Agnes and began her descent to the foyer, where Mr and Mrs Fortescue were waiting. She linked arms with Mrs Fortescue and they walked out to the waiting carriage together.

"Are you ready?" her mother asked.

Amy looked into the eyes so like her own and nodded. "Yes, I am," she said, and she stepped up into the carriage.

∂∞∾

Several hours later, Amy settled in front of the fire with her husband, in the cottage that was their very own. The couch was a wedding present from the Fortescues, along with the bed they would sleep in that night.

Henry rose to stoke the fire and then smiled at her as he resumed his seat. "Are you warm enough, my love?"

The warmth in his amber eyes was enough to light a thousand fires inside her. She nodded. "Very cosy. Thank you, Henry." Nerves and anticipation pulsed through her veins. What would happen now?

The fire crackled, and the dancing flames illuminated Henry's features, bright with adoration.

He reached over and took one of her hands. He turned it over and undid the top button on her glove with slow deliberation.

He glanced up warily, and she smiled at him. She was his; the least she could do was let him have her hands. The very thing which had kept her paralysed with fear – his skin on hers – was now a curiosity rather than a concern.

He continued releasing the buttons, moving slowly down her wrist to her palm. His fingers brushed the base of her hand as light as a feather, and she sucked in a breath.

The last button undone, he moved to her thumb and tugged gently to loosen the sheath, repeating the process for each finger: a soft caress for her fingertips.

Finally, keeping his eyes on her face, he grasped the glove and slipped it off her hand. Then, as he cradled the back of her hand in his, he dropped his head and tenderly kissed her palm.

It was… delicious. She shuddered as pleasure rushed through her.

He felt the movement and immediately let her go, his expression panicked. "Do you want me to stop?" he asked huskily.

Amy held his eyes and found only love and admiration there, not possession or greed. She felt wanted, cherished, and she trusted him completely.

"No," she said, standing. Taking a deep breath, she moved forward and sat down on his lap, offering her other arm.

A bemused smile tugged up the corner of his mouth as he accepted it.

"Touch me again."

Author's Note: Thank You

Thank you for reading *Gloved Heart*. I very much hope you enjoyed it.

I would greatly appreciate it if you would leave a review for this book at Goodreads or Amazon.

Visit my website www.charlottebrentwood.com to sign up for my email newsletter to find out about my next releases and other news about my books.

Ways to connect with Charlotte:
Email: charlotte.brentwood@gmail.com
Facebook: www.facebook.com/charbrentwood
Twitter: www.twitter.com/charbrentwood
Pinterest: www.pinterest.com/charbrentwood
BookBub: www.bookbub.com/authors/charlotte-brentwood

What's next?
I am busy working on the next book, *Heart of a Gentleman*. I have many more ideas for connected books as well!

Don't forget to sign up to my email newsletter or follow me on Facebook to get any announcements.

About the Author

A bookworm and scribbler for as long as she can remember, Charlotte always dreamed of sharing her stories with the world.

She lives in Auckland, New Zealand and loves exploring her beautiful surroundings. Her "day job" was in digital marketing, but she is currently a stay-at-home mother to two tiny tyrants and married to her real-life hero.